SWEPT AWAY

SWEPT AWAY

ARNOLD JOHNSTON

atmosphere press

Deborah, always.

Time is a sort of river of passing events,
and strong is its current;
no sooner is a thing brought to sight
than it is swept by and another
takes its place, and this too will be swept away.

Marcus Aurelius

"Lookit here what's happenin' to Romeo."

Bob Emory (as played by Ben Johnson)
One-Eyed Jacks

BRIXTON

"*You're* pissed off?" I shifted myself in the snug passenger seat of the Celica, trying to ease the pressure on my hip, and in the process, banging my right knee on the glove compartment. I was already irked, stewing in my own sweat as we sped south on the Coastal Highway down the Delmarva Peninsula. Eileen Moriarty's little blue roadster closed around me; with my height, I didn't so much get into it as put it on. "You have two *books* coming out," I said. "*I'm* the one who's scrambling to qualify for tenure."

"Don't change the subject." Her left hand on the steering wheel, Eileen jabbed the air sharply with her right index finger, her helmet of curly black hair lending her words an air of electric energy, despite the slightly lazy vowels of her North Carolina drawl. Moving her right hand back to downshift as she stopped for a traffic light, she added, "Two books coming out and no word from Finsterwald about a raise. Half the senior faculty don't have two books on their résumés. It's ridiculous. Sexist bullshit, too." She ended with one of her ever-ready Southern pronouncements—"It'd make a bishop mad enough to kick in a stained glass window."

"At least you'll have a job next year," I said, unwilling

to surrender the low ground. "If something doesn't break for me soon, you may be sharing an office with somebody else." I blew an exasperated sigh that wasn't entirely for effect. With few immediate career prospects, and not long divorced, I had difficulty matching Eileen's sense of outrage, probably because she at least had someone to blame besides herself. She didn't do the flashing eyes thing, but her ice-blue stare could be daunting. I was in no mood to back down, though. "I just got a letter from the Tenure and Promotion Committee," I went on. "From that horse's ass Neil-fucking-Christman, to be precise. He's gotten himself appointed chair of the subcommittee assigned to my file."

"When did you get it?" she said, sparing me another sidelong laser shot and managing to look annoying and attractive at the same time.

"In this morning's interdepartmental crap collection. Very formal. *Dear Dr. McCutcheon.* Latex glove but no Vaseline. Telling me if I can't look forward to placing a book in the near future, I'd better see about getting a production with a significant theatre company. And he had to add, 'Even though the permanence of a book would be far preferable.'" I felt my face becoming warm, despite Eileen's being well aware of my situation.

"Fuck the TPC and the horse's ass Christman rode in on." Eileen gunned the Celica away from the light on its way south. "That's why we're headed for the shore. We need something to take our minds off academe. Off the stodgy Georgian campus of Brixton University and all those who languish there, pretending a little Pennsylvania college town is Oxford or Cambridge. Something completely different."

Eileen was always good at changing the subject. I capitulated. "So, Monty Python, what's the plan?"

"It's a surprise."

I gave her a look, not quite up to her laser eyes. "The last time you surprised me, I wound up having to jump headfirst out of a kitchen window so Finsterwald's wife didn't catch us drinking his twenty-four-year-old Balvenie."

Eileen laughed. "For a man who recently played El Gallo in *The Fantasticks*, you seem to have mislaid your sense of adventure, buddy."

"El Gallo's a character in a play, kiddo. Right now, you're stuck with the offstage version. Much less adventurous."

"No kidding."

She had succeeded in distracting me. Two could play that game. "You know who played El Gallo in the original production? Jerry Orbach."

"Pre-*Law & Order*?"

"Yep. Back when he was an off-Broadway song-and-dance man. The original production ran so long, the *New Yorker* quit printing its capsule review and replaced it with a weekly excerpt from *Ulysses*."

"You're full of random information, aren't you?"

"Playwright's stock-in-trade," I said.

Eileen gave me a glance she would probably call impish. "Capsule review in the *New Yorker*. Gives you something to shoot for."

I snorted. "Right now, I'd settle for *any* capsule review. Maybe in the *Scranton Times-Tribune*."

Eileen's tone turned serious. My precarious perch in the department didn't lend itself to our usual banter.

"Maybe you should look into a dual appointment in Theatre. Or move over there altogether. After all, they were delighted to have you as a guest artist. Students liked you. Reviews were good. English may not be the right place for a playwright. Hell, it's barely the place for a film scholar. Not to mention a woman. Most of the senior faculty think *film scholar's* an oxymoron. And they're deathly afraid I'll start agitating for LGBTQ rights."

Eileen wasn't saying anything I hadn't thought before. "Yeah," I said. "They have trouble coming to terms with the *march of progress*, all right. But my degree's in English. And English is where the job is—and the creative writing classes. Teaching playwriting is just a bonus. Besides, neither English nor Theatre knows what to do with playwrights. Both departments prefer their writers dead—English because they don't really think playwrights are writers, and Theatre because if they're dead they don't have to pay them royalties."

"In Hollywood, all the writers are alive and pitching," Eileen said. "Makes for better company at lunches. And after they deliver the goods, the producers just throw money at them so they'll go away."

"Don't I wish." I exhaled, but couldn't stop myself from going on. "And lots of academic directors think they can stage plays any way their egos dictate. Shakespeare in penguin suits. *School for Scandal* with cellphones. Never mind the Dramatists Guild guidelines."

Eileen chuckled. "Movie directors win the ego contest hands down. Not to mention producers who think they know best."

Again, I couldn't stifle myself. "Then there's the turf issue. The younger Theatre faculty are leery of more competition. Especially from a playwright who acts." I shifted in my seat to ease the growing ache in my right hip. "Sorry about the whining. But you brought up the subject."

"Well, screw all that for today," Eileen said. "For now, we're free spirits!" As if to reinforce her point, she shifted gears swiftly from third to fifth, and cut around a windowless white van of the kind favored by serial killers in B-movies.

"I guess if we do something free-spirited enough to land us in jail, we at least won't have to go to Dean Rimmer's party tonight."

Eileen laughed again, the alteration in her features reminding me I was being chauffeured by a beautiful woman. Her look wasn't boyish. It was just all clean planes, devoid of makeup. "You might get a one-act out of the Rimmer extravaganza," she said. "Silver linings. They're everywhere."

"So where are we headed?"

"Ain't that the question that puts pepper in the gumbo?"

As we continued down through Delaware, skirting tidal wetlands and sand flats, I kept wondering what sort of surprise Eileen could have planned. She clearly wasn't about to spill the beans. After all, I was the one who had gone to graduate school at U of D. The odd little state was full of memories, places I had taken pleasure in showing Deirdre during my final year there when our relationship and marriage were new and still hopeful.

Playing the roles of carefree newlyweds, we had gone to the Brandywine River Museum at Chadds Ford next door in Pennsylvania, to see the collection of Wyeth paintings, including pieces by N.C., Andrew, and Jamie. We had visited Winterthur, originally the enormous estate of the du Pont family, but since the 1950s a museum of Americana, and whiled away a couple of hours wandering its sixty acres of gardens. We spent part of one afternoon in May watching thousands of horseshoe crabs emerge from Delaware Bay to spawn on the sand flats, looking like a miniature invasion of armored vehicles from a science-fiction movie. Then we drove *down by Smyrna*—as the locals say—to Sambo's Tavern on the Leipsic River, to sit at rough-hewn tables covered with newspapers to crack open steamed crabs with wooden mallets and wash down the crabmeat with ice-cold beer. All of our excursions were followed by frantic lovemaking in various cheap venues, as if we wanted to convince each other how crazy about each other we were.

We had also laughed together about the believable tale of the old *Candid Camera* TV show's having set up roadblocks at the two highways leading into the state from the north with signs that said, "State Closed for Repairs." Delaware was such a strange governmental entity that most people, so the story went, had believed the signs and driven away without protest. To me, at this point, as I cruised down the highway next to Eileen, laughing with Deirdre seemed almost as apocryphal in my memory as the *Candid Camera* story.

"Here we are." Breaking my reverie, if that's what it was, Eileen swung the Celica off the highway into a grubby-looking parking lot with a sign that said Emory's Live Bait & Boat Rental. A shack that probably hadn't been painted since the Nixon administration stood near a rickety dock on a tiny inlet leading out into Delaware Bay.

"We're in Rehoboth, for God's sake." I gestured back at the highway. "When you told me to bring along my towel and swim-suit, I thought we'd be headed for bunnies in bikinis on the beach and the boardwalk."

"Bunnies in bikinis? You? I wish. I don't think you've gotten laid more than two or three times since the divorce."

"You should talk," I said. "Anyway, three-and-a-half years with Deirdre would make anybody a little wary. And maybe I'm looking to do more than just *get laid*, as you put it so delicately." I realized how priggish this sounded, but at least it deflected the truth of Eileen's shrewd reckoning.

"And to think I could have invited my maiden Aunt Florence on this outing. Like I said, actors and playwrights are supposed to be livelier. Shakespeare would be ashamed. Hell, Thornton Wilder would be ashamed." Eileen popped open the Celica's trunk, which always had a Pandora's Box air about it, full of junk and unexpected items with the potential for mischief. She reached in and took out a roll of heavy-duty nylon rope attached to what must have been a fishhook, though its size went far beyond anything I had ever seen.

Peering into the mess, I said, "Jesus Christ, Eileen, what's your forty-four Magnum doing in there? And a box of ammo? What the hell do you plan on shooting in a resort? Robbing a bank is a little more excitement than I need."

Hefting the big hook, Eileen said, "Keep it down, Dennis." She jerked a thumb at the bait-shop. "You and I are going to catch ourselves a shark. Something big, anyway. The Magnum is for contingencies."

"Contingencies like in *Jaws*?"

"Speaking of which, let's see about bait and boat." Eileen glanced at the sign. "I assume we buy the bait and rent the boat."

Before I could comment further on the semantics of the sign, the door of the shop opened and a leathery, ageless-looking guy with a stubbly beard and a volleyball-sized potbelly walked out in *Deliverance*-style dungarees and teeth to match. He eyed us, giving me a cursory glance and taking more time with Eileen, her hair, her lean small-breasted body, her tropical shirt, the shorts that showed off her long shapely legs, and her chunky masculine sandals. Then he saw the hook and rope in her hand and sniffed.

"Don't tell me," he said. Since neither Eileen nor I did, he went on. "You two"—he paused, obviously searching for an appropriate word. He settled on, "You two *buddies* figurin' to hook yourselves a shark?"

"Yep." Eileen gave the guy what she probably hoped was a disarming grin. Then, pushing it, she said, "Is Emory your first name or your last name?"

"Em'ry's long-gone," the guy said, giving the *o's* the full Tidewater orchestration. "I'm H'ard."

Another grin from Eileen. "A hard man is good to find."

He wasn't disarmed. "H'ard," he said. "Aitch-oh-double-yar-dee."

Probably figuring she'd pushed far enough, she said, "Well, Howard, we'd like to rent a boat with a motor and buy some bait."

"Seen *Jaws*?"

"We have." Eileen soft-pedaled the grin. "Good movie."

Howard stabbed a callused finger at the hook. "And that's what passes for your plan?"

Eileen inclined her head toward the trunk. "We have a forty-four Magnum. For contingencies."

"Contingencies." Howard beckoned to us. "Come here with me a minute." He turned and ambled toward the dock, trailed by Eileen and me. He pointed down at the dark oil-slicked water. "See that?"

We all looked down at a flat-bottomed wooden boat. The starboard gunwale was missing an eighteen-inch wide, eight-inch deep crescent-shaped chunk unmistakably the result of a bite. Eileen and I looked at each other, then back at Howard.

"Couple boys like you rented that boat last summer." Howard grinned at us, evidently pleased by the *boys* reference. "Had a nice little hook like that one you're luggin'. Heavy-duty line and ever'thin'. They fastened onto a hammerhead. Said it was a twelve-footer. Bit through their damn nylon line, then started in on the boat. They was happy to get back here in one piece. Paid for the damage. Decided they might wanna spend the rest of their day-trip on nice safe barstools."

"You didn't fix the damage," I said.

Howard jerked his thumb toward the dock. "I got plenty a' boats out here. Decided whatcha call a *visual aid* might be quicker than havin' to explain the facts of life to any other suicidal beer-bongers. You gotta admit, it gets your attention."

"Never bonged a beer in our lives," Eileen said cheerfully, swinging her big hook like a pendulum. "And as a matter of fact, more people are killed every year by vending machines than by sharks."

Howard snorted. "Vendin' machines cain't smell blood in the water."

Eileen held up her hands in mock surrender. "We take your point. Maybe we'll go body-surfing instead. I brought my bikini."

Not content to surrender the last word, Howard said, "If you're body-surfin', you're a lot closer to a shark than you think you are. I'll go for the beer-bong every time."

2

"Do you actually have a license for that hunk of artillery?" I jabbed a thumb over my shoulder in the general direction of the Celica's trunk. "Not to mention all the other firearms stored in your arsenal at home?"

Eileen finally spoke, eyes fixed on the road ahead. "Varmint-shooting and more serious hunting require a careful calculation of precision and power."

"Try to remember that when the ATF agents swarm your apartment."

We were on our way back north, having spent several hours body-surfing in the bay instead of shark-fishing. And though disappointed not to have hooked a large predator, Eileen had foresightedly brought along an attractive one-piece, not a bikini—and a good thing, too, because our skin was reddened by the sun despite liberal applications of SPF-30 sunscreen, and further abused by scraping across wet sand, propelled by three-foot waves that added salt to the mix.

"I am, in fact, fully-licensed," Eileen added, "even for concealed-carry. To paraphrase Turkey Creek Jack Johnson in *Tombstone*, 'Law and order every time, that's me.'"

"Concealed carry? Other than the trunk of your Celica,

I'd like to see where you could conceal that smoke-wagon," I said, continuing Eileen's allusion to one of our favorite Western movies, scripted by the late Kevin Jarre, who, like me, was the product of a Detroit upbringing. "But since we only had a couple of beers, at least we won't get arrested for drunk driving."

"Law and order every time," Eileen said, grinning. "But we might've skipped Dean Rimmer's party and driven back tomorrow after a night of beach bunnies and bacchanalia."

"Very alliterative," I said. "You know, some of those bunnies may very well have been Brixton students. Better to deal with a rimmer-job at the party tonight than sometime later after he finds out we've had an ill-advised romp with random young women."

"Rimmer-job? Is that some kind of clumsy homosexual reference?" Eileen glanced at me archly.

"Ho-ho." I gave her a look of my own. "I'm just saying we need to watch our step. We're already on Rimmer's watch-list. Besides, we're not exactly each other's ideal wingmen."

"Wing *persons*," Eileen said, grinning. Then she gave me a pitying shake of her head. "I keep telling you to think about rewards instead of punishment."

"Virtue is its own reward." I touched the palms of my hands to my shell-like ears and felt, rather than heard, the sea somewhere in there. "I don't know about you," I said, "but after all that surfing, my head seems more like a water balloon than a source of rational thought."

"At least it ain't a beer bong."

3

"Ah, it's the odd couple." Corinne Rimmer, the dean's wife, twinkled at her own wit in welcoming Eileen and me to her palatial nineteenth-century pile of granite, nestled in one of Brixton's wealthy enclaves adjacent to campus. The place featured enough mahogany and expensive bric-a-brac for a *Masterpiece Theatre* episode; the Rimmers' money obviously came from some source other than academe. "Nice party outfits," Corinne added, looking at our tropical shirts, shorts, and sandals with a mixture of amusement and disapproval. "I told Bart we should have gone with a South Seas motif."

"Sorry about that," Eileen said, though she didn't sound sorry.

"We were at Rehoboth Beach all day," I said, trying not to give any more offense than we had evidently done already. "If we'd stopped off to change, we'd have been late getting here."

"You *are* late," Corinne said, though she certainly didn't seem overly insulted.

Some ten or fifteen years younger than her mid-fiftyish husband, she wore an improbably short *little black dress* that came close to revealing what my dear-departed mother would have called her *wim-wam*, and which sported a neckline that drew attention to her other major assets. She seemed well aware that Brixton students, staff, and faculty—not to mention spouses—wasted time almost daily on speculation as to why she had married Dean Barton Rimmer, who looked less like an academic and more like someone who might be cheerfully denying loans to widows and orphans.

"Enjoy," Corinne said in a murmur barely audible above the buzz of the already crowded party. "You know where the drinks are, I'm sure."

After flashing a knowing smile, she sashayed off, hips swaying, evidently intent on engaging a group of female faculty who were eyeing with covert disapproval the shiny high-heeled black boots that completed her ensemble.

"Always tasteful," Eileen said. "That dress is so short you can just about see her religion."

I shook my head and felt salt water shifting somewhere inside. "I wonder if a whip came with the outfit."

Eileen grinned. "I'm having a sudden vision of the dean on all fours with a choke collar around his neck."

As if he had heard his name mentioned, Dean Rimmer detached himself from a gaggle of senior faculty and fixed his toothy Cheshire cat smile on Eileen. "Professor Moriarty," he boomed, extending his right hand, complete with a pinky ring worthy of a Mafioso. "You look quite fetching, if a trifle incongruous." Eileen smiled noncommittally, so he went on. "Allow me to congratulate you on your forthcoming tomes. *Film* criticism, I understand."

Eileen glanced at me to show she hadn't missed the dean's inflection, then added, "And an introductory literature textbook."

"Yes," Rimmer said. "Much more solid ground. Potentially lucrative, too."

Eileen reluctantly took the dean's proffered hand, while I thought to myself, *Christ on a crutch*—had Rimmer really said *tomes*?

But before I could even catch Eileen's eye, Rimmer waved his arm expansively. "I think Moriarty has bested his—I should say *her*—rival for once. You've earned the right to partake at the high table, Eileen." The dean glanced at me like a horse-buyer appraising a spavined nag. "You, young Sherlock, will have to find refreshment over there, as usual, while you consider how to catch up professionally with your arch-nemesis, if you'll forgive a bit of Holmesian jocularity." Again, Rimmer flashed the Cheshire grin, making me wish the dean would follow through by disappearing into some Lewis Carroll phantasmagoria, preferably one full of Bandersnatches and Snarks.

Eileen and I had often groused with other young Arts and Sciences faculty over Rimmer's barbaric custom of setting up a table of premium wines, liquors, and beers for associate and full professors and another with cheap drinks for junior faculty and graduate students. And now Eileen was being escorted to rub elbows with what passed for the college's elite, leaving me to choose among half-gallon jugs of Almaden, cans of Miller Lite, and fifths of Jim Beam or Vat 69.

To her credit, Eileen did manage an eye-roll before Rimmer propelled her to the heavily ornate mahogany table laden with imported beers, vintage wines, and single-malt scotches, and surrounded by some of the most pretentious bores on campus, including the pale and pudgy Professor Neil Christman. The chairman of my TPC subcommittee eyed me briefly like an entomologist ready to skewer a negligible specimen, then turned to more important matters, like metaphorically kissing the asses of his senior colleagues.

I made for the cheap drinks table and poured a few fingers of wine the color of a urine sample. A sip of the stuff confirmed, at least, that it was wine, barely drinkable, but free. I quickly downed the contents of the plastic cup as if administering a dose of medicine and poured myself another. Even the slight tilt of my head involved in swallowing set off a tidal sloshing between my ears, making me think of the dank hold of a nineteenth-century whaler.

"Are you going to favor us with a song or two tonight, Dennis?" The voice was that of Lawrence Durwood, another junior faculty member, like Eileen, a part of Brixton's Southern contingent.

Despite the season, Durwood, a Victorian scholar and Anglophile, was wearing a tweedy sports coat, heavy twill trousers, and tan-colored wingtips with a silk paisley Ascot tucked in the neck of his blue Brooks Brothers shirt. Obviously, pretentiousness wasn't limited to the senior faculty table.

I was somewhat queasily disarmed by Durwood's almost fawning admiration, obviously based on my recent appearance in *The Fantasticks*. Hard for an actor to shrug off any kind of praise, whatever the source.

"Your El Gallo was magnificent, Dennis," Lawrence said, raising his glass and causing its neon-colored contents to slop onto one of his blue shirt-cuffs. "When you launched into *Try to Remember*, your voice was like spun honey."

I was saved from more of this by the sudden appearance of our department head, Dr. Raymond Finsterwald, tall, thin, and bald, with gray and cadaverous features that always made me think of Ichabod Crane.

Ever formal, Finsterwald gave a slight bow. "Good evening, Dennis—Lawrence." The department head looked me up and down and closed his eyes for a moment, but made no further comment on my tropical shirt and shorts. Instead, favoring us again with his hyper-thyroidal gaze, he said, "Regrettably, I have to let work intrude on the festivities for a moment. With Professor Christman and the other freshman writing staff attending the College Composition Conference next week, I'm afraid I must ask you to join Lawrence and Eileen in monitoring the multi-section freshman writing exam on Monday morning."

Lawrence was nodding even before Finsterwald stopped speaking. "Of course, Dr. Finsterwald. I'll be glad to help in any way I can."

I merely inclined my water-filled head and smiled. *Christman*, I thought. Obvious where this assignment had originated. Still, I took a little perverse satisfaction in noting that Eileen's two tomes weren't going to exempt her from this latest bout of academic scut-work.

Having accomplished his mission, Finsterwald headed back to the first-class drinks table, where I saw him accosting Eileen, who had just succeeded in detaching herself from conversation with the dean or, more accurately, from Rimmer's always-difficult-to-interrupt monologue about himself and his plans.

A few minutes later, Eileen looked across the room and

made a Chinese dragon face at me. She had obviously just gotten the news about the freshman comp exam.

"I look forward to working with you and the lovely Eileen." Lawrence raised his plastic cup of neon and took a sip. "I often envy you the insights that must derive from enjoying her unique perspective as an office-mate."

I raised my eyebrows, trying for what looked like agreement rather than irritation, and sipped from whatever swill I was drinking, El Gallo, no doubt. A moment later I broke eye-contact with Lawrence, looking down at the Rimmers' expensively-distressed hardwood floor. This slight movement of my head caused a trickle of seawater to slosh from my sinuses and down through my nostrils, dripping onto the toes of Lawrence's wingtips. Thank goodness I hadn't managed to drench Finsterwald's brogues.

Lawrence looked aghast; then, grinning like a zombie, he excused himself and headed for a small knot of graduate students arguing over Matthew Arnold.

Eileen and I apparently discovered the seawater phenomenon almost simultaneously. For the rest of the party, individually or in tandem, we found ourselves able to escape the invariably boring conversations that always dominated a Rimmer gathering by exercising the simple expedient of inclining our heads toward the floor. My only regret was that Christman left the party before I had a shot at dribbling on his suede loafers.

As midnight approached, Corinne Rimmer bore down on me with a glass in each hand; actual glasses from the senior faculty table. Corinne gestured toward my plastic cup, which, like my head, had developed a leak. "Get rid of that thing."

I did as I was told, and Corinne handed me one of the glasses. "Cheers," she said. "So long as you promise not to dribble snot all over my feet the way you and your charming *pal* have been doing to people all evening."

"Eileen and I were body surfing all day," I said. "Apparently our sinuses are still full of salt water. Apologies." I sipped from my glass, the contents of which tasted like a decent New Zealand Sauvignon Blanc, a nice change from El Gallo.

"Never mind," she said. "Watching you two work the room was worth it." She took a healthy swallow from her own glass, which I guessed was filled with scotch, neat. "Too bad you didn't bring your guitar," she added. "A song or two would have lightened the mood."

"We came directly from the beach," I said, "but I guess we mentioned that before." I couldn't tell if she was drunk, but the odds were in favor of it if she had been drinking scotch all night.

Corinne struck a pose, canting one hip in a way that enhanced the effect of the little black dress. Maybe she was just trying to find a balance-point. "I've always wanted to learn the guitar," she said. "Maybe you could give me some lessons." She smiled at me, making lots of eye-contact, then finished her scotch. "Another?" she said.

I raised my still half-full glass. "I'm good."

"I'm sure you are," she said and, turning, made for the drinks table. Maybe she had recently seen *Who's Afraid of Virginia Woolf?*

A short time later, as Eileen and I stood beside the Celica outside chez Rimmer, I said, "We'll probably pay for this. We must have dribbled on half the guests, including everyone on the TPC. Unfortunately, not including fucking

Christman."

"He's wet enough without our assistance. Have you ever shaken hands with him?" Eileen made a gargoyle face. "At least we weren't playing with fire."

"I'm not so sure," I said. "I just hope the Dean didn't overhear Corinne's request for guitar lessons."

Eileen shook her head, her expression registering both pity and amusement. "You'd just better hope there are no strings attached, and I don't mean guitar."

"And what about you? Did you talk to Finsterwald about your raise?"

"Talk to him? The *Artful Dodger*?" Eileen blew a raspberry. "After he delivered the news about the freshman comp exam, he wouldn't even meet my eye."

4

Sauntering between the broad A-V platform and the green board, I surveyed the lecture hall in which over a hundred students were packed into long curved rows of seats, heads bent over bluebooks, pens scratching away.

Standing nearby, Lawrence Durwood consulted his massive wristwatch, its face the approximate size of a Mason jar lid, checking it against the hall's notoriously unreliable wall-clock. Durwood was tweedy and professorial-looking as usual, the major difference between this and his party outfit being suede, rather than tan, leather wingtips, and a striped tie instead of an ascot.

"Ten minutes!" he shouted.

Tipped back in a wheeled desk-chair, Eileen gave every sign of being asleep until Durwood's announcement caused her to jerk forward with a clatter, eliciting wild-eyed head-swiveling from the students, accompanied by a scatter of nervous tittering.

"Jesus," Eileen said, glaring at Durwood. "What's up?"

"*Time's* up." Durwood pointed at his watch. "Almost, anyway. Under ten minutes to go. And you know Professor Christman. No extra time for any reason. And six-by-nine-inch bluebooks only. The man runs a tight ship." Durwood grinned and dropped his voice to a stage whisper. "Though after your liberal sprinkling of seawater at Dean Rimmer's party, perhaps nautical allusions aren't entirely appropriate."

"Ho-ho. We'll give Christman a tight ship all right." Eileen got to her feet, looking professional and attractive in close-fitting gray slacks, a darker gray sweater, a navy blazer, and gray suede chukka boots. "Start wrapping it up!" she shouted to the students. Then she pointed at the wall-clock. "When the big hand hits twelve, it's over. No exceptions. And don't forget to put your names and section numbers on those essays!" She sat on the corner of the A-V platform, arms folded.

"That's right," Durwood echoed weakly. "No exceptions."

Almost immediately, students began filing forward with their bluebooks, setting them down in a stack next to where Eileen was perched.

One kid, sporting a scruffy three-day beard, greasy hair, and clothes he had likely picked up off his dorm-room floor, started to add an eight-and-a-half by eleven-inch bluebook to the growing pile.

"Hold it, my friend." Durwood pointed at the kid. "Six-by-nine-inch bluebooks only. Per Professor Christman's express instructions."

The kid regarded Durwood like the caveman in *2001: A Space Odyssey* looking at the extraterrestrial monolith. Then, suddenly, he flashed what he probably hoped was a disarming grin. "All I could scrounge up this morning was the big bluebook," he said in a stoner drawl. "No prob, eh, bro?"

Before Durwood could respond, Eileen took the book from the kid. "No prob, bro," she said cheerfully. Then she picked up one of the proper-sized bluebooks, set it against the larger one, and tore off enough of the kid's book so it roughly matched the rest of the books in the pile. "No prob," she said again, dumping the residue in a nearby wastebasket, and waved the kid toward the door.

Stunned and slack-jawed, the kid managed only an extended, "Woah. Dude." Then he walked out of the hall, pausing at the door only long enough to give Eileen a look that somehow combined both fear and admiration. The other students buzzed a bit, but continued filing out after adding their books to the stack on the A-V platform.

Eileen rose and winked at Durwood. "One of life's little lessons," she said. Merely a spectator, I was enjoying this.

At last, the clock on the wall clicked the end of the exam period. Durwood started for the pile of exam books, but before he could scoop them up, another student, clean-cut and no doubt freshly showered, walked up hastily with a blue book in his right hand.

"No, young man," Durwood said sternly. "No extra time. You've missed your chance."

The student opened his mouth, then closed it. Then he said, "I'm only a minute late," and extended the book toward Durwood.

"No, sir," Durwood said. "No exceptions."

The kid took a deep breath. Then, in an outraged tone, he said, "Do you know who I am?"

Durwood's expression reflected satisfaction at this opportunity to face down a blatant attempt at using some evident extra-curricular connection to evade a just penalty and, incidentally, show Eileen how tough he could be. Fingering his striped tie like a talisman of authority, Durwood said, "Not only don't I *know* who you are, I don't *care.*"

"That's what I thought," the kid said. Then he buried his bluebook in the anonymous middle of the pile and walked quickly out of the lecture hall. Eileen and I did our best to keep straight faces.

Nonplussed, Durwood looked at the stack of exam books, then from Eileen to me. "Did you see where he put that bluebook?" Getting no response, he said, "Do you have any idea who he was?"

"I don't know," I said.

Eileen shrugged. "And I don't care."

5

As we watched Durwood trudging up the hallway toward the freshman comp offices balancing the load of exam books, I said, "Well, that was almost worth having Christman force us to monitor his exam."

"Almost," Eileen said. "But I'm definitely facing up to Finsterwald about salary today. Before he finds out I *adjusted* that kid's blue-book. Even though it's what the little shit deserved."

"*Facing Up to Finsterwald*—good title for a one-act." I tried to keep my voice low amid the between-class crush of students in Harriman Hall.

"Ho-ho," Eileen said without conviction. "I actually left him a note. Something he can't ignore."

"At least you've got some leverage," I said. "How many of us can say we have tomes due to come out within a couple of months? Certainly not me."

"Not the kind of grammar Dr. Christman would expect from one of his freshman comp exam monitors," Eileen said. Before she could respond to my dig about tomes, a slender *au-lait*-hued woman called to her.

"Dr. Moriarty? I have a couple of questions about tomorrow's test."

The young woman, Maxine Kuhn, was a fourth-year

senior, well-known to younger English Department faculty for her fashion-model looks and incisive intelligence, result of the marriage between a U.S. Army officer and a linguistics professor from the University of Essen by way of Ethiopia. I had always harbored the hope that Maxine would decide to sign up for one of my playwriting workshops, though her interests inclined more to the eighteenth and nineteenth-century prose stylists and to Eileen's class in film studies.

"I'll see you at the office," Eileen said to me, then started toward the doorway of the empty classroom where Maxine stood waiting.

"Professor Moriarty!"

Both Eileen and I turned toward the reedy sound of our department chair's voice. The man seemed to have been conjured from his office by Eileen's declaration of intent to confront him. Finsterwald nodded to me, then fixed his protuberant eyes on Eileen.

"I need to discuss a couple of matters with you, er, Eileen. Relative to the note you left me." Finsterwald waved his long fingers vaguely toward the department's main office.

Eileen's eyes darted back and forth between Finsterwald and her waiting student, as she weighed the conflicting demands of courtesy and duty. I tried to remain inconspicuous.

Eileen finally spoke, nodding toward the classroom. "Right away, Dr. Finsterwald. As soon as I've finished speaking to Miss Kuhn."

Finsterwald's hyperthyroid glare widened momentarily. Then he about-faced and strode back to his office. Eileen shrugged and started for the classroom, leaving me feeling like a spectator at an aborted tennis match.

6

I sat at my elderly walnut desk in the office I shared
with Eileen, hurriedly checking my email before starting
on a folder of several new student one-acts, though my
time would have been better spent submitting some of my
own work to theatre companies and journals to keep
Christman and his subcommittee at bay.

Senior faculty members were housed at the end of the
quad in Harriman Hall, site of the freshman comp exam.
Eileen, most of the other junior faculty, and I, occupied
cramped quarters in adjacent Winfield Hall, well away
from the departmental nerve center. With two people
crammed into offices that barely accommodated two
desks, four chairs, and two small metal file cabinets, young
faculty members had to work at making sure their student
conferences didn't overlap.

Fortunately, Eileen and I had hit it off immediately
after our random office pairing, and though we were
aware of the *Odd Couple* references, oblique or direct, both
of us were well-liked by students, in part because of what
Christman often referred to as our "semi-academic"
specializations. As for faculty, most were no doubt happy
to be relieved of the obligation to be politically correct
about sexuality, though they probably envied Eileen's and

my casual incorrectness.

I had over forty emails, most of which were from various fundraising arms of the Democratic Party. These I deleted swiftly, reflecting that when repeated pleadings managed to piss off even your strongest supporters, your campaign apparatus was in trouble. What I hated about them was the fevered subject-line adjectives— "Devastating," "Disastrous," "Heartbreaking"—and on and on. I wondered what behavioral consultant had convinced them people would respond to that sort of barefaced manipulation more than once or twice.

The next email might well have been from the Democrats, at least given the subject line, "How could you?" But the address identified my recently-ex-wife. She had somehow gotten hold of my latest short story, published in a relatively obscure literary journal. I reflected momentarily that *relatively obscure* was probably a redundant description of most literary journals. In any case, Deirdre had read my story, obviously combing it for any details that could be construed as referring to her.

"How could you violate the privacy of the marital relationship?" she demanded. "You've paraded parts of my life in public without so much as a second thought. Your vindictiveness is staggering. But I suppose your dyke office-mate only encourages that kind of attitude. How does it feel to be the male equivalent of a fag-hag? Or does she actually have you mincing around like a poof?"

The message went on in this vein for several more paragraphs while I combed my memory for what she could possibly have dredged up to be offended at from my brief story about a playwright caught up in a tense and not very successful opening night. The only thing I could manage to recall was my passing reference to the protagonist's childless marriage. Probably the real reason for the message, was her having come up with the fag-hag taunt and the reflexively aggressive questioning of my manhood. Manhood, I thought; what an increasingly quaint term. One way or another, fuck it.

Deirdre was attractive, perhaps not beautiful in conventional terms, but striking. She and I had fallen for—or onto—each other in a summer stock production of *Bell, Book, and Candle*, just before my final year of graduate school. I had played the Jimmy Stewart role from the film and Deirdre the part played by Kim Novak. I had been less swept away than distracted—by the play and the job-search—and I had failed to recognize that what I initially saw in her as uncomplicated and affectionate sexuality, would develop into fierce possessiveness that failed to dampen her own promiscuity. Or her narcissism.

Thinking about her anger over the short story, I thanked the random universe that Deirdre and I hadn't had any children for her to demand a Solomon's solution to satisfy her extraordinary antagonism toward me. Instead, she had simply been forced to settle for getting a judge to halve my relatively puny retirement fund from the college. That had been the price for her waiving her initial demand of half the rights to my past, present, and future plays and other work. She was damned lucky, I thought, that I hadn't included any reference in my story to the lead actress's clandestine affair with the lead actor. In her *husband's* play.

I hadn't learned about Deirdre's infidelity—another quaintly Victorian-sounding word—until after she had discovered my own brief and incandescent liaison with one of my recently-graduated students. And now, between roles, Deirdre could fall back on that chunk of my skimpy retirement fund, not to mention the degree in arts administration I had financed for her.

I thought back to the three years of high-maintenance, the meltdowns I had tried to ameliorate. Had I ever loved her? Liked her? I took a deep breath and deleted the message. I should be more like my students, who regarded email as a quaint means of communication soon to disappear into the *oubliette* of pop culture, along with cursive writing. But I couldn't see texting and tweeting editors or trying to send lengthy scripts via smartphone. Oh, well.

Before I could examine any further emails, Eileen entered the office, shut the door behind her, set down her briefcase, and threw herself into the desk chair she'd picked up at the university's surplus warehouse. The chair dropped about three inches on its central post. Her knees elevated almost to chest-level, Eileen glared at me.

"Jesus H. Christ," she said, more exhalation than speech.

I widened my eyes. "That bad?"

Eileen sighed and hauled her chair back up to its normal height. "Not good. Not as well as it went with Maxine."

"Watch out for students," I said. "At least while they're still in your classes."

Eileen snorted. "Maxine's graduating at the end of the summer session. That's what she wanted to let me know. For future reference."

No wonder Maxine hadn't signed up for one of my

workshops. "Congratulations," I said. "To both of you."

"Trouble with you is you need to get laid. How about Corinne Rimmer and those guitar lessons?"

"That's all I need. Another crazy woman. And the dean's wife, at that. Especially when Deirdre keeps stalking me electronically." I gave Eileen a brief account of the recently-deleted message.

"Dyke office-mate, eh?" Eileen shook her head. "That woman needs to find another hobby. Just hope she keeps it electronic."

"And by the way," I said, "for future reference. What *is* the male equivalent of a fag-hag?"

She smiled and winked at me. "Your education has been sadly neglected. And you a theatre person. I'll have to undertake remediation."

"You're stalling," I said. "What is it?"

"It's a *les-bro*." She laughed.

"I'll have a difficult time forgetting that," I said. Then I had to ask, "So what about Finsterwald? Did you face up to him?"

"Well, not before he faced up to me." Eileen grinned lopsidedly.

"What do you mean?"

"Well, as soon as I walked into his office, he looked up from his desk and fixed me with that popeyed glare of his. 'I do want to discuss how to recognize your pending publications,' he says. 'But first we need to talk about that little scene in the hallway just now.' "

"I was baffled," Eileen continued. "I figured he'd be after us about our sinus attack on Rimmer's party guests. But no. So I asked him, 'What scene was that, Dr. Finsterwald?' He looked as if his head were about to come to a point"—Eileen frequently paraphrased Angela Lansbury's line from the Frankenheimer version of *The Manchurian Candidate*. "Then he says, 'Eileen. I know you're from the South. But up here the appropriate term is *African American*.' "

I let out a laugh. "He thought you'd called Maxine *this coon*? You're kidding!"

"Nope," Eileen said. "He was absolutely serious. I had to explain to him that Maxine's last name was, in fact, Kuhn. He's probably checking with the registrar as we speak. Maybe he'll find out that Maxine is German African American."

"So. Did the Kuhn-hunt postpone your salary confrontation? That's Kuhn with a *K*, of course." I looked as innocent as I could manage.

"*Kuhn*-hunt? Seriously?" Eileen tried to sound outraged while suppressing laughter.

"You *are* the quintessential gun-toting Southern belle."

"Tell me this isn't going to show up in a story or a play."

"Not while I'm working here," I said. "Which may not be too much longer. And I'll take care to disguise it well. But don't try to dodge the question. What about the face-off?"

Eileen shook her head and scowled. "I brought up my books. He said the department would have me do a presentation in September, followed by a reception. I asked about a salary increase. He said *that* was something for next year, after the books were out. I said all I wanted was what I'd earned, what I deserved."

"So, what did *he* say?"

Eileen snorted. "He tilted his head back, the way he does when he makes pronouncements. Then he said, 'As Hamlet tells Polonius, "Use every man after his desert, and who should 'scape whipping?"'"

I laughed. "One thing you have to admit—this place is an endless source of material."

"Jesus." Eileen got up from her chair, which produced a pneumatic hissing sound. "Let's head to the Deer Park, have an early lunch and a couple of beers. Or just a couple of beers."

Normally I would have been delighted to join Eileen and commiserate, but half a dozen unread one-acts lay waiting in a folder on my desk. "Maybe I'll catch up with you in an hour or so," I said, gesturing at the folder. "I'd better make some inroads on this stuff first. Not that it'll help me 'scape whipping. Or Christman and the TPC. Or having to find a job as a waiter, leaving you with an office to yourself."

"Maybe you can land a musical gig at the Deer Park." Eileen made for the door, leaving her briefcase sitting beside her balky chair. "Summer session's almost over," she said as a parting shot. "And all we have is one class apiece. Loosen up, Dennis."

"Says the happy camper with two tomes in the works." I jabbed two fingers at her.

Eileen twirled one finger in reply. "See you in an hour, les-bro," she said, closing the door behind her with a click.

7

After Eileen left the office, I stared at the folder of student plays, though my thoughts kept drifting to comparison of my office-mate's career with my own. No matter how frustrated Eileen might be about the department's failure to bestow instant rewards on her for her double-dip publication coup, next year would certainly bring those rewards—a special salary increase, and undeniable advancement toward tenure and promotion.

I was pretty well-liked, well-tolerated anyway, by students and colleagues, except for a couple of senior faculty members like Christman, who as a rhetorician had little patience for *creative* writing, and Bert Sorensen, a Chaucer scholar who didn't seem to like anyone who wasn't moved to tears of laughter at the Reeve's Tale. My record of publications and productions was respectable, if not quite respectable enough for the TPC. True, I'd had one genuine off-Broadway production that had gotten a limited run and mixed reviews, and a long-running hit show at a non-Equity Chicago theatre. But otherwise, my work had appeared in small-circulation lit-mags and onstage at relatively small regional or off-off-Broadway theatres. Well, the only answer was to keep teaching, keep writing, and get more stuff published and produced; then

I could have my own face-off with Finsterwald.

For a while I entertained myself by typing up for future use a story recently related to me by Albert Greenbaum, a psych professor with a reputation for scholarly eclecticism and a wicked sense of humor. As Al told it, he'd given a lecture on the rhetoric of deception and its psychological components. After the lecture, Christman had cornered Al and suggested that their intersecting interests might make for a useful collaborative essay. Al reluctantly agreed to a meeting for further discussion, at which point the always parsimonious Christman asked whether he should bring his lunch to Al's office, or vice versa. "I told him to bring his lunch to my office," Al said.

When Christman arrived at the appointed time, clutching his brown paper lunch bag, Al's secretary, Bonnie, knocked on his office door and asked if he'd take lunch now. Receiving the go-ahead, she ushered Christman in. As Christman was unwrapping his wax-paper-wrapped sandwich, Bonnie returned with a silver tray bearing a covered metal dish and an ice-bucket with a bottle of white wine and two glasses. Setting the tray on Al's desk, she removed the metal cover to reveal a plate of fresh fruit, croissants, and pâté. Then she poured wine for Al and offered the astonished Christman a glass, which he accepted in lieu of opening his thermos of who-knew-what. After the discussion of the prospective article, which Al hoped might evaporate in the coming weeks, Christman rose to leave. Pausing at the office door, Christman said, "I have to ask you, Albert. Do you eat lunch like this every day?"

Al had looked at me and grinned. "I told him, 'No, Neil. I occasionally like to eat *out*.' I'm not sure he ever got the joke. Talk about the rhetoric of deception."

I shook my head sharply, trying to clear my mind of such unhelpful thoughts; at least the seawater was long-gone. I closed the short document, which might make a ten-minute play. Academe provided and endless supply of comic material. Nonetheless, I flipped open the folder lying reproachfully in front of me. Then I removed the top from the fine-point roller-ball pen I preferred, ready to begin scribbling marginal comments on the first play, when my desktop computer's email signal dinged. The sound annoyed me, but I had to admit I'd never switched it off because I usually preferred the distraction to whatever else I might be doing in my office. My laptop, on which I did most of my serious writing, was blessedly silent. I clicked the mouse, and the screen came alive.

I didn't recognize the name on the message, but I did note the wsu.edu address. Wayne State University, my alma mater in Detroit, which I still regarded as my hometown. Probably some alumni association or departmental plea for a donation. But the subject line said "Good News" in boldface. Just read the goddam thing, I told myself.

Turned out it *was* good news, almost as if my envious disgruntlement at Eileen's success had conjured the message from the ether, or the cloud, or whatever the hell it was calling itself these days.

"Dear Professor McCutcheon," it read, "As an alumnus of Wayne State University, you and your work are known to us here in the Theatre Department, even though you were not a theatre major during your time on campus. We take great pleasure in asking that you allow us to mount a fall production of your full-length play *Swept Away*, which came to our attention through its limited off-Broadway run at the Minetta Lane Theatre in New York. We would stage the play at the 100-seat Hilberry Studio Theatre. If the prospect of a production at your alma mater interests you, I am sure we can work out further details in the coming weeks. Your director will be Professor Edward Friend, one of our best young faculty members. He's highly talented and very excited about the opportunity to work with you on your fine play."

More stuff followed about royalties, proposed production dates in the coming fall, travel expenses and lodging and so forth, but I barely registered any of it beyond noting that the message came from the Theatre department chair, Dr. Genevieve Addante. The air in the dusty office seemed to hum around my ears, as if this intersection of my past and present had occurred at some molecular level. Strange attractors, indeed.

I decided I would walk back to Harriman Hall and face up to Finsterwald to request approval for sufficient release time for a trip to Detroit during fall semester. Then I would catch up with Eileen for a celebratory Rolling Rock—or two, or three—at the Deer Park. Take that, Christman! Take that, Tenure and Promotion Committee!

8

Dr. Finsterwald widened his eyes. Normally, the effect would have caused me to store the moment away for later conversational fodder with Eileen. At this point, though, I simply registered the nearly translucent skin at Finsterwald's temples, and realized how vulnerable the man seemed, how weighed down by his job. I had often noted how high-level administration turned good teachers out of the classroom and converted them into nervous and unhappy department heads.

"Well," Finsterwald finally said, intertwining his long bony fingers, "I can't say I greet this turn of events with the unbridled joy it no doubt deserves. Your missing a significant number of classes at the start of fall semester will certainly require adjustments and extra duties for some of your colleagues and will perhaps create distress on the part of a number of students."

I felt the hard wooden seat of the chair pressing on the bones under my glutes, like the passenger seat of Eileen's Celica. The discomfort of Finsterwald's chairs played a well-known part in the brevity of his audiences with visitors, particularly faculty members. "I'm sure people will pitch in." I tried to keep a note of desperation out of my voice. "After all, it is an honor for the department, and

I've subbed for others in similar situations."

"No doubt. I didn't realize I'd have to contend with both you and your office-mate this morning." Finsterwald closed his eyes for a merciful moment, then opened them again and flashed his large teeth in an unexpected smile. "Ah, well. You're right, of course, Dennis. A production at a major university like Wayne State is no small thing. It may help your, ah, cause with the TPC. I'm sure Professor Christman and his subcommittee will be suitably impressed. Congratulations. We'll make the necessary arrangements." As I rose to leave, Finsterwald raised a bony finger. "A word of advice, Dennis. You'll no doubt find yourself in gatherings with distinguished academics, not to mention representatives of the press—or the media, as they style themselves these days. I'm sure I needn't caution you about appearing in a get-up such as the one you arrived wearing for Dean Rimmer's party. But let me counsel you to invest in some attractive calf-length dress socks of a conservative hue. No one wants to be confronted in a serious conversation by several inches of hairy shin."

I suppressed a burst of hysterical laughter, thanked him—trying not to seem too ebullient, not to mention amazed—and left the department head's office. As I closed the door behind me, though, my expression obviously betrayed me.

"Win the Lotto, did you?" Ellie Endicott, Finsterwald's secretary, looked at me from her desk, her smile accenting her small perfect teeth and the hazel eyes that could reduce undergraduates, faculty, and administrators alike to the status of awkward suitors.

I, along with the rest of the junior faculty, including the always-hopeful Eileen, often griped at the injustice of the beautiful Ellie spending so much of her day in the disinterested presence of her happily-married and strait-laced boss. But none of them could muster the courage to ask her out, so her free time remained a mystery and the subject of extravagant speculation. Nonetheless, I caught myself thinking that the difference in looks between her and Eileen was mostly a matter of makeup and wardrobe.

"Cat got your tongue, or is that a canary stuck in your throat?" Ellie said, with breezy disregard for the mixing of metaphor.

"It's good news, all right." I flashed her what I hoped was an enigmatic smile, unwilling to surrender my own small mystery. "But you'll hear about it. Eventually."

"If not sooner. At least you seem to have gotten a happier result than your buddy Eileen."

I left the outer office, my hairy shins prickling, with the sound of her soft laughter trailing me. So much for discomposing her well-known serenity.

Ten minutes later I had made my way to the almost ridiculously spacious bar-restaurant section of the Deer Park Hotel. I paid the bartender for two ice-sheathed mugs of Rolling Rock and joined Eileen at a table in the middle of the room, sliding one of the mugs to her. Then, after letting her know about the unexpected email, I gave her a blow-by-blow of my meeting with Finsterwald.

"Boy," Eileen said, leaning back in her chair, "we really gave Finsterwald the old one-two, eh? Coordinated hotshots!"

"I'm not sure I believe he actually approved my trip to Detroit."

"Well," Eileen said, "it doesn't represent a permanent investment, like giving me a decent raise—especially since

Wayne State is footing the bill for your residency there."

"Point taken. Anyway, it does feel good." I surveyed the array of deer-heads on the walls with more affection than I had felt in months. Their glassy eyes often made me feel as if I were about to be incorporated in some pagan ceremony, especially as my alcohol intake mounted. "Makes even this stuff taste better," I said, taking another swallow from my frosty mug.

"I'm just happy I don't have to keep making excuses for my good fortune in getting a couple of books published. Thank God you're finally managing to eke out a little recognition for yourself and get off my back."

I raised my mug. "Fuck you very much."

Eileen raised her own mug. "Somebody has to keep you humble," she said. "Seriously, though, *Swept Away* is a damn good play. I've always thought it would make a good film, too, certainly better than the Madonna remake of the Wertmüller original. Maybe better than Wertmüller's. Totally different, of course."

"You're too kind."

"When it comes to movies, I don't do kind."

"Good thing titles can't be copyrighted."

"Amen. And I like the stuff you included about the museum director's lesbian daughter."

"I wondered if I'd gotten those references right."

"You bet. Just what I'd expect from a *les-bro*. One who pays attention. Who knew we sexual deviants argue about how long to boil an egg, just like regular folks."

"Touché," I said, grinning, knowing she meant us.

"And all those short scenes," she continued. "Very cinematic. And lots of chances to open it up for location shooting. I still have some film-school friends out there in

La-La Land. Ben Talbot, to mention a few."

"I know, I know," I said. "Your famously handsome pal."

"Famous, handsome, and bankable," Eileen said. "And always looking for another star vehicle. Asshole." Then, after a pause, she added, "You know, Ben was always good-looking, but he didn't become *People Magazine*-handsome till he had his first box-office hit."

"Regular features, a personal trainer, and able to open in cities worldwide. Everybody's Hollywood dream," I said. "And now you can offer him the chance to shoot a film in Detroit."

"*Dee*-troit's certainly the place for shooting of one kind or another."

"Ho-ho," I said. "And it's Detroit, not *Dee*-troit."

"Think I don't know that?" She flicked some Rolling Rock at me.

"Or sometimes the Big *Day-twah*," I said, flicking her back from my own mug. "And it's not everybody's can of Stroh's. You know who was supposed to star in *Beverly Hills Cop*?"

"Enlighten me."

"Sylvester Stallone. Then his mother, the astrologer, told him a winter location shoot in Motown was a bad idea. Bingo—bring on Eddie Murphy."

Eileen winked at me. "Doesn't exactly take an astrologer to keep people out of Detroit in the winter. Anyway, don't you worry your little regular-featured head. Ben trusts my judgment."

"Let's not get ahead of ourselves," I said. "First things first. Onstage before on-location. But I appreciate the thought. You just never know when somebody hundreds of miles away will suddenly decide to haul out a magic wand and wave it in your direction. When I left Finsterwald's lair, Ellie said I looked like I had won the Lotto."

"This can't be totally out of the blue, can it? After all, you're a Wayne State alum."

"But I was an English and Education major. Never took a theatre class. Never did any acting until after I left. Or any real writing, either, beyond a few parodies in the school newspaper. Everybody I knew in high school just figured I was a lousy science student and class clown by default. Nobody figured I might parlay that into writing and acting. But I guess there's no point in checking a gift-horse's dental work."

"Somebody from those days must have been keeping tabs on you." Eileen mimed keystrokes with her non-mug hand. "Googling."

"I can't imagine who. Or is it *whom*?"

"Whom cares?"

I shrugged. "I guess I'll find out whom cares when I get there."

"Well, when you do get there, for Christ's sake try to have a good time. You and your hairy shins."

9

I started for Detroit a couple of weeks into the start of Brixton's fall semester. I had been able to get my classes going before turning them over to colleagues. My introductory creative writing workshop, which combined instruction in poetry and fiction, would be handled in my absence by Lucy Gant, a new hire with an MFA from Ohio, who welcomed the chance to teach something other than freshman comp and introductory lit, even on a temporary basis. Lucy was shopping her MFA thesis, a novel drawing on a summer she'd spent working on a cruise ship. I hoped she'd find a publisher, but not too soon.

My playwriting workshop was another matter, being the only playwright in the department. But for the few weeks I would be gone, Brixton's resident novelist Paul Zimmerman had volunteered to pinch-hit.

Zimmerman had half a dozen books published by reputable literary presses, and even a couple of useful reviews from the *New York Times*. And like most writers— non-writers, too, for that matter—Zimmerman assumed that playwriting mostly involved adding nuts and bolts like dialogue attributions to the structure of fiction. No doubt he would turn one of his short stories into a one-act and ask me to take a look after my trip to Detroit. Fair enough.

After pulling out of my apartment parking lot that morning and heading for the highway, I called Eileen on my cellphone.

After a few rings, I heard Eileen's groggy-sounding voice. "Dennis? What time is it?"

"Nine o' clock." I had left Eileen and the lovely Maxine Kuhn the night before at the Laughing Gargoyle, where we had celebrated Maxine's summer graduation and my imminent road trip. "I'm on my way," I said. "And you're missing the best part of the day."

"God," Eileen said, "what are you—a rooster?"

I heard a muffled voice in the background with a distinctive female timbre and just a hint of German accent. "Are you sure *you're* not the rooster?" I said. "Or whatever the appropriate term is."

"Give it a rest," Eileen said. "In fact, give *us* a rest. And have a wonderful time in Detroit."

"You and Maxine have a wonderful time, too, if I'm not being redundant."

"Send me a picture of the big Joe Louis fist," Eileen said. "I've always admired a city that threatens a potential punch in the mouth as one of its landmarks."

Before I could think of a suitably smart-assed rejoinder, she broke the connection.

Smiling, I pulled onto the highway. Feeling a buoyant sense of freedom, I realized I didn't have to push through to Detroit in one day. On a whim, maybe because of memories stirred by Eileen's and my trip to Rehoboth Beach, I decided to stop off at the Gettysburg battlefield, another of the places Deirdre and I had visited in happier times.

As I drove, I thought about Eileen and Maxine, or more

particularly about how the relationship would affect Eileen. Despite our continual banter about my romantic life, I knew Eileen wasn't doing much better, no matter how attractive she was, or how she might thumb her nose at convention in the safety of our office. Her opportunities were limited by her sexual orientation as a faculty member in a relatively small college town that didn't even have a gay bar. And though my divorce from Deirdre might be the cause of recent pain and whining, I knew Eileen had demons in her own past: sexual abuse as a pre-adolescent by the seemingly inevitable uncle; parental accusations and recriminations when she had decided to come out. Anyway, I hoped Maxine would prove to be a happy development in the life of the woman I realized had become something more than just my best friend.

Gettysburg wasn't much longer than three hours away from Brixton on US 30, the aptly-named Lincoln Highway. Just as at the Chesapeake and Delaware Canal, I had found there a piece of the past, a minié ball from a muzzle-loading rifle I'd kicked from under a clump of weeds and had surreptitiously carried off.

Once on the road, I didn't intend to stop until I reached Gettysburg. But as I drove through the Lehigh Valley, past signs for towns like Ephrata, Blue Ball, Bird-in-Hand, and Intercourse, always good for a snarky laugh, my eye was caught by a Pennsylvania Dutch diner Deirdre and I had discovered years before, so I decided to make time for breakfast.

The place was much as I remembered it, the gift shop full of chintz and *tchotchkes*, the menu sprinkled with quaintly Teutonic imagery and catch-phrases of the *throw-Mama-from-the-train* variety. The proprietor, a stout, seventyish guy with close-cropped white hair, would have evoked thoughts of a Nazi *Stalag* guard had it not been for his being decked out in a gingham bonnet and apron more appropriate for a farmer's wife.

As I watched the man shuffling around, treating patrons to a heavy-accented, cornball spiel, I recalled Deirdre's scathing comments, uttered at a level difficult for people at other tables to ignore.

"A barnyard transvestite with a nose like a rutabaga and an accent out of *Hogan's Heroes*," she had said.

That was one of the many signs I had ignored of Deirdre's desperate need to find people to feel superior to, compounded by her equally desperate need to be admired and catered to. I had actually put Deirdre's remark into the mouth of a not-very-pleasant character in a one-act, until she had made me take it out. Had I known the old guy in the bonnet and apron would still be at the restaurant like a comedy ghost from the past, I might well have reconsidered stopping there.

Deirdre's neediness in our relationship, I now knew, was exacerbated by her conviction, accurate I had to admit, that her looks weren't quite of leading-lady quality and her undeniable talent was tinged with the same edge of desperation for approval that could undermine her efforts both at auditions and onstage.

I, on the other hand, could turn to writing, which I knew made my approach to auditions and performances more relaxed. And because several directors had told me, and several reviewers had implied, that I was simply more talented than Deirdre, I was pretty sure I hadn't been manufacturing my own version of reality. Such opinions must have been difficult for her, and certainly hadn't helped our relationship. Now, years later, I still felt a twinge of guilt. Deirdre compensated for the situation by becoming increasingly strident in her opinions about me and everyone else.

I finished my breakfast and paid at the counter, getting a jovially guttural *"Danke schön"* from the old guy in the bonnet. Then I got into my Highlander and drove back onto US 30 with a gastrointestinal payload of eggs, scrapple, potato pancakes, toast, and apple butter that I realized was surplus and probably antithetical to my daily maximum caloric requirements.

Maybe I should just push on to the Motor City, I thought, especially with the memory of Deirdre's mean-spiritedness fresh in my mind. But some part of me felt I should give her another chance, as if she were sitting in the shotgun seat of my mind radiating need. So, Gettysburg it would be.

10

As I approached Gettysburg, I reflected that the entire town had been pretty much the heart of the battlefield, though much of the heaviest fighting had taken place southwest of the population center, such as it was in 1863. Again, I found myself retracing the route Deirdre and I had taken on our one visit to what was properly known as the Gettysburg National Military Park, operated by the National Park Service. Admission to the sprawling battlefield was free, though visitors were encouraged to pay for various guided tours and exhibits.

I steered the Highlander into town, past the railway station, then turned left to find a spot in one of the spacious parking areas to the south of the Visitor Center. Leaving the SUV ticking in the lot, I hiked down to the southwest among knots of other tourists along Cemetery Ridge, making for the most familiar sites where the battle had been decided: Plum Run, the Wheatfield, Little Round Top, and beyond them the tumbled lava rock formations of Devil's Den. The air was cool, the sun dazzling, and the grass and foliage still green, though not so green as it would have been on those few fateful days in July.

Slowing my pace a bit, I felt my collarbones grow clammy under my shirt, and made my way among the boulders into the cool, still shade of maples and poplars, away from the hum of voices and the sound of Leicas, iPads, and cellphones slicing the landscape into frames to be carried away. Among the trees and weeds and brambles, I felt, once again, the spell of the place, and the tension of my own response to it, the same hushed sense of violating a sanctuary I'd experienced years earlier on a trip to my parents' native Scotland at the battlefield of Culloden.

Places where many lives had been taken violently, the earth soaked with their blood, seemed to create vibrations like a tuning fork within me, nothing so obvious as the spirits of the dead, but *something.* I, who had never shed blood for any cause, felt a kind of shame at my own petty ambitions and carping criticism of other people.

Shake it off, I thought. All you had to do was look at the history and biographies of the principals in this drama, and you would find enough pettiness and mean ambition to be getting on with. Getting lost in the alleged romance of it all distracted tourists from the reality that the essential cause one side fought for was the continued freedom to use other human beings as slaves. States' rights, my ass. I began climbing back up through the shade of the trees, realizing that I must be close to the spot where I had found the minié ball.

And with a sudden rush of blood to my ears and cheeks, I also recalled Deirdre's pushing me against a tree-trunk, her tongue shoving into my mouth and her hand groping my crotch. Even back then, when our passion for each other was at its strongest, she had tried to push the limits, as if needing proof of my willingness to make passion public, as if playing a scene.

The past continued to vibrate within me, whether prehistoric sharks' teeth, battlefield relics, or other images from the filmstrip of my own memory. Crunching twigs and leaves underfoot, brushing through a stand of fiddlehead ferns, I emerged into sunshine, blinking and shading my eyes.

Far down the slope of Cemetery Ridge, on the now-deserted field where Pickett's men had charged into a barrage of artillery and musket-fire fierce enough to turn the human form instantaneously into a red mist and fragments of flesh, I saw a distant figure emerge from the waving grass. A long-haired man in dark, bulky-looking clothes and a hat with one side of its brim pinned up, he was carrying what could only be a muzzle-loading musket, its shoulder-strap dangling. As I watched, he raised his weapon and seemed to sight it, not in my general direction, but right at me. My skin tingling, I fumbled for my cellphone and hurriedly thumbed at the screen to activate the camera, snapping a series of shots with only perfunctory aim.

Swiveling around, I glanced farther up the slope to where a man in cargo shorts and a photographer's vest stood holding a professional-looking camera with what looked like a telephoto lens.

"Did you get a clear shot of that re-enactor down there?" I called to the man, waving my cellphone toward the field.

He frowned at me. "Ain't no re-enactment scheduled for today," he said. "I got some great pictures of the field, though."

I persisted. "But didn't you get a shot of the guy down there? I snapped about five or six, myself."

Again, the photographer frowned, then shook his head. "Didn't see nobody down there."

I moved up the slope to where the guy stood with his expensive camera. I clicked my cellphone to show him the series of pictures I'd snapped. The photographs showed nothing but grass, trees, and a long wooden fence.

"See," the guy said. "Nothin'."

I spun and looked back down at the field. It was empty.

DETROIT

After spending the night at a Gettysburg bed-and-breakfast, where the landlord favored gingham and chintz décor, but not cross-dressing, I fortified myself with coffee and a cinnamon roll and got an early start toward the Motor City. Through breakfast and pulling onto the highway I couldn't shake the image of that re-enactor—or whatever he was—on the battlefield. I must have snapped my photos too quickly and missed what I was aiming at, even though I was positive I had seen the guy framed on my screen. The spell of the battlefield, I finally decided, and my clumsiness with the cellphone. I turned my attention to the road, punched on the car radio, and found an eclectic FM pop station.

The rest of the drive was blessedly relaxing. On the last leg of the journey on I-75 north through Toledo and on into Michigan, I felt no urgency to find my hosts right away. After driving through Mexican Town and past the Ambassador Bridge and the MGM Grand Casino, I steered the Highlander off the expressway near Comerica Park and the Fox Theatre then made my way to Woodward Avenue. I could have taken time to stop off at Hart Plaza and snap a picture of the Big Fist for Eileen, but I figured I'd get settled in my lodgings first. Synchronously, Bob

Seger began to rasp *Against the Wind* on the radio.

Even after years away from Detroit, I knew my way around downtown and the Wayne State campus, though I hadn't counted on having to negotiate the new Q-Line streetcar construction project on Woodward, apparently a way to encourage travel between New Center and the heart of the city. Large sections of Motown looked like some post-apocalyptic nightmare. The campus and its surrounding cultural center, however, still looked alive, at least the main layout, despite the many changes made since my undergraduate days some twenty years earlier.

Back then, I had seemed likely to end up teaching high school English in Redford or Royal Oak, trying to kindle the love of literature in gangly teenagers who had no more sense of culture than I'd had myself as I bumbled my way through to my diploma at Cass Technical High School. And now my students at Brixton, like countless others, looked at the world through the lenses of film, television, Google, Facebook, YouTube, Twitter, Instagram, Wikipedia, and the rest, giving them only a schizophrenic and tenuous hold on the distinctions among past, present, and probably future. The musings of an incipient old fart, I thought.

My father, who had always wanted to be a chemical engineer rather than an immigrant factory worker in a rivet plant on Vernor Highway, had coerced me into a science-heavy curriculum—three years of chemistry, two of physics and metallurgy, even a year of foundry, for God's sake, where the older of two teachers, Mr. Horn, had taken sadistic pleasure in stepping on my clumsily-wrought sand molds—"Do it over, McCutcheon"—and where I had always been afraid I would wind up pouring molten metal on my feet or somewhere even less appealing. My father had even tried to get me a summer job alongside him at Rix Manufacturing in an effort to awaken what he probably hoped was the dormant tradesman within me. I could still smell the scorched oil from the rivet machines and see the curls of metal shining on the factory floor. But the plant manager, who could have been Mr. Horn's younger brother, with square jaw and gray hair like a wire brush, had been able to sense my lack of passion for metal fasteners, even if they might wind up holding together a space shuttle. So I'd continued delivering *The Detroit News* on Eastside streets through the rest of my undistinguished high school years.

I had managed to graduate merely by the grace of Dr. Jarrow, the ancient head of the Chemistry Department. The old man looked at the pathetic thirty-percent score I had racked up on my final exam in organic chemistry, and said, "Don't worry, son. I've never failed a graduating senior in all my years at Cass." Department heads dispensed diplomas at the school, and when I marched across the stage amid the mob of fifteen-hundred high school seniors, old Jarrow waved the ribbon-tied escape certificate over his thin white crew-cut and actually winked at me as he handed it over.

I had skinned my way into the freshman class at Wayne State by passing the entrance exams. I wasn't stupid, and I didn't really hate science; I just hated science classes. But the three-year humiliation of high school persisted into my sophomore year in college, when I discovered that my instinctive retreat into an English major had actually allowed me to find something I was halfway decent at. In the dusty academic-non-chic of the classrooms in State Hall, and the offices of the few English professors who were impressed by my clumsy working-class intellectual groping, I found something like a calling. People who got paid to decide on such matters told me I could read and write better than most, so I figured being a schoolteacher would give me a career by default.

And even though Professors Gray, Golden, and Leopold convinced me I could get into graduate school, then helped get me a fellowship at the University of Delaware, I had still thought teaching would be my only option. I certainly never imagined winding up being a writer, much less an actor and a playwright. I did eventually wind up teaching, but creative writing rather than high-school literature and career English. Even a relatively successful writer had to make a living.

And, as I discovered, even relative success as a writer attracted good-looking, though often complicated, women who were difficult to resist. As one of my almost-famous actor friends had remarked, "The thing about adulation is, it goes straight to your dick."

The night before I'd left Brixton, Eileen reminded me of that story, saying, "Let the wild adulation begin." Well, here I was, ready and willing.

2

Having a play produced at my alma mater still felt like an incredibly unlikely development. After all, I never acted until starting on my doctorate at Delaware, never wrote a play until after I had compiled a modest publication list of fiction and poetry, and, of course, I never was a theatre student.

For years after I started writing for the stage, after my work began being published and produced around the country, I had resigned myself to being an unknown quantity in Detroit, except to my relatives and old school friends with whom I was never quite able to shake my image as a personable fuck-up. But here I was, about to attend rehearsals at Wayne State's Hilberry Studio Theatre, not to mention being lodged at the swanky Inn on Ferry Street just across Woodward from campus.

My parents had sold their bungalow in St. Clair Shores ten years earlier to settle in St. Petersburg among the palm trees and geckos. My visits with them in Florida had always struck me like being on a film set, with glaring sunlight and pastels everywhere, and they both appeared to feel isolated and aimless in the cut-rate luxury of their stucco ranch with its orange trees and lanai-sheltered pool. True to my father's pragmatic approach, they had gotten rid of almost all their Michigan possessions, right down to the Christmas and Halloween ornaments, so their new home held few memories for me. Then they were both suddenly gone, killed instantly on their way north to visit me at Brixton when the right front tire of their Pontiac had blown out on I-75, plunging them off the highway into a wooded ravine. Like an amputation, the trauma of their deaths had cut me off from the rest of the widely-scattered and never gregarious family.

After their Florida funerals, I had disposed of their generic furniture and their unfamiliar house, feeling not only grief, but also that I didn't deserve to profit from their passing. My father had imposed his Scots frugality on the household, so I had inherited a surprising six-figure bank account that Deirdre had somehow felt entitled to part of, even though we'd been divorced for a couple of years by then. I certainly wished my parents were still around to enjoy their retirement, perhaps even to take some pleasure from such success as I had enjoyed, especially this production. My mother had usually applauded my various accomplishments without reservation. The only unalloyed compliment I could recall from my father was a terse acknowledgement of my skill at parallel parking. Hoping for compliments from him was always a waste of energy. As my mother had often noted, true to her Scots-Irish heritage, "If wishes were horses, beggars would ride." I had to admit, though, to a certain guilt-tinged gratitude at being free from my parents' inevitable interrogations into my personal life.

When Deirdre and I had gotten divorced, my mother said, "I don't think you can blame your father and me for your troubles."

I was irritated enough to say, "If you want any credit for everything good that happens to me, maybe you should take some responsibility for the bad stuff, too." She had looked so stricken, I immediately apologized. And for all my father's attempts to push me into science, I had to acknowledge that my mother's love of music and encouragement of my singing at family gatherings—including my gift for mimicking various accents—had probably done more to set me on a theatrical path than I realized at the time.

Now, as I neared my destination, sunlight broke through the fall overcast of dirty-looking clouds that hung overhead. Dirty clouds, dirty city: what everyone expected when entering the nation's model for urban blight and fiscal hopelessness. But despite the dusty chaos of Q-Line construction on Woodward, the campus, the Detroit Institute of Arts, the medical complex, and the rest of the cultural center were a welcome island amid the predominantly dismal Detroit landscape, and the sunshine gave an attractive sheen to the streets and buildings. Even back when I was in high school and college, taking three buses back and forth on my daily commutes from the East side, the city's appearance and atmosphere varied sharply with the seasons.

I remembered the damp, marrow-chilling winter walks to the bus stop on Warren Avenue and the occasional painful sidewalk tumbles into wet, partially frozen snow under mottled gray and white clouds. Returning to the present and Bob Seger, now singing the Eugene Williams song, *Tryin' to Live My Life Without You*, I decided I was finally running *with* the wind, at least for the time being. I was certainly trying to live my life without, well—almost everyone.

As Eileen had told me so many times, I needed to loosen up. I turned off the radio and made a right turn through the construction zone onto Ferry, noting off to my left the Merrill-Palmer Institute, where, as an undergrad, I spent several weeks observing and recording the interactions of preschoolers for a sociology class. Almost immediately on my right was the bed-and-breakfast I'd be lodged in for the next few days. The Inn on Ferry was actually a collection of six buildings, four impressively-restored Victorian mansions and two no-less attractive carriage houses. After parking my SUV, I lugged my overnight bag up the few stairs that led into the main building.

Behind the reception desk, a cheerful, golden-skinned African American woman introduced herself as Latrece, the Inn's manager. When I gave her my name, she nodded and smiled proprietorially. "You're our distinguished playwright and actor from out East," she said. "Welcome to the Motor City. Apologies about the construction project. We hope it doesn't inconvenience you too much during your stay."

"I'm an old Detroit boy," I said. "I'm used to threading my way through digs and demolition."

"Which part of town are you from?"

I knew she would expect me to name some suburb safely outside city limits. "East side. Grew up just far enough out of Grosse Pointe not to be rich," I said. "Went to Cass Tech and the big school over there on the other side of Woodward."

Her smile broadened. "That's just how my own education went, though I grew up near Eight Mile. You know, like in the movie with Mekhi Phifer."

"I thought that was Eminem."

"Maybe that's how *you* remember it. Mekhi was *fine*. Even though he wasn't from the Motor City. Harlem's a pretty good place to be from for a brother." She grinned with good humor and a glint of mischief in her eyes.

"Wasn't he in *ER*, too?"

"That's right." Her inflection reminded me for an instant of the Tigers' recently-fired TV broadcaster Rod Allen.

"*ER* was set in Chicago," I said. "The Midwest's been pretty good for Mekhi."

"Maybe you'll write something for him in your next play." She waved off my reaching for my wallet. "Everything is all set for you. People from the Theatre Department took care of your accommodations. We have a special relationship with the university. You'll be in our Owen House. I'll be happy to show you to your room."

3

Ten minutes later, Latrece had given me a quick introduction to my Victorian-style room with its bay window and conveniently placed writing-desk, its inviting queen-size bed, flat-screen television concealed in the armoire, and complimentary bottle of water and oatmeal-raisin cookies on the nightstand. I had also duly admired the Jacuzzi tub in the bathroom, though if Victorian toilette design had to be flouted, I would have preferred a walk-in shower. I thanked Latrece, closed the door behind her, slung my bag on the luggage stand, then unpacked my laptop and set it on the desk, confident in the manager's assurance that the Inn's Wi-Fi was strong and required no password.

Besides the usual thirty or so unfiltered junk messages from dunning Democrats, come-ons from Nigerian bankers and widows promising me millions in exchange for my personal information, Facebook notices and the like, there was the inevitable message from Deirdre, with the subject line, "Screwed Any Good Coeds Lately?" I sent it to the trash bin, unread. So much for romantic memories.

I hoped Deirdre wouldn't launch into another remote attack on *Swept Away*, as she had done during its off-

Broadway run. I'd been careful to skirt or alter any biographical content, but she went berserk simply because the plot dealt with an adulterous relationship. She even went so far as to consult with her divorce lawyer on the feasibility of a libel suit. The lawyer had pointed out that she would be wasting her time and money, earning her contempt for what she called his cowardice and misogyny. She finally had to content herself with her own libelous emails, though Facebook had mercifully removed her postings as abusive. But I knew she was, however ironically, quite capable of showing up at an audition for some future production, convinced that her status as ex-wife-of-the-playwright constituted some special qualification for whatever role she might want.

The only other email of note was from Ed Friend, the director of my play, letting me know his schedule for the rest of the week. This included rehearsals, social gatherings, and appearances in classes, one of which would be mid-morning the next day, followed by a public talk and Q-and-A about playwriting.

Ed added, "I'll drop by and pick you up for rehearsal tonight. We could do dinner first, then go out with the cast and crew afterwards, maybe head to the Cass Café. I thought you might want to relax this afternoon. Rehearsals are going well, but I'm sure the cast will have questions. Great play, by the way. I like it even better the more we work with it."

The text of the email was free of cuteness—no Emojis, little faces, cryptic symbols, or other electronic rubbish—a small but encouraging sign of the director's good sense.

I replied, agreeing to Ed's plan for the evening. After the drive from Gettysburg, the chance to relax seemed like a wise choice. I took another deep breath and leaned back in my chair, which I would have liked to cart off as a replacement for the clunker in my office. I valued these transitional periods between arrival and entry into the fray, when I could simply enjoy looking forward to a production without the apprehension or tension that inevitably accompanied such a complex human enterprise.

In a moment of clarity, I realized I was in much the same position with respect to the rest of my life. And here I was, back in Detroit, as if I were starting over. As I sat there noting the way the sunshine set off the Victorian architecture and artfully placed stained glass windows, I sensed a silent presence behind me.

Then, startling me, a soft voice said, "Be careful." Latrece with a message, or news of some amenity she had forgotten to mention? A maid?

I turned my chair toward the door, where a plain-faced young woman, perhaps in her twenties or early thirties, stood on the threshold, smiling slightly, as if I had just said something mildly amusing. The door had been closed, and I hadn't heard it open.

"Can I help you?" I said, and rose from the chair.

The woman backed out of the room without a word and turned soundlessly to her right, disappearing around the doorjamb. I moved toward the door, realizing as I did that she had been wearing some sort of nineteenth-century costume. Perhaps she was an employee, hired to enhance the historic ambience of the place. "Wait," I said.

But when I reached the doorway and looked down the hall, the woman was nowhere to be seen. She couldn't have disappeared so quickly and without a sound, short of ducking into a secret passage. A chill hung over the threshold, like the feeling when someone opens an outside door on a winter day. I felt the hairs on the back of my neck stiffen, and my eardrums clicked as with a sudden change of air-pressure.

Be careful. Was that what she'd said?

I went back into the room, closed the door, and turned on the flat-screen television for something prosaic to counteract the strangeness of what had just occurred. The Tigers wouldn't be playing until later in the evening, by which time I'd be at rehearsal, so I settled for reruns on HGTV. I leaned back on the bed, propped up by pillows, thinking about the man with the musket who had walked out of the woods into the Wheatfield at Gettysburg. Images of Deirdre, my departed parents, the Detroit of my childhood, flitted through my mind like random photos spilled from an envelope.

Finally, as I watched an affluent young couple arguing over which house to buy, I surrendered drowsily to the effects of the drive and the unreality of all that had happened over the last two days.

4

I woke to the perky inconsequence of yet another *House Hunters* episode. Feeling a little silly about my own apprehension, I turned off the television, got out of bed, and checked around the room, but found nothing amiss. I went into the bathroom and splashed water on my face, which, reflected in the mirror, looked like a mug shot. Then I decided my best course of action was my usual one. Write something.

I roused my computer and started a new document. Typing as rapidly as my self-taught fingers allowed, I pecked an account of my drive from Brixton, including the equally haunting stops at the diner and the battlefield; then I added a description of my encounter with the young woman at the door of my room. I also appended some notes about the death of my parents, which seemed like a part of the puzzle. I tried to keep the prose as matter-of-fact as possible, without speculation or introspection. For months, I'd been concentrating determinedly on my present; now my past was reasserting itself.

When I finished typing, I hit save, then copied the document into an email and sent it to Eileen, with the subject line "Ghosts" and an introductory message that simply said, "Talk about the dead hand of the past. I'll catch you up on other stuff later. Say hey to Maxine."

I put the computer back to sleep and decided a shower and a change of clothes would help me to refocus on the present and the future. One question still nagging in my mind was why someone here at Wayne had suddenly decided my play would be a worthy addition to the Theatre Department's season. The answer to that one certainly couldn't be supernatural.

5

When I walked into the Inn's main lobby to wait for Ed Friend, I greeted Latrece, then in a deliberately casual tone asked, "Do you have any kind of special event going on right now? A reception? A wedding?"

"Nothing right now, Mr. McCutcheon," she said, her penciled eyebrows arching quizzically.

"You don't have employees who dress up in Victorian costumes to enhance the atmosphere?"

"No, sir," she said, her tone guarded. "Why do you ask?"

"Earlier today, a young woman in a long dress with all the trimmings opened the locked door to my room while I was at the desk. I didn't hear any sound at all. She said, 'Be careful.' When I asked if I could help her, she backed out and disappeared. There was nowhere for her to go, not that quickly." I looked at her steadily. "She just disappeared."

Latrece's mouth tightened. "I'm so sorry, Mr. McCutcheon. Our security is excellent. We try to ensure that our guests won't have to worry about intruders or disturbances. No one else is supposed to be in Owen House at the moment." She picked up a pen and began fiddling with it. "What can we do to make it up to you?"

I shook my head. "Oh, don't worry about that. No harm done. It was just a little theatrical moment. Maybe an acting student playing a trick on the visiting writer."

She set down the pen and managed a smile. "We're not big on tricks at the Inn, sir." As I turned to head for the door, she said, "Oh, speaking of young ladies reminds me. This came for you before you checked in, and I forgot to give it to you." From a cubbyhole behind the desk she withdrew a small pink envelope and handed it to me. "A woman hand-delivered it this morning."

"In modern dress, I assume? She wasn't transparent?"

She nodded and smiled indulgently. "Not even a little bit. She was very beautiful."

I thanked her and moved to the door, where I opened the envelope with my tiny Swiss Army knife. Then I unfolded the card, which bore a small reproduction of an Edward Hopper South Truro seascape. The message was written in violet ink. Its flowing cursive read, "Dear Dennis, I'll be at your talk tomorrow. See if you can pick me out." There was no signature, just a small ink-drawn heart.

I didn't recognize the handwriting, though it seemed somehow familiar. Someone from my Detroit past? Another ghost? God, I thought, could Deirdre possibly have gotten someone to write the card? I sincerely hoped not.

6

As I sat in the lobby waiting for Ed Friend, my cellphone trilled. I quickly checked the screen—Eileen.

"Not even gone for a couple of days and you've already logged two paranormal encounters," Eileen said. "Who you gonna call?"

"Not you, Buster. Anyway, that's not all." I filled her in on the Edward Hopper card and its brief message.

"My oh my," Eileen said. "Two ghosts and a mystery woman. And you haven't even gotten to the real point of your trip. I said you needed to jump-start your life, but this is an embarrassment of riches. My advice is, forget the ghosts and go with the mystery woman."

"Yeah," I said. "But I need to stay focused on the production and avoid too many distractions."

"Dennis, buddy," Eileen said, "relax. Go with the flow. You've done all the work already. Just enjoy the fruits of your labor. You're the man. And just remember, 'If there's something weird, and it don't look good, who you gonna call?'"

"Right," I said. "I'll keep it in mind." As I spoke, Latrece caught my eye and pointed out the window at the parking lot, where a red SUV had just pulled in. "Nobody drives sedans any more, do they?" I said.

After a momentary silence on the other end of the line, Eileen said, "Not unless they manage to snag a vintage Celica. Or is that just one of your dramatic non-sequiturs?"

"Sorry," I said. "My ride's here."

"Don't forget to stay in touch. And let the current sweep you away." She disconnected before I could respond.

Ed Friend walked into the lobby, grinning when he saw me. He stuck out his hand. "Dr. McCutcheon, I presume."

"Dennis will do nicely," I said. The handshake was dry and firm.

Ed was in his forties, with tousled, gray-flecked black hair, and the beginnings of a small pot-belly. He was dressed for rehearsal in jeans, WSU sweatshirt and work boots, and seemed encouragingly normal.

A few minutes later, introductory small talk out of the way, and after he'd snagged one of the inn's complimentary oatmeal-raisin cookies, the two of us walked down the steps from the Inn to Ed's Ford Escape. I buckled my seatbelt and briefly described my encounter with the young woman at the door of my room.

Firing up the Ford, Ed finished chewing his cookie and grinned at me. "The Inn's supposed to be haunted. At least a couple ghosts I've heard about. Latrece obviously doesn't see the story as an attractive feature, no matter how much it appeals to the local press. Innkeepers and real-estate agents probably rank ghosts just below rodents, roaches, and bedbugs." He winked and patted his stomach. "I do love those free cookies."

As we pulled out of the parking lot, I glanced back at the building where I was supposed to be the only guest. In one of the windows, I thought I could see a pale oval face looking down at me.

7

My preoccupation with the apparition, if that was even a marginally appropriate description, and with the mysterious Hopper notecard, faded quickly once Ed and I arrived at the Theatre Department in Old Main for an introduction to Dr. Addante, the department chair.

"Genevieve," she said as we shook hands in her office. She was a short woman with bobbed hair and wire-rimmed glasses. Her clothes, tweedy and academic, looked more like those of a scholar than a theatre artist. I knew from my visits to the departmental website that her primary focus was theatre and drama criticism—she'd written books on *commedia dell'arte* and Sartre—though she kept a hand in the game by directing one show every season.

I thanked her for including *Swept Away* in their current lineup. "Oh," she said, "I can't take credit for that. Actually, the suggestion came from our Associate Dean of Fine Arts, Wily Fox."

"Wily Fox?" I said. "Really?"

"No." She tilted a shoulder. "His name's actually Willy."

"But around here that's close enough for a nickname," Ed said.

"I'm sure you'll meet him in due course," Dr. Addante said. Then she waved her hand around apologetically at her office and reception area. "We're in the middle of a campaign to build a new version of the Hilberry. Right now, we're pretty scattered, with offices in Old Main and classrooms here and there. There's the Bonstelle, of course, on Woodward. The new construction will give us our offices, classrooms, and mainstage in the same building. We'll convert the existing Hilberry into a multi-use black box. We have the plan. Now all we need is the money."

"So says every arts organization in the world, I guess." I gestured over my shoulder. "I actually took a fencing class in Old Main from a former Hungarian Olympic coach, Istvan Mihalyfy. He used to hit us on the helmet with his epée and say, 'Lowerr *en garrde!*' At least it kept me from having to take a bowling class. He's not still here, is he?"

"Retired years ago," Addante said. "Went back to Hungary, I think."

"That's right," Ed said. "But I understand he used to help out the department with stage combat. You never graced the stage here, though, did you?"

"Back then, I was an English major with no theatrical pretensions."

"That's okay," he said. "You're still an alum. Genevieve will probably put the bite on you for a donation."

"Good luck with that," I said to both of them. "I have a plan. Now all I need is the money."

The Studio Theatre was an easy walk from Old Main, in the basement of the Hilberry Theatre, a former Christian Scientist Church at the corner of Cass and Hancock, complete with Ionic columns and other Greek revival architectural touches. I would have been pleased if my play were being produced upstairs on the main stage, but I was realistic enough to know that filling a hundred seats a night for a short run would be more likely than filling five hundred. And if I hadn't been realistic enough, Dr. Addante had pointed it out in one of her follow-up emails and again before we left her office.

"Every time I talk to an administrator," I said, "I wonder how I ever got a job in academe."

"Me, too." Ed led the way down to the theatre, laughing. "At least we're doing what we love."

8

The rehearsal was pretty typical. They had gotten beyond early slogging through lines and blocking, but the proceeding showed only a few glimpses of any magic that might develop by opening night. I had seen the process from both sides, as actor and writer, so I was able to discern the real play lurking in the rehearsal version, especially considering the four main characters, two couples in their thirties, were being played by actors ten years younger.

I could tell, though, that the performers and I were in good hands with Ed. He was a gentle and good-humored director, but one who insisted relentlessly on his cast's following Hamlet's advice to the players, especially, "Speak the speech as it is written," advice I have never seen improved upon.

I always quailed a bit when sitting in on rehearsal for the first time, anticipating the inevitable questions from actors looking for deep back-stories on characters or for authorial disquisitions about theme, and of course for tips on performance. The only recommendation I was tempted to add to Hamlet's was, *louder, faster, funnier.* No one seemed to know the source of that one, and actors often felt insulted by it, but I was amazed by its relevance to almost every production I had ever been involved in.

After the rehearsal, I applauded sincerely. The actors were growing on me, and were doing as well as I could have hoped with a play full of brief scenes that called for real concentration from moment to moment. And Ed was guiding them toward an ending that I hoped would be genuinely moving without losing an element of humor. *A Serious Comedy*, I had subtitled it.

My only mental reservation was with regard to Anna, who was portraying one of the play's two deceived spouses. I had tried to write her as genuinely attempting to cope with her betrayal, making her ultimate act of vengeance all the more poignant because it is unexpected. Anna's pale complexion and almost neurasthenic good looks seemed perfect for the character, but her performance so far seemed to project an initial querulousness that could make her husband's turning elsewhere seem almost inevitable.

As usual, I wondered if the fault lay in my writing, if somehow my retrospective anger at Deirdre had subconsciously taken control. I discarded the notion. I had worked too hard on getting the character right. Perhaps I could give Ed a private word to the wise. But I knew Eileen would tell me to keep my trap shut.

After the customary exchange of compliments, and before heading for after-rehearsal drinks, we all sat down onstage for twenty minutes or so of back and forth about the play.

Mark, the tall and earnest young man who played one of the illicit lovers, jumped right in with the most obvious question. "My character has the same first name as you. Are you drawing on your own life here?"

I shrugged. "Only to the degree that I use scraps of experience here and there. Like Dennis in the play, I've been through a divorce. But the play's not auto-biographical. Using my own first name just amused me." They all looked at me. "Hard to believe, I know. But it's nothing more profound than that."

Paul, a stocky twenty-five-year-old with a gray-shot beard, played the oldest character, a museum director who perhaps had to deal with the play's most challenging complications—not only being cuckolded, but also having to describe, then deal with his failure to avert the death of a character never seen onstage. "The story involves a number of offstage deaths that affect the four of us onstage," Paul began. The other actors murmured assent; they all wanted to know more about this. "What's your thematic intent with those developments?"

The question I dreaded most of all. But I reminded myself that what you had to do with a bullet was bite it. "I actually never think about theme when I'm writing," I said, with what I hoped was a disarming shrug. "I just try to get the stuff right and pay attention to construction. My reasoning is, if you do that, you can't avoid having a theme. If you threatened to drop a sandbag on me from the flies, I guess I'd say I felt the characters needed to deal with larger complications—and death's the big one—besides their relationship issues."

This, thankfully, seemed to satisfy everyone. Then Anna said, "I'm curious about your decision never to have the four characters onstage together, and to let the lovers and the abandoned spouses appear together only in the final scene."

"Well," I said, "that's where the stuff and the

construction come in. With this play, I set myself the task of dramatizing the affair's effects on the original two couples. I also decided I'd try to write the play in lots of scenes and make each one like a short one-act, even though that's not the usual way of constructing a full-length drama."

Anna pressed the matter. "Why did you decide to do that?"

"It's like writing a sonnet," I said. "You hem yourself in with a set of restrictions, then see how they affect your original intent. In my experience, they pull things out of you that you didn't know were in there, things you might never have come up with otherwise."

Mark, the tall and earnest young man, said, "Doesn't that risk taking some of the magic out of it?"

"Not for the audience. *They* get to believe in magic. All of *us* believe in practice and technique—the *illusion* of magic."

The other lover, Rachel, whose unruly red hair went well with her artist character, nodded wistfully and said, "So. No magic."

I shrugged and spread my palms upward. "That depends. If you've ever seen Baryshnikov or Fred Astaire dance, you know they believe in technique and practice. But do *you* believe in their magic? You decide. I know I do."

Rachel smiled, nodded, and gave me one of those *I'm available* looks I had seen from women in other productions I had written or acted in. I reminded myself to stay professional. Too many writers wound up reinforcing clichés and leaving bad feelings behind them. And students were off-limits. Rachel was attractive, though—she was an actress, after all—and for quite a while now, my life had been devoid of simple female companionship, other than Eileen, let alone anything more physical. I nodded and smiled back.

Later, at the restaurant, Ed said in an undertone, "I like your bit about magic and illusion. I may steal it."

"Feel free," I said. "I probably stole it, too."

9

Back at the Inn, after leaving a wakeup call with the night-clerk, my head buzzing a bit from the effects of too much mediocre Pinot Grigio on an empty stomach, I realized I was looking around the room for evidence of another presence. But all I could see were the cookies left on my nightstand by the maid, the obvious result of practice and technique, rather than magic.

I decided to check my email messages while nibbling on one of them. Almost all of the messages were advertising or politics, eminently deletable. Happily, I saw nothing from Deirdre. But there was one from Eileen.

"Hey, buddy," she said. "I did a bit of Googling after I spoke with you earlier. Your current digs *are* supposed to be haunted, but it all reads like the typical newspaper and tourist hype. As for the battlefield, you can find tons of videos, so-called guided tours, and other loony stuff about *the ghosts of Gettysburg*. It's pretty much a cottage industry there. What you saw—if you saw anything at all— was probably someone from the Visitor Center having a little fun. I'll submit my bill for ghostbusting in due course." She had signed the message *Dr. Peter Venkman*, the Bill Murray character from the movie.

I typed in a quick answer. "You have a better chance of

getting slimed by ectoplasm than collecting on any bill you send me. But thanks for the report." I smiled as I sent the message zipping into the ether.

Even so, as I stood at the bathroom mirror brushing my teeth, I kept glancing at the door reflected behind me, reminded of random mirror moments from horror films. And when I settled down in my enormous-seeming bed and switched off the bedside lamp, I lay awake in the semi-darkness for some time. My senses were attuned to any slight shift in what little light seeped in from the windows or some untoward click or creak from whatever might be walking the night. But nothing manifested itself, natural or supernatural, except the sound of my wake-up call when morning came.

My ablutions accomplished, and fortified by coffee and a couple of croissants, I used the free morning to walk over to State Hall, where I tried to look up my favorite English professors, Esther Leopold, Philip Gay, and Aaron Golden.

My quest led me first to the office of the current chair, Ariadne Jamison, who—like chairs almost everywhere in academe—was protected from casual visitors by an administrative assistant, in this case a full-figured African American woman wearing a multicolored caftan and a turquoise turban. The nameplate on her desk read "Queen C. Digby," and when I coughed discreetly to get her attention, her raised eyebrows and appraising stare discouraged me from making any smart-assed remark about her first name.

Once I explained who I was and why I was there, however, Ms. Digby smiled broadly and said, "Welcome back to Wayne State." She then raised her considerable bulk from behind her desk, tapped on Dr. Jamison's door, and announced me as a distinguished alumnus.

Dr. Jamison was also African American but, in contrast to Ms. Digby, was small, wispy-thin, and dressed in a conservative, expensively-tailored pantsuit. Not surprisingly, she confessed herself previously unaware of me or my reason for being on campus. She also let me know that Phil Gay—who first let me know that my writing was not merely serviceable, but gave evidence of talent and a good mind—had retired three years before; the dry-witted Shakespeare scholar and his wife were now soaking up Florida sunshine in a bayside condo in Naples. Esther Leopold, who encouraged me to think about applying to graduate schools, was on sabbatical, having just left Detroit with her husband for a year in England, where she was probably just finishing a day's research for a book on the Brownings. I remembered saying to her, "I can't afford to go to grad school."

Dr. Leopold had smiled and said, "They'll pay you." So off I went, my incipient career as a high school teacher receding in the rearview mirror.

"Well, nothing for two so far," I said to Dr. Jamison. "I'll have to email them both. I just took a chance on dropping in."

But Dr. Jamison then told me that Aaron Golden was not only still teaching, he was actually in his office, the same one he occupied when I was in his eighteenth-century poetry class. "Go on," she said. "I'll try to get to your talk, and I'll be sure to see your play. Watch for a piece about you in the next issue of the department newsletter."

Before I left the outer office, Ms. Digby, who had overheard her boss's last remark, said, "Watch for us to ask you for a donation to the creative writing program, too. We never waste a chance."

I flashed her a grin. "That's show-biz."

I made my way down a flight of stairs and along the once familiar hallway. Aaron Golden's office door was open, as it almost always was during my undergrad years, and Golden looked up immediately from his desk when my shadow fell across the threshold.

"I'm not sure I'd have recognized you after all this time," Golden said, "if I didn't keep up on theatre news on campus." Bald, swarthy, and stocky, Golden rose and grasped my hand firmly, then gestured toward a chair. "Sit, sit." I did so, and Golden resumed his place behind his desk. As he sized me up, I noted that he seemed younger than he had in my student days, when everyone on the faculty had looked elderly. I was obviously catching up. "So," he said, "the prodigal returns, eh? And who'd have imagined you'd be back as a playwright?"

"The last time I saw you, Dr. Golden," I began.

"Aaron. Aaron," Golden said. "We're colleagues now."

"You had a lot to do with that, Aaron," I said. "The last time I saw you, I told you I had offers of fellowships or assistantships at three different grad schools. You remember what you said?"

"Probably asked you which of 'em was offering you the most money."

"Bingo. And when I said, 'What about comparing programs, faculty, stuff like that?' you said—"

"You can be a bum anywhere. And if you're any good, it won't matter where you go, so take the money." He shrugged. "It's advice I've given to a pretty long line of promising students."

"Well," I said, "I took it. And bum or not, I've certainly turned out a lot different from the kid you saw in your office that day. I never really expected to wind up writing—or acting—much less teaching at a university."

Golden poked a stubby finger at me. "I do remember you showed me a play you'd done some work on."

I laughed. "You have a good memory. It wasn't a play of mine. I was taking a French class. We were reading Racine's *Andromache*, so for practice, I thought I'd try translating it."

"That's right," Golden said. "In rhyming couplets, I recall, like the original. I think I said you had a long way to go before Richard Wilbur had any cause to worry."

"Yep. I abandoned it after about five pages."

"But you did keep writing. I'm looking forward to your presentation. And I'll be at your play on opening night."

"That's great," I said. "What I really dropped by for was to thank you. Your class made me see literature as more than just a puzzle to be solved, and your advice actually changed my life."

10

Buoyed by my visit with Aaron Golden, I decided to see if I could track Wily Fox to his lair and thank the Associate Dean of Fine Arts for recommending *Swept Away* for production.

I checked my map app for the administration building of the cumbersomely named College of Fine, Performing, and Communication Arts. I found it was located a few blocks away on what, in my undergrad days, was the northeast corner of Second Avenue and Putnam, but was now 5104 Gullen Mall, named after a recent WSU president. Dating from 1904, Linsell House was one of the numerous restored historic homes on and around campus, many of them now refitted for offices.

I found my way from State Hall to where Linsell House sat across from the University Bookstore near the massive and incongruously modern Adamany Undergraduate Library, named for an even more recent president. I stopped for a few seconds on the front path to admire the fine arts building's Federal Revival architecture, with its peak-roofed porch and second-floor Palladian window. Trust the administration to find a suitably distinguished place to spend the working day.

Unfortunately, when I approached the Dean's

secretary, Ms. Scott, an attractive blonde in the mold of Ellie Endicott, I found that I had tracked the fox to the wrong den. "Associate Dean Fox's office is on the third floor of Old Main," she said. "It's 304-B. But I doubt that you'll find him there. He's had a series of meetings off-campus this month." She seemed a little discomposed, maybe because she wasn't able to fulfill my request. Then she smiled. "I'm sure he'll be delighted to meet you in due course, though. His academic specialty *is* theatre."

After thanking Ms. Scott and finding out that her boss, the Dean of the College, was also involved in the off-campus meetings, I decided I would head for Old Main anyway. I hadn't been inside the building for years, though I knew the little gym where Coach Mihalyfy had hit me on the head in fencing class was now subdivided and transformed into office space like the innards of so many other timeworn buildings.

But despite the changes, the echoing space of the old pile, with its terrazzo floors, high ceilings, and ornate beams and lintels, took me back to my days under Coach Mihalyfy's sardonic tutelage. I learned the rudiments of the rapier, the epée, and the saber, and I recalled that the coach's final exam was an elimination tournament pitting both male and female students against each other, with course grades depending on the order of finish. The most aggressive and least chivalrous guy in the class, Lionel *something*, had won by attacking every opponent like a berserker, completely ignoring the aesthetics of fencing. Though I managed to last long enough to earn a decent grade, I remembered Lionel's dispatching me with a whack on the helmet from his epée. So, Coach M wasn't the only agent of assaults on my brain-pan.

I had preferred the rapier (or as coach Mihalyfy insisted, "Not ze *rapier*, but ze *foil*), the most delicate of the three weapons, dependent on thrust and parry, rather than the more extreme swings of the other two blades. Though I took the course mainly to avoid bowling or swimming, it stood me in good stead after graduation, when I had discovered acting and had been cast as Hotspur. I was a long way from Stewart Granger crossing blades with Mel Ferrer in *Scaramouche*, but choreographed fencing with Prince Hal was far preferable to dealing with crazy Lionel.

I made my way through dimly-lit hallways and finally found myself standing in front of an office door identified as 304-B. Beneath the frosted glass pane, a small plastic sign plate proclaimed that I'd come to the office of Dr. William Fox, Associate Dean of the various arms of Fine Arts. If anyone was in there, he was saving on the light bill. I tried the handle. Locked. I knocked. No response. Fox evidently had no secretary, which seemed odd. At Brixton, this sort of isolation would have looked like some kind of administrative punishment. But perhaps he just liked being elusive. Very wily.

When I decided I'd had enough useless fox-hunting and nostalgia for one morning, I took out my cellphone and Googled the associate dean. The process took longer than I expected, starting with the Wayne State homepage. I finally discovered Fox's own staff page, from which I learned the man's degrees—from Harvard and NYU—were in contemporary theatre, and that he had actually done a fair amount of acting and directing. He was also, surprisingly, a trustee of the DIA. Quite the Renaissance man. Surprisingly good going for a college administrator.

More to the point, the page had a photograph of Fox, dressed appropriately in a dark suit and tie, but with an assertive purple shirt befitting his theatre background. His hair was cut expensively, a touch longer than administratively necessary, and his handsome, tanned face was highlighted by a smile that flashed white teeth regular enough to suggest a considerable investment in dental care. Well, at least I would know him when, if ever, I met him face to face.

Reflecting that the Old Main connection would give me something to talk about with the hard-to-corner Wily Fox, beyond offering him obsequious thanks, I walked out of the building into a light drizzle and headed through the raindrops toward the Inn.

My public talk took place at eleven a.m. in the Studio Theatre, and I was grateful again to be in the small space. Literary readings could be embarrassing for all concerned, readers and organizers alike, when the audience turned out to be the organizers, a few would-be writing students, and the occasional savvy street person who wandered in for the free refreshments. At least the drizzle had abated, which was all to the good.

"Any chance of Dean Fox being here today?" I asked, as Ed Friend and I walked to the theatre. "I tried to drop in on him this morning, but he was off at a meeting. I'd like to thank him for suggesting you take on the play."

"I think he has some sort of administrative gathering today," Ed said.

"So I hear from the dean's secretary." I pictured Fox flashing his male-model smile among a bunch of fusty administrators.

"Ah, yes, the attractive Ms. Scott." Ed shook his head wryly. "Not much interested in dating academics."

I thought immediately of Ellie Endicott back in Brixton. "My department chair has a secretary with the same kind of looks and the same opinion of faculty members. Maybe Dean Fox doesn't care for those of us in the peasant class, either."

Ed looked vaguely embarrassed. "I'm sure he's looking forward to meeting you."

I shrugged. "I'm surprised he's stuck over in Old Main. And without a secretary, so far as I could tell."

Again, Ed seemed hesitant. "I guess," he finally said, "he likes playing hard to get. Values his independence."

"No doubt," I said. Ed looked relieved to get off the subject. Academic relationships, I knew from bitter experience, could be fraught.

I realized I had no reason to feel anything but gratitude to Fox, but I couldn't help wondering why such an obviously hotshot administrator had singled me out for special favor. Something just didn't seem to add up. Well, in administrative phraseology, I would no doubt find out *in due course.*

When Ed and I entered the auditorium, I was relieved to see a sizable crowd already assembled. If I managed not to alienate them, perhaps the play might even bring out enough theatregoers to justify the production expenses. I glanced around to see if I could spot the mysterious woman who had left the notecard at the Inn but, aside from Drs. Golden, Jamison, and Addante, I saw no one who looked familiar. Mysterious females were becoming a motif.

Ed introduced me and got a scattering of polite applause. Then we both sat back in the front row while the cast presented two early scenes from the play. Ed had picked scenes that didn't run the risk of being spoilers for opening night. They generated some laughs, too, which couldn't hurt box-office, and the audience response afterward was encouragingly enthusiastic.

I resisted making notes on my iPhone, remembering a director I worked with who insisted on sitting in the house making rehearsal notes on an old portable typewriter. For the actors, the effect had been like someone firing a small automatic weapon at the stage. I turned off my phone. While waving me onstage again to a podium just left of center, Ed referred to me as "Detroit's own, Dennis McCutcheon," which now garnered a genuinely warm reception.

I thanked Ed, the actors, and everyone else I could manage to think of, including the elusive Wily Fox. Next, I dealt briefly with Mark's question about autobiography from the night before, figuring I needed to get that out of the way. Then, I let the audience ask questions. These were surprisingly acute, covering much the same territory as the actors' queries, though with more interest in general biographical and broader professional matters.

"How does being a Detroiter influence your work? Or have you, like so many other former residents, gladly turned your back on the city?" This from an earnest-looking man with a fringe of gray hair, a high forehead, and the Asperger's-like mien of so many university faculty, though the brevity of his question might have argued otherwise.

I wondered when the man himself had taken up residence in Detroit. But I answered dutifully. "I left town because I got a fellowship at a good grad school out East. Then I went where I could find a job. As you know, announcing a job opening in academe these days is like throwing chum to a lagoon full of sharks." This drew a ripple of amused acknowledgement, and I went on, "I'll always think of Detroit as home. And I'm still a fan of the

Tigers, the Red Wings, the Pistons, and—God help me—the Lions"

This got a laugh, though not from the questioner, who was more concerned with keeping the floor. "I know you were an English major here at Wayne," he said, establishing his research credentials. "Did that experience plant the seeds of your writing career?" Then, before I could respond, he continued. "And what creative writing classes did you find particularly helpful?"

A faculty member, no doubt. "Actually," I said, "I've used my Detroit experiences in several plays, including this one, as I'm sure you can tell from the scenes you just saw. I had several wonderful professors in the English Department who introduced me to lots of outstanding works of literature. But I actually had only one creative writing course, and I didn't exactly knock the socks off my teacher—pretty much because I had very little to say, and very little idea of how to say it. My ignorance didn't seem to stir his interest in showing me how. He and I did wind up going to the same barber on the East Side, though, so he became sort of a friend, if not a mentor. I'm sure if I'd had more training, I might well have wasted a lot less time. Who knows?

"The best I can tell you about my writing, is that I've read a lot of great writers and watched quite a few good actors and directors. Then I worked hard to learn technique and practice it. The rest seems to have come from relaxing and realizing I could only write like myself about things that fascinated *me*, rather than writing like people I admired about things that fascinated *them*."

A well-dressed middle-aged woman with expensive-looking hair asked, "What about your theatre experience?

You went to Cass Tech, a high school with a renowned performing arts curriculum, and then attended Wayne State, of course."

I shrugged. "I wish I could say those experiences were crucial to my acting and playwriting. The truth is, I stumbled through a science curriculum at Cass Tech without a shred of performing arts instruction. My only performing there was clowning around in class when I should've been taking notes. And here at Wayne, I was a working-class kid who'd never even seen a play onstage. The first live play I ever saw was a performance of Shaw's *The Devil's Disciple* at the Bonstelle."

These admissions drew surprised murmurs from the audience, so I went on, "I got into acting because I always enjoyed singing, and that helped me discover I had a facility for accents and mimicry. Finally, the combination of indiscriminate reading, then acting onstage and writing poetry and fiction, encouraged me to try my hand at playwriting. Luckily for me, it's worked out pretty well."

The woman, whose outfit looked like Neiman Marcus, or at least J Jill, went on. "Who were your primary influences? And whom would you say your work resembles most?"

I was ready for this one. "Well, I do value imitation as a way to learn craft, and I'm not arrogant enough to believe my voice is unique, but I obviously try to pursue my own obsessions and try to produce my own take on things. What I've found most flattering was a review that compared my approach to Chekhov's. Way too kind, but appreciated. Mostly, I leave decisions like that to other people. My influences, besides Chekhov, are probably Shakespeare, Pinter, Edward Albee, Stoppard, Alan Ayckbourn, maybe Noel Coward. You know—the usual suspects."

This got a bit of a laugh. But a thin African American woman, in a startlingly blue suit and a violet turban reminiscent of the one favored by the English Department's secretary, was waving her hand in the third row. "I notice you didn't include any women or minorities on your list. Any comment on that?"

I nodded. "You're right. All white guys, mostly not even Americans at that. And I'm obviously a white guy, too." This drew another scattering of tentative laughter. "The previous question was about my influences, though. As a working-class kid, I've been playing cultural catch-up all my life, and I think that explains the influence part. My early cultural ignorance was profound.

"So far as my admiration goes, and with apologies for any gaps in my memory, I'd add Lorraine Hansberry, James Baldwin, Theresa Rebeck, Amiri Baraka, Kia Corthron, Wendy Wasserstein, OyamO, Charles Smith, Paula Vogel, and Anna Deveare Smith. And I have to say, guy though he was, I think August Wilson is one of the great American playwrights, with a voice and a vision that cut through all the crap. He gives us all something to shoot for."

Warm applause greeted this. I glanced around at the crowd, pleased to have dodged a confrontation of the kind Deirdre would have enjoyed. Like, "How do your own sexual transgressions contribute to your work?" I knew my list of playwrights had been sycophantically long, and even a bit show-offy, but it was a question I had been asked before, so I'd had time to think about it.

I fielded a few of the inevitable questions about theme,

as well as a couple about the Wertmüller film and the remake by Madonna's squeeze, Guy Ritchie. Then someone spoke up in an indeterminate Slavic accent. The moment reminded me instantly of the literary Q & A endured by Graham Greene's Holly Martins in *The Third Man*, and Kingsley Amis's nod to Greene in a similar scene from *One Fat Englishman*, in which a heavily-accented interlocutor demands to know the protagonist's opinion of several renowned writers, including *Shem Shoyce* and *Grim Grin*.

In this instance, the questioner asked me, "Vat iss joor offerall wision?"

Trying not to chuckle at Amis's rendering of James Joyce and Graham Greene, I said, "I'm not sure I have an overall vision. I just start off with characters and situations that intrigue me and go from there. I try to stay open to whatever may develop, and I make sure the beginning, middle, and end have enough connections to be coherent."

This brought a follow-up from the man, whose unnaturally gleaming black hair nearly merged with his equally dark eyebrows, which formed an almost unbroken line across his forehead. "So vat zen are ve to tek avay at ze ent off ze ewenink? You haff no intress in poley-tiks?"

"Well," I said, concentrating on a serious tone, "you'll probably notice my characters have stronger opinions than I do. But they don't usually think of themselves as heroes or villains. And if I had to boil my convictions down to a phrase, I'd probably admit to agreeing with E. E. Cummings, who said 'love is the every only god.' These days, that may qualify as a subversive view."

A young man with a skinhead buzz announced himself as a writing student and asked, "How do you handle plotting? Do you start off knowing exactly where your story will end?"

"I sometimes wish I did. But no. I start with something that fascinates me—character, setting, situation, scraps of dialogue. Then, early in the play, I try to think of something unexpected for the characters to deal with— preferably something *I* didn't expect, either. I call it a modified version of the Passover question: what makes this day different from all other days? That helps me decide what the characters want or need. Then I pretty much listen to them, follow their lead."

"That sounds pretty simple," the young man said. "What if you run into a block?"

"That happens pretty often. I find the best guide to making sure you can keep going is to look back to the beginning, to your original impulse, which is always strong. Whatever's there, I try to find ways to connect to moments throughout the play, particularly at the end."

A bit more of this sort of thing got me through the session to more applause than I expected. As Ed and the cast joined me onstage for bows, Rachel sidled next to me and whispered, "I appreciate the idea of Q & A, but like today, the A's are always better than the Q's."

I smiled and nodded; but I always felt like a bit of a fraud, pontificating about my work and my views. Not that I didn't believe what I was saying, but I was, after all, just a writer, just one in a dauntingly large throng. I wrote as well as I could, and I wanted people to read or pay admission to see the results. I even supposed, like Shakespeare, I wanted to live forever through my work.

To distract myself from more of this writerly angsting, I turned my gaze outward. And this time, as I scanned the crowd, I saw her.

12

"You're sure this isn't taking you away from something more important? Like the redhead?"

"Everybody connected with the show, including Rachel, is busy with classes or meetings. And it *is* lunchtime."

We were seated in the Cass Café, surrounded by an academic lunch crowd: women in various unfashionable but impossible-to-ignore ensembles; men who looked as if they had dressed in the dark; and a few students looking either earnest or manic. I was reminded of my mother's usual observation when she saw someone in an ill-conceived outfit. "It's amazing what you see when you don't have your gun."

After my talk, and some obligatory chit-chat with audience members, I had thanked Ed and the actors, then made my excuses and headed for the tall, willowy woman standing at the rear of the auditorium. Her blonde hair was shorter, but something else about her looked different from the long-haired young woman I remembered from my graduate student days out East.

"Wow," I said. "Andrea. What a surprise. I got your note at the Inn, but I couldn't imagine who sent it. And I certainly didn't expect someone from back East. You did send the note, I assume?"

She smiled and extended a hand, pale, with long tapered fingers and pink nails. "I did." Looking at her smile, I recalled the little parentheses at the corners of her mouth. She was beautiful enough to stop conversation. I took her hand, noting how soft and smooth it felt, as if she'd just applied hand-lotion. Her startling gray eyes widened, and she said, "It's good to see you, Dennis."

Now, looking at her across the table, I said, "I'm not sure I'd have recognized you if I hadn't been looking for you. Other than to appreciate how amazing you look. But there's something different about you, besides a new hairstyle."

"It's the boobs," she said. "I had them reduced. Larry made me get saline implants right after we got married. I was just out of high school and easily pushed around. I finally got tired of having them enter places before I did and distracting everyone from anything else about me."

The breast reduction had done nothing but make Andrea even more spectacular. I weighed my response carefully. "You look wonderfully . . . proportionate," I finally managed.

She laughed. "Just the way Mother Nature intended," she said.

Again, I considered what should come next. "So," I said, "what brings you to Detroit? A business trip? Or have you discovered you're a Lions fan and you're planning to follow them all the way to the Super Bowl? That's a joke, by the way."

She laughed once more, softly, looking at me with those piercing gray eyes. "Larry got a job offer with Chrysler. Now that the auto industry is making a comeback, they need computer experts. And that's Larry."

"So," I said, "you're living here?" This relieved me of having to ask if she and Larry were still together.

"We have a house in Indian Village," she said. "I guess, being from here, you know where that is."

"Lots of great architecture there, mostly early twentieth-century, by great architects. Albert Kahn, Louis Kamper, William Stratton. Mostly built for Detroit bigwigs of the period. Popular again for yuppies, if that term hasn't passed its useful life."

"Yuppies like Larry—and me—I suppose." She shrugged. "We wouldn't be there if a lot of the houses weren't reclamation projects."

In graduate school, my housemate Arnie Rivkin and I often wondered why our beautiful next-door-neighbor ever married Larry Durant, a tall round-shouldered, wide-hipped man with a large square head, an autocratic conviction of his own importance, and a strident way with an opinion. Several times we speculated about the likelihood that Larry physically abused Andrea, but we never actually saw any evidence, except for her occasional, unsettling lack of affect, which I had been reminded of by her flat demeanor in announcing her breast reduction.

Back then, even without incontrovertible evidence, the always blunt Arnie said, "I don't care. I still think the blockhead knocks her around. He certainly does it emotionally."

"Dennis?" she said, startling me. Her gray eyes widened.

"I'm sorry," I said. "I was just thinking about the past. And about synchronicity. Indian Village actually figures into the play. One of the offstage characters has a place there."

"We have a Victorian house. Tudor, really." She took a sip of the tea our nose-ringed waitress had finally brought. "Well, everything in the neighborhood is pretty much Victorian. We had to do quite a bit of renovation."

"Yeah," I said. "A lot of places there fell into disrepair over the years. But I guess it's a real-estate hot-spot again."

"Speaking of neighborhoods," Andrea said, "do you ever get back to any of your old haunts in Delaware? Brixton's not that far away."

"Not too often. Last time I was there I saw our old houses were gone, replaced by an apartment complex. My office-mate and I just drove down to Rehoboth Beach, though. She planned to surprise me by taking me shark-fishing, but we finally decided, wisely I guess, on body-surfing instead."

"She?" Andrea said. "Anything happening between you?"

"No," I said, grinning. "Just good friends. Eileen's not into men—not romantically, anyway."

Andrea's gray eyes seemed to be looking at something inward. "Remember when I took you to look for prehistoric shark teeth where they'd been dredging the Chesapeake and Delaware Canal? All those fossils."

"I still have a cardboard check-box full of stuff from that day, sharks' teeth, a Mosasaur tooth, a couple of Trilobites." I thought back to that bright clear morning when Andrea and I lay side-by-side on our stomachs, she pillowed by her then more than ample breasts, picking among grass and Cretaceous debris. I remembered sensing an attraction between the two of us and doing my best to keep my own feelings in check. "I haven't thought of that day in a long time," I said carefully. "I did write a poem about it, though. Even managed to get it published."

She looked at me and smiled. "I know. I Googled you. Then I read you were coming back to Detroit."

I hoped my flushed cheeks weren't as obvious as they felt. "I guess I owe you a belated apology for raiding a part of your life. It's what writers do. But I figured you'd never see it."

"I thought it was beautiful," she said. "I felt quite flattered."

"I actually did think about sending you a copy. But I felt kind of awkward about it. And I didn't want it to cause a problem for you. I never imagined you'd find it on your own."

"The Internet makes secrets hard to keep these days." She smiled, then went on. "When I told Larry where I'd been that morning, he wasn't happy. He thought there might be something going on between us. So, by the time the poem appeared, it wasn't really an issue. But Larry's not a reader. He's never seen it. Anyway, back then, I told him you were all about sharks' teeth. But I was glad to learn that wasn't quite true." Before I could respond, she took another unexpected conversational turn. "I'm working on my bachelor's degree here. I'll probably wind up with a teaching certificate, but I'm enjoying a whole different range of courses—art history, archaeology, literature. It's like waking up after being asleep for a long time, like Rip van Winkle."

The waitress arrived with the salads we had ordered, after which I said, "I got a teaching certificate here, too. Never used it." Then, in attempt at a conversational turn of my own, "Children?"

She looked down at her salad, then back up at me. "There won't be any. We got married out of high school because I got pregnant. Then"—she paused as if considering what to say—"there was an accident. So, no more pregnancies. No kids."

Once again, she had surprised me with an affectless revelation. "I'm sorry," I said. "I had no idea."

She smiled, almost pityingly. "You wouldn't have. Not something we talked about back then. But it's just as well it happened. A child, children, would have been a mistake."

While I digested this, I took a bite of my house salad, which, as the menu put it, I had been able to *beef-up* with salmon. Only one of the beef-up choices actually involved beef.

As I chewed, realizing I had nowhere to go with her last revelation, she saved me by saying, "Larry wants to take you out for dinner. Well, we both do, of course. If you have the time."

Grateful for a relatively neutral subject, I said, "Of course. That would be great. Most nights I have rehearsal. But tomorrow I'm free, if that works." I wasn't really eager to see Larry, especially after hearing about his long-ago suspicions, but how bad could it be? A couple of awkward hours, at worst.

"Wonderful," she said. "And if you're free during the day, I'd love to show you some of what I'm learning about art at the DIA. And I've never seen the famous inn you're staying at. Maybe you could give me a tour."

"Sure," I said. "A belated payback for your taking me on the fossil field-trip." Then I added, "Unless you're afraid of ghosts. I think I saw one yesterday, not long after I checked in."

"Sounds interesting." She treated me to one of her parentheses-accented smiles, then threw me another curveball. "You and—Deirdre?—are divorced now. Something else I read about when I Googled you. Was it awful?"

"Sort of like one of those outdoor magazine stories about an animal gnawing off a limb to get out of a steel trap." I smiled to suggest I was joking, even though I wasn't.

Andrea gave me her gray-eyed, serious stare. "She was never right for you."

"I'm beginning to wonder if anyone is."

Her gaze continued to meet mine. "That seems a bit extreme."

"At the moment," I said, "there aren't too many people who'd miss me if I vanished in a puff of smoke."

"Family?" she said.

"My parents are dead. I'm not close to the few relatives still around, half of whom are in Scotland. And I don't think being despised by Deirdre really counts." Why, I wondered, was I laying all these personal details before her?

"What about your office-mate—Eileen, is it?"

I shrugged. "I guess she's about the only one who wastes much time thinking about me."

Her pink lips curved into a smile. "Besides me," she said.

I managed a smile of my own. "Besides you."

"And your ghost, of course."

I grinned. "And my ghost."

13

The next afternoon, as I shaved at the bathroom mirror, readying myself for dinner with the Durants, I had the sense of being watched that I hadn't felt since my first day at the Inn. Twice I turned quickly but detected only a faint stirring of air that could have come from the heating registers. Once, hearing a floorboard creak, I actually moved toward the open bathroom door. When I returned to the sink, I saw a curling streak of steam on the mirror. Readily explicable, of course, if I had been running hot water. Which I hadn't been. I felt an increasingly familiar tingle at the back of my neck.

I set down my razor and started filling the tub. Stepping in, I thought about the aftermath of the previous night's rehearsal. After post-show notes and a drink or two at the café, I had started walking back to the Inn. And as I'd half-expected, red-haired Rachel caught up with me, her Western boots clacking on the pavement. She was dressed in a skin-tight leotard—was there any other kind?—and a long pleated skirt, and as I turned toward her I couldn't help but notice the way her nipples stood out in the cool air under the taut fabric.

She touched my arm lightly. "Dennis," she said, narrowing her green eyes, "it's so nice having the playwright directly involved in the process."

"Thanks," I said. "Everything's coming together well."

She looked directly at me and drew a finger across her lips. "I have to say, I'd like to get to know you better." She watched me register this, then added, "My apartment's not far. Perhaps another glass of wine."

I was certainly tempted, and even now, lounging in the tub, my erection reminded me how long it had been since I had seen a woman's naked body, rather than an image on a page or a screen. I had to say something, though. "I really try not to take advantage of students," I managed.

She inclined her head. "I'm not your student," she said, her tone neutral. "And no one takes advantage of me unless I decide to let them. Sometimes *I'm* the one taking advantage."

"Point taken," I said. "I just wouldn't want to upset the delicate balance of relationships a production depends on. Besides, I have a writing deadline, and I need to get some work done before tomorrow morning." I actually was working on an article I hoped might interest *The Dramatist*, but I realized my explanation sounded stiff and priggish.

She took a moment to process my refusal. Then she said, "I'm sorry. My radar's usually pretty good, unless somebody's deep in the closet."

I laughed and assured her I wasn't gay. And a memory flashed into my mind of an opening night party at which a fellow actor had told me, "Dennis, you're too butch to be true."

"Another time, then," Rachel said, not seeming unduly upset. As an artist, she was no doubt used to rejection, as I was myself. Probably with more regret than she, I watched her swinging away down the sidewalk, her boots clicking assertively as she went.

And now, I had to admit to myself that the image in my head was not Rachel, but Andrea, an even less professional notion. When I got out of the tub and reached for a towel, I noticed my shaving cream and razor had somehow found their way into the sink. I certainly hadn't left them there, and I hadn't heard them fall. Again, I felt unsettled. I just had to continue taking notes and find a way to use all this. Including whatever it was that had happened in Gettysburg. Maybe I could get a one-act out of it, or a short story.

I dressed quickly, which was good, because I didn't have long to wait. The Durants picked me up at the Inn, and I persuaded them to make a slight detour down Woodward on the way to the restaurant so I could get a photo of the giant Joe Louis fist hanging from its heavy chain.

That done, we headed for Fishbone's Rhythm Kitchen Café in Greektown, apparently one of Larry's favorite places. As we drove the few blocks to the relatively concentrated downtown ethnic enclave, Andrea turned to where I sat in the rear seat of Larry's silver Chrysler Town and Country. "I didn't realize you were a boxing fan," she said.

"It's for my office-mate," I said, noting how her flawless skin was set off by her hooded black coat.

"Is he a writer, too?" Larry asked. Andrea glanced at me to see where this would go.

"Well, *she* writes," I said, "but she's a film scholar."

"She?" Larry said with a man-to-man leer. "Good-looking?"

"She is. But mostly to other women."

Larry let out a small grunt that might have been a laugh. "Lesbian roommate, eh? Sounds like a TV series."

I felt myself flush. "*Office*-mate," I said. "And she's a good friend."

Fortunately, Larry occupied himself with parking the car, so further discussion of Eileen was curtailed. She wouldn't have cared, I knew, but I didn't want the conversation to turn derisive and inevitably contentious.

Despite the persistence of the acne scars that pitted his cheeks and neck like pores under a magnifying lens, Larry Durant had gained some superficial polish since moving to the Midwest. Mostly it added up to more expensive clothes and an unnecessary augmentation of what I recognized as his habitual overbearing and largely unearned air of confidence.

He still broadcast his Eastern Pennsylvania origins whenever he made one of his frequent pronouncements. I remembered Larry's references to the *loan-more* when he was cutting grass, or *wutter* as in *scotch and*—and, most often, *na-ow* as in *I know*.

Now that we were seated in Fishbone's, orders placed and a second round of drinks before us, discussion was diverted to food. Though a fair number of restaurants in the neighborhood featured Greek cuisine, the presence of a gambling casino nearby insured an eclectic array of eateries. Fishbone's emphasized Cajun cooking. Andrea announced that her favorite restaurant in the area had been an Ethiopian place called The Blue Nile, now unfortunately relocated in a suburb.

"No way I'd a gone to that place again, even if it had still been open," Larry declared, lubricated by his second

Hurricane, an enormous pink New Orleans cocktail composed mostly of rum and fruit juice. His accent had become more pronounced. "Who wants to sit on the floor and eat with your fingehs? And drink yew-gurt?"

Andrea retreated into affectless silence as Larry maneuvered his conversational bulldozer through his current career success—"a hunner-eighty-thou a year" and "clueless administrators" he had to guide through the mysteries of IT. "They even popped for a two-mil insurance policy," Larry added, then grinned. "Can't afford to lose me."

"We have tickets for your opening night," Andrea put in quietly during a lull in Larry's monologue. Like me, she was sipping a New Zealand Sauvignon Blanc.

"That's great," I said. "I'll make sure you get an invitation to the after-party."

"Two good-looking actresses in your shew," Larry said. "Especially the redhead."

Andrea said, "Their pictures were in the *Free Press* preview article."

"Now that you're single again," Larry added, "she's fair game."

I shook my head. "Not someone in the cast of my production. And a student, at that."

Larry snorted. "That's crazy. You oughta make a move if she's available."

And surprisingly Andrea said, "Larry's right. I saw the way she looked at you during your talk. Besides, you'll probably never see her again after this month."

"Timing," I said, "is everything."

Mercifully, our waiter arrived with large platters of gumbo and dirty rice for Larry and me, and a shrimp remoulade salad for Andrea. The conversation veered first to food, then to recollections of our days as neighbors back East. I felt fortunate that the subject of sharks' teeth didn't come up.

When the check arrived, Larry picked it up of course, and paid with a ceremonious flourish of his platinum credit card. How in the hell could anyone actually be paying this guy a hundred and eighty thousand a year? Especially compared to the relative pittance I earned. And a two-million-dollar life insurance policy? Jesus wept.

Later, when the Durants dropped me at the Inn, Andrea said in an undertone, "I'll call you tomorrow about the Art Institute."

Larry, fortified by another couple of Hurricanes, was a stranger to undertone—and subtlety. After an ambivalent squint at the back of his wife's head, he blared, "Go feh the redhead, Denny!" Then he gunned the engine of his Town and Country. As I watched them drive away, I saw Larry waving an arm in evident reinforcement of some vehement observation.

I drew in a deep breath of the cool night air, then took out my cellphone and sent Eileen the photo of the Joe Louis fist, accompanied by the message, "Show going well. But I'm feeling a little punchy. More later."

As I entered my room, I couldn't shake the impression that someone had just left. The maid, I decided, and let it go at that. At least the oatmeal raisin cookies were intact.

As I unwrapped a cookie, my phoned *pinged* with an incoming message from Eileen. "Glad to hear all's well onstage. Thanks for the punch-pic. Gotta love a city with a big fist for a symbol. Hope you're finding something more to occupy you offstage than your own."

I couldn't let that go, so I typed in, "Ever wonder why we wind up all by ourselves, texting each other in the middle of the night?"

I waited for a rejoinder, but nothing came.

14

"It doesn't *look* haunted." Andrea glanced around the room. "Just expensive." All the same, her quiet voice was almost a whisper, as if someone other than I might be listening.

"Fortunately," I said, "Wayne State's picking up the tab. Probably coming out of your tuition."

We had just gotten back from an abbreviated tour of the Detroit Institute of Arts, which, thanks to the recent bankruptcy agreement, was no longer in danger of having its collection sold off to help pay the city's creditors. I hadn't been there for a long time, so I had depended on Andrea, who gladly took on the role of docent.

We began, like most DIA visitors, with the Diego Rivera murals. As when I first saw them, I was impressed by their sheer scale. They reminded me of Fritz Lang's *Metropolis* in their ambition, their power, their composition, their Deco stylization, and in the case of the Rivera work, his rendering of a vivid range of Meso-American colors. I had to admit, though, that neither Lang's film nor Rivera's murals moved me much beyond their aesthetics. Too much concern with message for my taste. Then again, I supposed, the aesthetics were impressive enough.

We moved on to the European collection, and I was newly amazed by how fortunate Detroit was to have a jewel like the DIA in its tarnished diadem. Truly significant and historic masterpieces, by artists from long before the Middle Ages to the present, graced the walls, pedestals, and platforms. Fra Angelico, the Holbeins, Rembrandt, Brueghel, Benzoni, Van Eyck, Degas, van Gogh, Renoir, Rodin, Sisley, Sargent, Picasso, Kokoschka, Feininger—the array of work was dazzling and, in the limited time we had to tour the galleries, was almost overwhelming to the senses. I was struck, too, by Andrea's obvious pleasure in demonstrating her knowledge, not just about the art, but about the range of subjects her belated foray into higher education had opened to her.

At one point, we stood before Degas's *Violinist and Young Woman*. Both subjects were seated, the bearded violinist slightly behind the woman in the act of plucking a string. The woman, in a long gray dress, her blonde hair gathered behind her head, seemed to be gazing at something unseen in the foreground, her expression serious and enigmatic.

"I can't quite pin it down," I said, "but somehow she reminds me of you."

"Because she's preoccupied with something other than the man she's with?"

"Maybe that's it," I said, wondering which man she meant.

"Larry never wanted me to go back to school," Andrea said, as we walked toward the exit. "But now that he's busy with his"—she took a small ironic breath—"career, he can't keep me safely at home. I've agreed to be decorative at social gatherings, but otherwise, I'm free. I'm my own person."

Unsure how to respond to this, I said, "You seem to be making the most of your opportunity to work on a degree. You certainly gave me a wonderful tour. Thanks."

She lowered her long eyelashes and bobbed her head in acknowledgement. "We could have spent much longer here," she said. "But I have a class this afternoon. And I would like to see your room at the Inn before then." As we walked, she said, "Looking at all those beautiful paintings—masterpieces—made me think about your talk. Those artists, just like you, believed in technique and practice, right?"

"Pretty much," I said. "But I'm a long way from writing masterpieces."

"You may, though," she said.

"Actually, there's more to it than technique and practice. You have to be obsessed. Driven."

"To succeed? You're not doing too badly at that."

"There's two kinds of success," I said. "One is getting rich and famous. Lots of people are driven to that. The other is actually being driven to produce the work. For either kind, you also need luck—or chance—or good timing."

"So, it comes down to luck?" She seemed genuinely interested.

"All four," I said. "Technique, practice, obsession—and luck. And it's not always what people would recognize as luck." Talking too much, I thought, as we walked down Woodward to Ferry, but I went on. "Take van Gogh. He had the first three, obviously. But the masterpieces came because he was lucky enough—or unlucky enough—to have almost nothing else in his life. Allowed him to concentrate. Cervantes? Would he have written *Don Quixote* if he hadn't been thrown in prison? Melville? He had a boring job—almost like being in prison—so he could focus on *Moby-Dick*. Then, later on, the timing shifts. Same writer, same gifts, same drive. But he writes *Pierre*, which almost everybody agrees is terrible, and hardly anyone has ever heard of outside of graduate school."

"Timing," she said.

"Timing."

"It's everything." She smiled.

Remembering something, I wondered, or thinking ahead?

15

And now she stood in my room, making tea for us at the anachronistically modern machine on my Victorian sideboard, while I sat watching from a well-upholstered love-seat. Still thinking of the gallery tour, I mused that with her now-slender stature and almost translucent complexion, she looked as though she could have stepped out of a painting by Sargent.

Conscious of my gaze, she turned from pouring tea and said, "You're so thoughtful, Dennis. Sympathetic. I guess because you're a writer. Or maybe you're a writer because of how you are."

"Actually, in my experience," I said, "most writers are pretty self-absorbed. We take stuff in to process it for ourselves, which is pretty narcissistic when you come right down to it. Self-interest isn't exactly a novelty in the business. Lots of assholes." This sounded like something Deirdre might have said, I thought.

Impassive, as if what I had said simply confirmed her good opinion of me, she handed me a mug of black tea. "The reason I can't have any more children is that Larry punched me in the stomach while I was pregnant way back at the beginning. I had a miscarriage."

She made this revelation with the same tone as if she'd

asked whether I wanted sugar in my tea. Realizing that Arnie Rivkin's long-ago assessment had been right after all, I could manage no more than, "I'm sorry. That's awful."

"No," she said. "It was for the best. Who'd want Larry for the father of their child?"

"Does he still hit you?"

"No. Not for a while, anyway. He realizes I'd be gone in a heartbeat. And I will be when I finish my degree." She took a sip of her tea, then set her mug on the sideboard. "You know," she said, "back then, I wanted to have an affair with you. But I guess you weren't interested." She hesitated for a moment. "You're not gay, are you?"

I felt blood warm my cheeks. Two women asking the same thing within a couple of days. "No," I said. "I'm not gay."

She spoke in what seemed like an embarrassed rush. "I mean, I know your marriage failed, and you're in theatre—and you had a roommate when you lived next door to us—what was his name?"

"Arnie Rivkin? House-mate. Definitely not gay. Neither of us."

"And your lesbian office-mate."

"Eileen has her life. I have mine. We're just good friends."

Her long lashes momentarily concealed those unusual gray eyes. "Then I guess you must not be interested."

I took a deep breath. "I wouldn't say that." I realized I was on the brink of something potentially disastrous, with a woman who might well be damaged. But when I thought of it, wasn't I damaged, too? Give it a rest, I thought.

She quickly joined me on the love-seat. "I'd like you to

kiss me," she said.

I did so, meeting those soft full lips with my own, my arms around her. Her tongue found mine, and her lilac perfume, faint but heady, enveloped me. Sober reflection fell away.

Then, shocking me, her hand was on my fly, opening my zipper, grasping me. I was immediately hard; breathless. She broke from the kiss and whispered, "I have to be at class soon, but I want to taste you. You can come in my mouth."

And before I could respond, she had bent to my lap, and those soft lips took me in.

"Wait." I took hold of her shoulders. She released me and looked up, confused. "Let's not do this in such a rush. Let's wait till we have more time, till I can do more than just stand by."

"Pick me up after my class tomorrow," she said, touching the point of my nose. "It ends at eleven. I'll be on the sidewalk outside the DIA. We can go to the house. Larry won't be home until late." Then she added, "You're quite a surprise, Dennis. And definitely not gay."

I said nothing, reflecting that life was becoming more complex by the minute. She went to the bathroom, and when she emerged, her mood was subtly altered. "I think going to the house is a good idea," she said. "She may not want me here."

She left quickly, and I remained to ponder her final words. I walked to the bathroom. My complimentary shampoo bottle lay on the floor, and the mirror was smeared with pearly-white shampoo.

16

That night during dress rehearsal, I had difficulty concentrating on the play. I kept thinking of what had happened in my room at the Inn, but especially the shampoo dribbling down the bathroom mirror. "She may not want me here," Andrea had said.

Could the shampoo really have gotten on the mirror while Andrea and I were occupied on the love-seat? Was I really taking this ghost stuff seriously? And I actually caught myself thinking that my ghost wouldn't have done such a thing, as if the ghost somehow deserved the benefit of the doubt. Common sense dictated that Andrea must have put the shampoo on the mirror. But what did that say about Andrea? And what did it say about me that I passed up a blowjob? *A blowjob*, for Christ's sake. Or, on second thought, probably not for Christ's sake. Archaic good manners, maybe. Slow on the uptake. But definitely not gay. If I ever mentioned the moment, Eileen would certainly have something caustic to say.

I shifted in my seat and tried to focus on the stage. The costumes were unobtrusively effective, executed by a young woman named Carey, whose sense of design fortunately trumped her own flamboyant style, which fell just short of a clown at a child's birthday party. I'd often thought someone—certainly not I—should write an article or a short book lavishly illustrated with shots of the outfits worn by costume designers.

Nonetheless, Carey had found just the right look for the characters, as had the set and lighting designer, Robert, who had gracefully handled the staging requirement of two separate living rooms and another multi-use area without calling attention to his own virtuosity or mucking around with symbolic touches.

This rehearsal was better. The actors were undeniably finding their way with the characters and dialogue. And the pacing was almost there. Anna, in particular, had finally captured the requisite strain of anger underpinning her character without overdoing it.

After rehearsal Ed said, "All right. We've done all we can do. Now we need an audience." Everyone in the cast and crew applauded, and I joined them. "Just remember to hold for laughs."

"Let's hope we get some," I said. I looked at everyone, then added, "Well? I'm holding."

They all laughed. "Thank goodness you wrote better laugh lines than that one," Rachel said, brushing her red hair from in front of one eye. This, too, got a laugh, though a small shiver of tension passed from her to me.

"Question." Mark, the illicit lover of Rachel's character, raised an index finger. "I know I'm not supposed to ask stuff like this. But that last scene, when Rachel and I are finally together, feels like such a release of tension. Were you building on real experience there?"

Thinking about the day's events, I was glad my flushed face was unlikely to show up in the dim light of the auditorium. "No," I said. "I've never had an experience quite like that."

Rachel followed with, "So you've never been swept away by passion, as if you'd plunged into a river like Paul's character says when he's explaining why Mark and I fall in love?"

"No," I said, admitting it more to myself than to everyone else. "I've never been swept away."

"Even though that's the title of the play? You have a wonderful imagination."

"I guess writers write and actors act so they can have experiences they've never had. Or might never have."

Rachel smiled. "Well, you certainly had me convinced."

After a beat or two, Paul said, "Now all we have to do is convince the *News* and the *Free Press*."

"Let's concentrate on convincing the audience," Ed said. "Then the *News* and the *Free Press* will take care of themselves."

17

I spent a restless night, waking almost every time I turned over in bed, less concerned with a female poltergeist than with the real woman I had agreed to meet the next day. Andrea's air of detachment from herself unsettled me, but that very quality, combined with her beauty, exerted a force I couldn't seem to resist. My own situation, too; divorced, alone, far from the place I now called home, my apprehension about opening night, all of this made me feel untethered, without a point of reference. Was I being swept away at last? Or did being swept away mean you didn't think about it?

Larry Durant weighed on my mind as well. No matter how despicable the man might be, no matter how much he had earned Andrea's contempt, he'd done nothing to me except present himself as a target for betrayal. And all I had was Andrea's side of the story. I could just imagine what Deirdre's side of the Dennis McCutcheon story might be, not that her continual emails concealed any of her thoughts on the subject.

Nonetheless, I rose in the morning and got ready to pick up Andrea outside the DIA, giving particular attention to grooming and personal hygiene. Before leaving my room, I checked my email, most of which was delete-able, except for one from a theatre in Wisconsin that wanted to produce one of my one-acts. After my night of soul-searching, the good news was welcome. I tried to shake off the feeling of guilt. In the arts, bad news was the rule, so I had better enjoy the good, undeserved or not.

As if I had conjured it up, I also saw a message with Deirdre's address and the subject line, "Gotten Laid Yet?" Unable to resist, I glanced at the first couple of sentences. It began, "Formerly Dear Whatever, I suppose you've lost no time in taking advantage of some slutty little actress. Some innocent who won't know till later what a scene-stealer you are—the scenes being parts of your victim's lives, which are always more interesting than your own."

I deleted the message without reading more. If she only knew, I thought. Evidently, Deirdre's own romantic drama was between acts, though I ruefully conceded that she had always been able to handle multiple roles.

My phone rang. Eileen. She really was a good friend, I thought, clicking the little green *talk* icon.

"So, how's Maxine?" I said.

"Probably in Essen by now. Her parents popped for a quick trip to celebrate her graduation." Eileen's soft drawl betrayed no disappointment.

"She *is* coming back, though? You two seemed to be in pretty enviable synch just a few days ago."

"Who knows? We'll see." Now a note of discomfort had crept into Eileen's voice. "I guess I can't help worrying about terrorists. Even though the odds are against it, she *is* going to be on planes and trains and in terminals and stations."

"Those places are full of guys in uniform with Uzis slung over their shoulders."

"What I'm worried about are the guys with Uzis who aren't in uniform. Or with knapsacks full of Semtex."

I realized my friend was serious about this relationship. And who could ignore the sense of foreboding that accompanied international travel these days? "Maxine will be okay," I said. "Hang in there. She'll be back. Give her a call."

After a brief silence, Eileen said, "I made *this* call to find out what's happening with *you*."

I gave her a quick summary of how the play was going, sketched the Q & A, and gave her the news about the one-act in Wisconsin. Then I filled her in briefly on Rachel and the Durants, minus the oral sex moment.

"My, my," Eileen drawled. "You have yourself a plateful, don't you? You've turned into a babe magnet. Who knew? But you better watch out for that big spouse. I bet his antenna's already tuned in."

"Right," I said, trying to sound dismissive, but silently agreeing.

"My advice is stick with the actress. Remember what Nelson Algren said in one of his memoirs. 'Never sleep with anyone whose troubles are worse than your own.' "

"Never mind the authorial quotes. Besides, as I remember, Algren didn't follow his own advice with regard to Simone de Beauvoir. And lived to regret it."

"I think that may have been where he learned the lesson," Eileen said. She went on quickly, "Well, some of us are still working. I have papers to read. You take care of yourself, hear?"

"Maybe you should think about a trip out here. Take your mind off worrying about Maxine. And you could help take some of these women off my hands."

"Speaking of hands," she said, "maybe you can visualize which finger I'm inviting you to twirl on."

Before I could think of a response, she broke the connection. Smiling, I walked over to the main building for coffee and pastry, dodging the considerable crowd of other guests and finding a corner by myself. I noted Latrece keeping an eye on me and, after finishing breakfast, I walked past the reception desk.

"Good morning, Mr. McCutcheon," she said. "I have a little confession to make. You may have Googled this for yourself, but there *is* a rumor that the Inn has a couple of ghosts, and one of them *is* a young woman in a long dress. I've never seen or heard anything unusual myself, but I can assure you no one's ever said she did anything harmful. If she even exists."

Keeping my voice low, I said, "I don't think I'll be calling out the Ghostbusters anytime soon."

She grinned. "That's good to know, Mr. McCutcheon. Good luck with your play. Or I guess I should say break a leg."

As I walked to my SUV, I couldn't resist glancing at the window of my room, where I saw something move almost imperceptibly behind the curtains. I felt a flash of irritation. Someone must be trying to bring some drama into the life of the visiting playwright. As if I needed it. And at that point, I realized something that had been hovering on the edge of my awareness since the previous afternoon. The young woman in the Degas painting looked uncannily like the one I saw on my first afternoon at the Inn. What was happening to me?

I climbed into the Highlander and fastened my seatbelt. The trouble with Algren's words of wisdom was that the only way to have a lasting relationship would be to find someone whose troubles were approximately the same as yours.

18

Andrea was waiting right where she said she would be, carrying a university book bag and looking like a runway model in a green trench coat and impressively high heels, her short blonde hair unkempt in a way only an expensive salon could achieve.

Before I could move, she opened the passenger door and slid in beside me. She kissed my cheek, and as I registered her faint scent of—what?—orange blossoms?—she buckled her seatbelt and reached over to touch the inside of my thigh.

I glanced at her. "You don't want me to have an accident, do you?"

She smiled. "The best way to get there is Jefferson. We're not far from Belle Isle. But you know that."

I followed her directions, driving east along the river on Jefferson under a typically cloudy Detroit sky. We passed the usual twenty-first-century mixture of preserved nineteenth and twentieth-century buildings; used car lots, liquor stores with Lotto and "We cash welfare checks" signs, riverfront parks, and upscale condos and apartments, both high and low-rise. Places that jogged my memory, like Sindbad's Restaurant and The Roostertail, where prom nights and wedding receptions had been going on for decades, as well as parties devoted to watching the annual hydroplane races on the river. We also passed Bellevue, a street that, a couple of miles west, intersected with Vernor Highway, site of the rivet factory where my father had worked for thirty years.

I mentioned this fact, and Andrea said, "Would you like to drive out there?"

"No. I saw it enough times riding on the bus to high school and college. Even visited there a couple of times."

"You've come a long way from your working-class roots," she said.

"My father's take was a bit different. After I published my first book, he said, 'Everything you do for a living now is a hobby.'"

She glanced at me and smiled. "Nice way to make a living."

I released a rueful puff of breath. "Walking through the DIA yesterday reminded me my father tended to forget that art's been around a lot longer than the Industrial Revolution and the drudgery he associated with *real* work."

"You still feel a bit guilty about it, though," she said, a flat statement I couldn't really dispute. She went on, "I notice you never say anything about what your mother thought. She must have thought something."

"You're right," I conceded. "She didn't express too many opinions, except in self-defense, though she had a Scots-Irish saying for every occasion. But when it came to me, her only son, she was pretty uncritical, other than wanting me to be happy. Whatever she believed that meant. Mostly to behave myself, I guess."

"But now you're free to do what you want. Like me. Free to misbehave." The sensation of her hand on my thigh radiated through me.

Now we were approaching the MacArthur Bridge across to Belle Isle, where I skated on the canals as a boy, and wandered through the aquarium and the conservatory. I pointed up the street east of the bridge. "There used to be a giant oven somewhere over there, an ad for the Michigan Stove Company."

"Too bad it's gone. What happened to it?"

"I think they relocated it to the state fairgrounds sometime back in the sixties. I've seen photographs of it. Advertising like that is the stuff of nostalgia now."

"Turn left here," Andrea said when we reached Seminole.

Seminole was a beautiful street, airy and tree-lined, far from the picture most people imagined, if they bothered to imagine Detroit at all. I thought of my high school and college years, when the neighborhood seemed exclusive, but something to which I might aspire, unlike the mansions of the real industrial barons out where Jefferson turned into Lakeshore Drive. At least you could see these houses from the street. "Here we are," she said.

The house, set well back from the sidewalk and surrounded by neatly-trimmed hedges, was a half-timbered two-story Tudor with a huge bay window.

"Why don't I let you off and park a bit up the street?" I said, already feeling guilty.

She smiled and said, "If you like. But no one will notice."

Nonetheless, as I drove up the block, I had the feeling I was being watched. The feeling persisted while I walked back to the house and up the path to the concrete steps, where she was waiting just inside the open door. She led me through the foyer, past the stairs that ascended to the second floor, and into the living room. "Quite a place," I said, registering the Victorian furniture, the tasteful art, and the leaded stained glass that accented the windows.

"Larry likes it," she said quietly. "He feels like the lord of the manor. He hired the decorator. I picked out the art. At least they're originals, not expensive Ethan Allen crap. The stained glass was already here."

"I like what you've chosen," I said. "You have a good eye."

"There's my prize." She gestured at a small sketch, well-framed and prominently displayed, of a beautiful woman in high heels and nothing else, seated on the edge of an armchair and looking out of a window. The image conveyed both vulnerability and exhibitionism. And a highly erotic charge.

"It's lovely," I said. "Theatrical, like a Hopper—like all of his pieces that include people."

"The gallery owner told me it could be a Hopper sketch," she said, "for one of his paintings, *Isolation*. But it's unsigned, and the provenance is hazy. Otherwise, it would have been unaffordable. And, even unsigned, it cost more than Larry wanted to spend."

"You must have been persuasive," I said.

"Larry doesn't like you," she said in a dismaying shift of focus.

"He hasn't seen me in years." Larry would like me a lot less at this very moment, I thought. "Or did I make that bad an impression at dinner?"

"He asked me about your Q & A. He said you sound

like a know-it-all."

"That's a pretty small sample to base an opinion on." I recalled my own fear about pontificating. Could I really be concerned about the opinion of the man whose wife I was about to fuck? I shrugged. "Maybe it's the way you told it."

"Nobody tells Larry anything." She smiled and set her book bag on an upholstered chair. "Welcome to my world."

I looked at her, realizing that, in her high-heeled shoes, she was my height. Before I could say anything more, she loosened the belt on her green trench coat and shrugged it off on the floor. Except for the high heels, she was completely naked, nipples erect on her beautifully reduced breasts, her golden pubic triangle almost as silky as her blonde coiffure.

"Jesus," I said. Whatever conversation I had imagined after our arrival evaporated from my mind, along with any thought of averting what was about to happen.

"My clothes are in the book bag," she said. "I took them off in the restroom at the DIA. Do you like it? Me?"

"Jesus," I said again, taking in her flat belly, her long shapely legs. "You're astonishing." I was struck by her almost childlike pleasure in my discomposure.

"Come into the guest room," she said, and her generous mouth curved in a smile. "I want to see you, too."

19

In the guest room, which featured a canopied four-poster and matching dresser, Andrea turned down the bedclothes, then turned to face me. "Would you like me to help?" she said and kicked off her shoes. Even her feet looked good.

"Are you sure about this?" I asked, conscious that I must sound like an idiot.

She spread her hands. "Do I look as if I'm not sure? Don't worry about Larry. *I'm* not. He knows I'm only here until I finish my degree. And I've done this before."

"You have?" I said, naively startled.

"Remember Doug Andrews?"

I hadn't thought of the man in years. An ex-marine with a homely, submissive wife—Marcia? Laura?—Andrews had lived two doors away from the house in which Arnie Rivkin and I had rented an upper flat. I had thought of Andrews as boorish. Why would this beautiful woman involve herself with someone like that? Especially after Larry. And why would she tell me about him now? It certainly wasn't doing anything to make me feel at ease.

As if reading my mind, Andrea said, "Not your kind of person, was he?" She shrugged. "Mine neither. I guess I thought if Larry found out, that would end things right there. I certainly wasn't careful. But it was as if Larry didn't want to see. Anyway, I ended it long before we moved here."

"Don't you worry about Larry's retaliating? Becoming violent? After all, you said he hit you and caused you to miscarry."

She closed her eyes and shook her head. "Things have changed. The balance of power has shifted. He needs me now more than I need him. And he knows the clock is ticking." She reached out and loosened my belt, then took hold of my zipper and opened my fly. "Oh, my," she said.

As I took my clothes off, feeling a combination of absurdity and desire, I reflected that at least we were using the guest room, instead of—in a phrase my mind wouldn't let go—*the marital bed*. I had never bought the notion that Shakespeare's leaving his wife the "second-best bed" had been anything other than an ironic jibe, never mind what the *Notes and Queries* crowd might think. The Bard was convinced something had been going on in Avon while he was gone, and, judging by the content of his plays and sonnets, his own conjectured adulteries apparently never eased his mind on that score.

As I stood naked before her, I felt as if I should keep checking behind me, almost as if I were still at the Inn. The Degas painting flashed in my mind. Then Andrea took hold of me and tugged gently, bringing me closer to where she sat on the bed. She reached behind my hips and pulled me down on top of her. Feeling my body touch the length of hers, skin to skin, was electric.

She threw her arms and legs around me and whispered in my ear. "After you come, you can watch me bring myself off with my fingers. I can't come any other way."

Bring herself off? It sounded to me like something out of a porn video. Then she pulled me inside her, and for a while, I lost all coherent thought.

20

Later, as we lay tangled in bedclothes and each other, Andrea again said, "Oh, my."

I stroked, then kissed one of her perfectly reclaimed breasts, not at all marred by the small pink scars underneath, and said, "Amazing."

She looked at me, her gray eyes and sober expression dissolving into a baffled smile. "That's never happened to me before," she said, and shook her head. "Not with anyone. I came twice."

I said nothing. I could hardly say something self-congratulatory. And I couldn't say what momentarily occurred to me—that this was the sort of thing women said in romantic novels. I could even hear Elaine in *Seinfeld* telling Jerry about her orgasms: "Fake, fake, fake, fake." I continued to stroke her left breast. Then I said, "I haven't made love to anyone in a long time. But I guess instinct takes over."

She made a small sound, not quite a laugh. "You didn't forget anything." She reached beneath the sheet and took hold of me. "God," she said. "You're still hard."

She began to work me with her hand, and now my turn came to make an indeterminate sound. I lost myself to the rhythm of her movement and our almost synchronized breathing. And when I climaxed with a cry I tried to stifle, I realized that she had maneuvered herself down on the bed so that I would come on her breasts. We lay back, her head on my right shoulder, my arm beneath her neck, and she massaged her breasts, as if she were trying to absorb part of me. She turned and kissed me, her tongue moving languidly in my mouth. Then she said, "Not with anyone."

We eventually rose from the bed and she said, "Let's have a shower, then go to Belle Isle."

All I could think to say was, "You're sure Larry won't suddenly turn up?"

"Don't worry," she said. "He's all the way up in Auburn Hills, keeping Chrysler's electronic infrastructure safe and efficient."

The walk-in shower was more than big enough for both of us. We soaped each other, which inevitably gave me another erection. She laughed with pleasure. Then, when we had rinsed off, she sat on the shower's built-in bench and completed the act she had begun at the Inn. Afterward, to her evident surprise and delight, I returned the favor.

21

"Belle Isle figures in the play," I said, as we stood in the parking lot of the Dossin Great Lakes Museum. "One of the characters is the director of the museum here. He's unable to save someone who breaks through the ice on the river."

"So, it's not just the lovers who get swept away in your play," she said. "It's obvious the image means a lot to you."

She was unsettlingly on target. "I guess it does," I conceded. "But for a writer, there's also a certain pressure to make connections, especially in a longer piece. I also did research on bootlegging in the twenties and thirties. There were black gangs and Jewish gangs as well as the usual Mafiosi. They ran booze across the river from Canada, sometimes driving over the ice in the winter. The Jewish mobsters were called the Purple Gang. For the play, I created a black bootlegger named Marvin Dietrich who's the subject of a book one of the characters is writing."

"You really are a Detroit boy, aren't you?" Andrea shielded her eyes against the glare from the water.

"Yep. But growing up someplace doesn't mean you don't have to do research. Thank goodness for the Internet."

"Is your black bootlegger based on a real person?"

"He's based on details I gleaned here and there. I just

liked the idea of a black guy running liquor across the river. The museum director finds out that he fell through the ice, too, but didn't get swept away." On the Canadian shoreline, traffic moved swiftly on Riverside Drive, bringing to mind the pivotal failed rescue scene in the play. "I used to come here a lot, summer or winter," I said. "I skated the canal all the way around the island a couple of times. Mostly on my ankles. Fortunately, unlike my bootlegger, I never fell through the ice." My memory briefly took me back to images of crisscross skate marks on the mud-colored ice, the smell of hot dogs and mustard in the pavilion, and the scalding cocoa that always tasted more like the cardboard cups than whatever chocolate might have been involved.

Andrea squeezed my arm companionably. "It's too bad the museum's only open on weekends. Same goes for the aquarium. We're not getting much for the new admission charge to the island."

"Well, it's a good thing the state took a lease on it," I said. "The admission charges will help to maintain it. Like the DIA, it's one of the good things about the city, one of the things that deserve to be saved. I'm not sure what anyone's doing to save the people."

"Like me," she said, "I guess the people will just have to save themselves."

"You're doing a pretty good job of that," I said, because I had to say something. "Let's hope they can, too."

"We'll see. Sooner or later, we all have to. Or go under."

The edge in her voice made my scalp tingle.

Later, under the great arching central dome of the conservatory, we strolled hand in hand through the warm

humid air amid towering palm trees. As with my
memories of the skating pavilion, the profusion of tropical
plants in the South Wing—fig trees, calamondin oranges,
bloodleaf bananas, pink powder puffs, and peace lilies—
took me back to my teenage years.

"One of my friends and I skipped school one day, not
long before graduation," I said. "The only time I ever
skipped in my life. We drove over to the island in his old
Ford and wandered around for a couple of hours. We
finally found ourselves here. Some guy in his forties or
fifties tried to pick us up." I recalled the man's short-
cropped gray hair, his expensively casual white cashmere
sweater, his pleated tan slacks, his soft brown loafers, the
air of wistfulness under his attempt to sound like one of
the guys. "I suppose he was just gay and desperate. I
remember he told us his address in Indian Village. Told us
we could drive over and have a good time. He was pretty
graphic about it. He lived on Iroquois, I remember, not far
from your place. When we got to our cars, my buddy,
George, said to him, 'If we don't get there, start without
us.' Teenagers are heartless, aren't they?"

"That man wasn't just gay," she said. "He was a
pedophile. You're lucky George was there that day."

"Why's that?"

"I think if you'd been here alone, you would have gone
with the guy just because you're so reluctant to give
offense." She smiled as if to soften the effect of this. "And
here you are, all these years later, still a target for
seduction by Indian Villagers."

"Lucky I got a second chance," I said. "With you."

Again, she smiled, more enigmatically. "We'll see."

And again, I felt a tingle that began in my scalp and

made its way down my spine.

When I dropped her back at the house on Seminole, she asked if I wanted to come in.

"Maybe we shouldn't push our luck," I said.

"I'd make it worth your while." She gave me that gray stare. Then, with a small shrug, she kissed me deeply and slid out of the SUV. "We'll see you for the opening," she said before closing the door. "And the party afterwards. By the way," she added, "I smeared the shampoo on your mirror."

"I wondered about that. It seemed like a strange joke under the circumstances."

"I'm sorry," she said, eyes downcast. "I was afraid you were brushing me off."

As I drove away, I knew she was still watching from the sidewalk, and I thought again about the second-best bed.

Back at the Inn, I checked my email, a habit I couldn't seem to break; curse of the hopeful writer. I had a terse message from Eileen. Without salutation or signature, it read, "Maxine tried coming out to her parents. They convinced her she'd made a terrible mistake. She has a fiancé she hadn't told me about. That's it. And I worried about terrorists. I suppose it's what I deserve for dating an undergrad."

I called her immediately, but got her voicemail message, tinny-sounding and aggressive. "Leave a message if you have anything worthwhile to say." The usual beep followed.

"Eileen," I said, "pick up if you're there." I waited for an answer, but none came. "I'm really sorry, sweetheart," I said. "You deserve only good things. And Maxine wasn't an undergrad. She wasn't even a student. She'd graduated. Please call me. We need to talk."

Part of me felt like leaving the Inn and driving back to Brixton. But I knew Eileen would be furious if I did. I sat down heavily on the desk chair and stared out at the parking lot, thinking about the shifting currents of relationships and our invariably futile efforts to exert any control over them. I would just have to keep calling and emailing until she responded.

At about midnight, after more attempts than I could count, I finally took a bath and went to bed. I expected to lie awake for hours, thinking about Eileen, about the situation with Andrea, and worrying about the play. Instead, I fell asleep almost immediately and didn't stir until morning light filtered into the room.

22

Opening night of *Swept Away* began with a reception in the lobby of the Hilberry. The place smelled of floor polish, perfume, and after-shave. I saw that the guests included a sprinkling of Theatre and other humanities faculty, their spouses or partners, assorted college and university administrators, a few students, potential and actual donors with interests in the arts, and representatives of the media. In the latter group, I suspected the assignment had gone to a fair percentage of second-stringers. I was glad I had decided to wear a tie, even though I had to keep reminding myself not to tug at the knot. I still wished I could talk to Eileen, but she had not yet responded to my numerous texts, emails, and voicemails, and I knew that I would have to wait.

Before disappearing backstage, Ed introduced me to most of the press people, but only two of them made an impression. Gloria Ammons, a WXYZ TV anchor with expensive hair, five-inch heels, and a short-skirted ensemble that looked a size too snug; and Terry DeVere from the *Free Press*, dean of Detroit reviewers, a dapper little guy in a perfectly tailored gray suit, a red tie accented with blue fleurs-de-lis, and tan designer shoes polished to a fare-thee-well. The Ammons woman murmured,

"Congratulations, Mr.—McCutcheon," gave me a reception-line finger-brush and moved on, leaving a haze of expensive perfume, as if she didn't want to be tainted by too much contact with the writer. DeVere had a surprisingly firm handshake for his size and said he had actually read the Samuel French script of *Swept Away* and looked forward to talking with me after reviewing the production.

I had difficulty processing it all, as I usually did on opening nights. Nonetheless, the atmosphere was encouragingly festive, and I was able to take a certain pleasure in realizing the amount of expense and attention being lavished on me and my work.

I eventually excused myself and made my way backstage to congratulate everyone on the professional quality of their preparation, sharing handshakes or fist-bumps with the crew and hugs with the cast and the two designers. My embrace with Rachel somehow ended up with her kissing my neck and whispering, "Your play is amazing. I hope we can stay in touch. I always think acting in a play creates a bond with the playwright. And it's especially true when you've actually met the writer."

Wishing her a broken leg, I detached myself and moved on. I found Ed again and let him know that his vision for the production, thankfully, had been in tune with my own from the beginning. We shared a high five and a knuckle-bump. Then I left them all to concentrate on their work. My own work now was at the reception.

Andrea and Larry were among those who showed up early enough to be included in the gathering, Andrea dressed in her hooded dark coat over a spectacular dress in a silvery hue. Larry wore the same expensively ill-fitting suit he'd had on at Fishbone's. But aside from introducing them to a few people, I was too busy meeting the confusing array of other guests to spend much time with the Durants, which was just as well with me. Andrea and I shared a conspiratorial glance, but nothing more. Now and then I thought I noticed the tall square-headed Larry eyeing me above the bald pates and expensive hairdos of the upscale non-academics in the crowd. Was Larry glowering? Maybe the collection of strangers made him uneasy. Or perhaps I, myself, was uneasy, a combination of opening-night jitters, guilty conscience, and concern about Eileen.

In a kind of *Macbeth's porter* moment that broke my mounting tension, a pudgy associate dean of something, balancing a plastic cup of some nasty white wine on a plate laden with shrimp tails and a smear of cocktail sauce, asked me if I was the writer. Receiving an affirmative response from me, the man went on, "So how does it work? You write these"—he paused—"*plays,* and then—what?—you try to get people to put them on for you? Is that the deal?"

I allowed as how that was, pretty much, *it*, after which he excused himself and went off to dump his plate and utensils in a trash can, evidently underwhelmed by *the deal.*

Among the crowd of unfamiliar faces and expensive suits, dresses, and hairstyles, I finally spotted Wily Fox, whose tanned features and dazzlingly-capped teeth were unmistakable from the photo on the college website. I threaded my way forward and, though Fox seemed to keep receding among the crowd, I eventually came face-to-face with my apparent benefactor. Fox raised his eyebrows as if expecting me to perform some acrobatic feat.

Extending my hand, I said, "Dean Fox. I'm happy to meet you at last."

Fox, an inch or so taller than I, had exactly the kind of manly grip suggested by his chiseled profile, but our handshake lasted no more than a millisecond. "Great to meet you, Dennis." His baritone voice was as manly as his handshake. "And call me Wily—everyone else does."

"I just wanted to thank you," I said, "for recommending my play. I had no idea anyone at Wayne knew anything about me these days."

Fox flashed his smile again, but his eyes were darting here and there as he spoke. "We keep an eye on our alums—even those from other departments, especially when they distinguish themselves in theatre. And *Swept Away* deserves to be staged. I'm just glad I could help."

"At some point I'll have to get the story on how you came to know about the play—and me." I still couldn't believe that Fox could have registered my existence. Though I felt mean-spirited at the thought, I reflected that he didn't seem like the kind who did things without an ulterior motive.

"You bet," Fox said. "We'll have to make time for a chinwag before you leave town. And now you'd better attend to your public." So saying, the associate dean melted away into the throng of first-nighters. He hadn't given me much more time than I had gotten from the TV anchorwoman.

Chinwag? I thought. Really? I'd have to save that for Eileen, sometime when she rediscovered her sense of humor. And again, I realized no one's opinion in the world mattered to me quite so much as hers did.

I craned my neck to scan the crowd, but Fox had vanished. Only his aftershave lingered in the air. I gulped down the barely-palatable Chardonnay a young man had handed me. Then, in relatively short order, I found myself, surprisingly, seated in the auditorium next to Andrea, with Larry on her other side, watching the lights fade to black prior to the start of action onstage.

23

During the first scene, Mark and Anna's characters—a mid-level auto executive and a journalist working on a book about a black bootlegger in Prohibition Detroit—prepared to meet the other two for the first time:

(*As the lights rise on the MACLEOD condo, we see KATHERINE kneeling on the floor, arranging stacks of books, manuscript, photocopied pages, and corresponddence in an attempt to create order. She is a good-looking woman wearing only a bra and panties.*)

KATHERINE: (*Calling off.*) Tell me their names again.

DENNIS: (*Off, preoccupied.*) What?

KATHERINE: Their names! What are their names?

(*DENNIS enters. He wears sharply-pressed khakis,and is putting on an equally sharply-pressed oxford-cloth shirt.*)

DENNIS: Ziehl! Willis-Ziehl, I guess. One of those hyphenated names. Jennifer Willis-Ziehl. And Ben.

KATHERINE: Jenny and Benny. And Denny. Jenny and Benny and Denny. Do you think that means something?

DENNIS: Where are my loafers?

KATHERINE: We rhyme! Except for me. Do you think that means something?

DENNIS: No. Katherine, for Heaven's sake, put your clothes back on. They'll be here any minute. Anyway, it's Ben. She calls him Ben. I suspect you don't call a stuffy museum director Benny. Where are my loafers?

KATHERINE: (*Playfully.*) I suspect your shoes are under the couch. Where I threw them in my desperate passion to get your trousers off.

DENNIS: I like your desperate passion.

KATHERINE: I like your liking my desperate passion.

(*They kiss. He picks her shirt off a chair.*)

DENNIS: They'll be here any minute. I'll pick up this mess. You put your clothes on.

At this point the characters' relationship had to seem both playful and untroubled. The actors caught the lightness of tone I had tried for in the scene, preparing the way for future complications without telegraphing them. The audience responded with laughter, but not too much, just as I had hoped.

Seated next to me, Andrea had contrived to drape her evening shawl over both our laps, and her fingers brushed my thigh, finally settling on my own hand. The distraction created in me a curious mixture of excitement and annoyance. Was she more interested in me or the play unfolding before us? I was conscious of a vague stirring beyond her that could only have been Larry shifting in his seat. This produced a corresponding movement from Andrea, and during the next few minutes, all three of us settled into concentrating on the action onstage. I exhaled, realizing I had been holding my breath.

The second scene introduced Paul's museum director, older than the other characters, and Rachel's artist, whose work had been commissioned for Mark's corporate headquarters, necessitating a relationship between artist and auto exec.

(*JENNY and BEN stand in the lobby. She is dressed with flair, in a long skirt; he is older than she and has the look of a professor, with a corduroy jacket and a beard.*)

JENNY: (*Pushing a button.*) How much do you suppose these places cost?

BEN: A canopy that cries out for a doorman in the lobby. Antique brass rails. Mahogany doors. It wouldn't be the cost that keeps us out. We'd be blackballed on general principles. (*Eyeing the telephone.*) Are you sure it's today?

JENNY: It's a good commission, Ben. Chrysler. And this is the guy in charge of the parts. *All* the parts, evidently. You met him at Cranbrook in August.

BEN: The one with the terminally neat haircut. Trying to pretend he was a Republican. I remember.

JENNY: Be good, Ben. Behave.

BEN: No artists' studios here. No smoke from welding to taint the exclusive air. (*Indicating the phone.*) I don't think just pushing the button will do it. I think you have to pick up the phone, too.

JENNY: (*Picking up the receiver, punching buttons, and listening. Then into receiver.*) Hi. It's Jenny Willis-Ziehl. I've come about the sculpture. About the pieces. (*Pause.*) Thanks. (*She hangs up; then, to BEN.*) He said he'd buzz us in. Behave, Ben. This is important.

BEN: Somehow, welding together automobile parts doesn't seem to me—doesn't seem worthy of your talent.

JENNY: You're talking about the money again. But just because someone is finally willing to do more than give me rave reviews doesn't diminish what I do.

BEN: Auto parts, Jenny.

JENNY: Actually, I really like the parts.

BEN: You think you can let a Big Three auto company be your patron and everything will be just fine. That, Jenny, is what Michelangelo thought when the Pope asked him to paint the ceiling.

As the scenes progressed, the performers increased the level of tension without sacrificing the comic moments. And the audience reacted appropriately, with amusement and focused attention, without the fidgeting and coughing I had learned to dread in any dramatic production, whether of my own plays or someone else's. And the packed auditorium meant that the crowd was reacting in concert, like a congregation, rather than in the independent clusters of response or non-response that inevitably developed in a house with appreciable numbers of empty seats.

Paul's big scene, in which the museum director recounts his unsuccessful attempt to save a man from drowning in the Detroit River, from being in fact *swept away*, had numerous audience members sniffling and dabbing at their eyes.

(*JENNY is seated at her studio's kitchen table, sketching on the large pad. The door opens and BEN enters, wearing his winter coat and holding a single glove.*)

JENNY: (*Preoccupied, sketching.*) Hi. Rough shift at the museum? (*Without replying, BEN takes off his coat and hangs it up. He crosses to a cabinet, lays the glove on it, takes out a bottle of single malt scotch and a glass, and pours himself a generous measure. He then crosses to the window with his glass and stares outside without drinking. Still sketching, JENNY nonetheless notes the bottle on the cabinet.*) My. It *must* have been rough. Wouldn't you rather open a bottle of wine? I'd take a glass, too.

(*He doesn't respond. She finishes another sketch and drops it on the floor.*)

BEN: Something awful happened today. You know how the ice forms along the shore of the island? Sometimes clear across to the Canadian side. It looks thick, but the current is so strong that it's thin in places. And it hasn't been cold enough to be solid yet.

JENNY: (*Gathering up her sketches.*)   So. Something happened.

BEN: (*Still not looking at her.*)   This man, a guy about thirty—from one of the high rises on Jefferson, I guess—he was jogging with his dog around the island. The dog—it was an Irish setter—it got away from him and ran out on the ice and broke through. (*A beat.*) I was in the museum parking lot—I'd just gotten back from lunch. The dog went right by me. There are signs everywhere telling people not to go out on the ice, but the dog broke through. This fellow ran by me to rescue his dog, and he broke through, too. It all happened in a rush.

JENNY: Into the river? Is he all right?

BEN: No one else was around. Just me. I ran down to the water—the dog was closest to me, sort of scrabbling at the edge of the ice. I was afraid I'd break through, too, but I took hold of the dog's collar and yanked at him, more to get him out of the way than anything else. The guy—his name was Jim—pushed the dog from behind, and out he came.

JENNY: You saved the dog.

BEN: Then I tried to reach the guy. But the ice was thin. And the dog was barking and jumping around behind me. I told the guy I'd go for help. We have life-preservers in the museum. But the man said, "No, I really need help now." His voice was calm, as if he were asking me for change. But he was panting. From the cold. And the current was pulling him away, to the downriver side of the hole. It was pulling him under the ice. (*He turns to face her.*) I yelled as loudly as I could. I thought somebody in the museum would hear me or be looking out the window. No one came. And I could see cars, across the river, in Windsor, driving along in the sunshine. (*A beat.*) I took off my coat. Then I went out—I slithered out—on the ice, on my belly. I held onto one sleeve of my coat. I tried to get the other sleeve to him. We were looking into each other's eyes the whole time. And talking, in these conversational voices. Even with the dog barking. "Can you reach it?" "No. The current's too strong." "I'll try to get closer." He had brown eyes. So did the dog. What a stupid thing to notice, eh? I slid farther out, closer to him. Then the ice started to crack again. And I flailed around and scrambled back, so I wouldn't go in. And when I looked for him, he was gone. He never made a sound. (*A beat.*) I was still holding onto the sleeve of my coat. I lost one of my gloves. (*He swallows all of his drink.*) He never made a sound.

JENNY: Ben. My God.

BEN: He drowned. He drowned.

JENNY: Ben. My poor Ben.

BEN: They found him at the end of the island. The Coast Guard. He was caught in the broken ice. (*A beat.*) I saved. The dog.

JENNY: (*Rising and moving to him.*) Ben.

This complication distracts the museum director from confronting the affair between his artist wife and the auto exec.

Meanwhile, Anna's journalist and Mark's auto exec effectively carried off an intense scene in which she forces him to confess the affair, which he has been covering not only by his assignment on the art project, but also by his negotiations with a Japanese parts supplier.

(*As the lights rise, DENNIS is seated in an armchair, reading the Free Press.*)

KATHERINE: (*Off.*) Dennis. What's this?

DENNIS: What?

(*She enters holding up a pair of boxer shorts.*)

KATHERINE: This? What is this?

DENNIS: Boxers. Boxer shorts.

KATHERINE: Whose, Dennis? Whose boxer shorts?

DENNIS: They're mine, silly.

KATHERINE: Why? I didn't think men wore boxer shorts anymore. You certainly don't. Didn't.

DENNIS: I like the free feeling.

KATHERINE: When did you discover you liked this free feeling? How did you decide this?

DENNIS: Jockey shorts are for little boys.

KATHERINE: Look at these. Plaid. Silk.

DENNIS: They're not silk.

KATHERINE: Sure they are. Where did you get them?

DENNIS: I stopped at Macy's. To pick up those mints you like. I just saw them on a rack and bought a box.

KATHERINE: Impulse buying. Something you never do.

DENNIS: Well, maybe it's time I started.

KATHERINE: Does this have anything to do with feeling free? (*Suddenly dead serious.*) All right, Dennis. What exactly does all this free impulse stuff mean?

DENNIS: (*After a pause.*) At the very first, I thought, This is crazy, but if I don't do anything about it, I'll be sitting on a porch someday and I'll be an old man looking at the sunset and rocking away, and I'll regret what I've missed.

KATHERINE: A porch? A rocking chair? What are you talking about?

DENNIS: (*Continuing.*) But that was only at the very start. It seems like it was only a few seconds, and then I quit thinking at all. There was no stopping. No slowing down.

KATHERINE: What have you done?

DENNIS: (*After a pause.*) I've fallen in love. I'm sorry, Kath. I'm in love. It just happened. Like a great wave washing over me. I was swept away.

KATHERINE: I thought *we* were in love.

DENNIS: I couldn't stop. There was never a moment after the very first when I could have stopped.

KATHERINE: It's that Jennifer, isn't it? Jenny and Denny.

DENNIS: We went out to the plant to look for parts for her sculptures, and we talked and talked, and when I came home, I kept thinking of more things to say to her. I couldn't get enough of her. And it's not just the sex. I love talking to her.

KATHERINE: Stop it. Stop it. I don't want to know any of this.

DENNIS: I'm sorry, Kath. I didn't mean for this to happen.

KATHERINE: (*Backing away.*) What would make you think I wanted to know all of this?

DENNIS: You're right. It's just that you're my friend, and I tell you everything. I've really wanted to tell you.

KATHERINE: This is awful, Dennis. I thought we loved each other. And you want to tell me about this artist. Oh, Dennis. How could you do this? Now we can't even be friends. (*A beat.*) And I said you have no sense of adventure. That you didn't like a good mess.

DENNIS: I *don't* like a mess.

KATHERINE: But you like this Jennifer.

DENNIS: Jenny. Yes.

KATHERINE: I'm going to bed. I don't want to talk to you anymore.

(*She throws the boxer shorts on the floor, then exits. The lights fade to black.*)

And so it continued through Act One. No missed cues, no flubbed lines, no malfunctioning props or tech glitches, just strong acting and efficient building of motivations and relationships. The numerous brief scenes had the intended effect of short one-acts, each ending with a point that propelled the forward movement. All in all, Ed had kept the action swiftly paced and left the audience with plenty to think and talk about during intermission, without giving much away about what was to come in the second act.

24

After the act closed to a pulse-quickening volume and length of applause, I decided I would stay in my seat throughout intermission. I said as much to Andrea, who squeezed my hand and said, "It's wonderful. I have to say I never expected it to be this good." While I was trying to think of a response she added, "I'd better follow Larry," then rose and moved after her husband who, without a backward look, was shouldering his way through the crowd toward the lobby.

Before I could do more than begin to wonder what might be going on with Larry beyond a sudden urge to pee, I saw Ed peering out from the wings stage left, giving me a thumbs-up, which I returned as unobtrusively as I could. Then I tried to shut out the buzz of voices around me, actually going so far as closing my eyes.

Finally, I felt Andrea settling into the seat next to me and heard a sack of potatoes sound that must have been Larry dropping into his place. Startled, I glanced at Andrea, who simply raised her eyebrows in silent comment. Something had obviously happened between her and Larry. He was staring straight ahead, but even in profile I could tell his closely spaced features were arranged in a pugnacious expression. I had no idea how to react, but I was soon relieved of the need to by the dimming of the lights and resumption of action onstage.

25

Act Two began with a monologue by Rachel, consisting of her character's responses to a committee of unseen and unheard auto executives questioning her about the project for which Mark's character has served as company liaison.

(*A spotlight rises on JENNY down C. She is dressed as usual, making no concessions to corporate style.*)

JENNY: (*Answering a question from L.*) Actually, I don't like to talk about theme. I like the auto parts. The shapes and textures. The structure. I'm not thinking about something like—say—Diego Rivera's *Detroit Industry* murals—the workers, the muscles. I'm concerned with how things fit together. How to make them fit into the piece as a whole. Just like you are when you put a car together. (*Another question from R.*) All three are like—pyramids. The individual figures build to the top. The apex. (*Another question from C.*) Who's on top? (*She laughs.*) At this point it's the figure with the tie. (*A question from R.*) No. It's not some sort of political statement. It just fits the feel of the piece. The shape is right. That's all. (*A question from L.*) I did my first welding in high school. Cass Tech. Right here in Detroit. Then I got my MFA at Wayne State. (*A question from C.*) No. I've never worked in a factory. Dennis—Mr. MacLeod—arranged a tour for me. (*Listening, then.*) Yes. The parts inspired me. Each has a function. Each is perfectly designed to do its job. Quite beautiful. (*To the same questioner.*) The man with the tie? Yes, I see what you mean. (*A beat.*) But, you see, it's the shape that's important. The woman with the welding torch is rounded. She fits here. The tie, the pen, the clipboard are all angular. They all point to the apex. The power in the structure. (*To a concluding remark.*) Well, yes, thank you, too. I do like talking about my work. I don't mind. I'll be glad to try to explain.

(*The spotlight fades to black.*)

Rachel expertly evoked both her character's confidence in her abilities and her growing disquiet about her questioners' motives. I realized the tone of the scene echoed my own recent Q & A session. I also realized that Rachel really was talented.

The thought was swept aside as the action moved forward, with Dennis and Katherine deciding to try salvaging their marriage. Then a series of scenes makes clear that neither can manage to overcome the obstacle of the affair, Dennis because he cannot deny his continuing love for the red-haired artist, and Katherine because, at heart, she can't forgive the betrayal.

(*As the lights rise dimly, KATHERINE is curled in a chair in her underwear. The outside door opens, and DENNIS enters.*)

DENNIS: You're still up.

KATHERINE: I'm still up.

DENNIS: I told you I'd be late. The meeting about the new sculpture went on and on this afternoon. And I can't afford to say too much, considering. I just sat and listened. (*A beat.*) And then I had the Matsu meeting. It's my baby, too. I couldn't leave.

KATHERINE: I believe you, Dennis.

DENNIS: Good. Because it's true. (*A beat.*) These were difficult meetings.

(*He sits heavily.*)

KATHERINE: I'm sure they were. I know everything you've told me is true.

DENNIS: The Japanese wanted to back off on all the compromises we negotiated.

KATHERINE: Do you want to know why I believe you?

DENNIS: What?

KATHERINE: Because fifteen minutes after you left, I got in my car and drove out past your office. And then after you called at nine p.m., I did it again. I also drove by *her* house, and she was there.

DENNIS: Katherine. That's crazy.

KATHERINE: I do it all the time, Dennis. I also push the redial button on the phone to see who you've just called. I pretend I'm your secretary and double-check your lunch reservations.

DENNIS: I haven't seen her. I haven't talked to her. I said I wouldn't.

KATHERINE: And you haven't stopped loving her.

DENNIS: I've tried, Kath. I don't know what to do.

KATHERINE: The time to do something was before it started. Now, it's too late. We can't put our life back together. I should have gone to an attorney before. I'm going now.

DENNIS: I've tried. I've given up a lot.

KATHERINE: Not as much as you're going to.

(*The lights fade slowly to black.*)

Intertwined with these scenes, a parallel series portrayed the relationship of Paul and Rachel's characters, Ben and Jenny. As if in punishment for the affair, Rachel's artist has learned that her sculpture for the auto corporation has been rejected. This sequence showed the museum director so profoundly shaken by his earlier failure to save the drowning man that his wife's affair—of which he's well aware—not only pales by comparison, but also seems more forgivable.

(*As the lights rise, JENNY is seated at the table with her sketchpad; the floor around her is strewn with crumpled sheets. She rips another sketch from her pad, tears it up, and throws the pieces down violently. BEN looks up; he rises, crosses to the sideboard, removes a bottle of scotch from its box, and carries the bottle and two glasses over to the table. He pours two stiff drinks, one of which he offers to her.*)

JENNY: You know I never drink that stuff.

BEN: I think it's time you did.

(*He sips from his own glass as if to demonstrate. She drains her drink in one swallow.*)

JENNY: (*Noting his surprise.*) I'm not drinking it for the taste. If I were, I'd pick something that didn't taste like varnish.

BEN: Another? (*She holds out her glass and he refills it.*) Losing the commission is rough. I know it was a real breakthrough for you. But you do have the money. And you'll find buyers. Galleries. It *will* get you the attention you want. You deserve. (*She drinks again, as does he.*) I know how you feel. I do.

JENNY: (*Obviously a bit drunk now.*) It's not just the

commission, Ben. I'm sorry about everything. These past weeks.

BEN: It's all right. I understand. I'm the one who's been crazy.

JENNY: No, you don't. I have to tell you something, Ben. Ben, I—

BEN: (*Holding up a hand.*) No, Jenny. Wait. *I* have something to tell *you*. Really. I need you to listen. I was nearly arrested today. (*She reacts to this but remains silent.*) Yes. I drove out to Bloomfield Hills again. To his parents' house. And while I was sitting there in my car, consumed with anxiety, a police car pulled up behind me.

JENNY: His parents called the police. Ben, I—

BEN: No. No. They're very nice. Besides, I don't think they ever knew I went out there. No, the policeman said that people in the neighborhood had noticed my car on several occasions. Bloomfield Hills doesn't tolerate strangers hanging around without good reason. Once he found out I was harmless—or at least didn't have any warrants outstanding—he asked me what I was doing there. I couldn't tell him. I realized how . . . crazy it sounded.

JENNY: What did you tell him?

BEN: I told him I was a museum director. That I was studying the architecture.

JENNY: In Bloomfield Hills?

BEN: He didn't believe me. He just told me that, from now on, I'd better do my studying in another municipality. Then he let me go.

JENNY: Ben—

BEN: (*Interrupting.*) The point is, he helped me to realize that I have to put this thing behind me. That I have to start paying attention to my life—to *our* lives. To the future.

JENNY: I'm glad, Ben. I've been so worried about you.

BEN: Come on. You need to get some rest. (*He starts to guide her offstage.*) We can talk about other things later. About the future. Face the music.

JENNY: (*Leaning on him, slurred.*) Ben. I don't think I want to—face the music. (*She does a clumsy pirouette.*) I'd rather dance to it.

BEN: (*Catching her in his arms.*) Don't worry, Jenny. Everything will be all right. You'll be dancing. Just not tonight.

JENNY: I care about you so much.

BEN: I know you do, Jen. I know you do.

(*He dances her offstage as the lights fade slowly to black.*)

Paul's work on this sequence again had many audience members reaching for tissues, and despite my usually critical eye, even I found myself moved. I was gratified to hear the audience murmuring receptively.

The action moved quickly toward resolution with Katherine finally initiating divorce proceedings against Dennis.

(*As the lights rise, KATHERINE is sorting through books, putting some in a box and others back on shelves. DENNIS enters from outside.*)

DENNIS: Katherine! Are you home? (*Seeing her, he waves a legal-sized document.*) What is this, Katherine?

KATHERINE: Wasn't the door locked? Did someone let you into the lobby?

DENNIS: Did you know about this? Katherine, I got this in the mail today from your attorney—who used to be *our* attorney, for Christ's sake. Did you know about this?

KATHERINE: What I do know, Dennis, is that this is my home, and you don't live here anymore. You need to ring and wait to be let in. In fact, you need to phone before you come over.

DENNIS: No-fault? What's all this stuff about "his lady friend"? It's supposed to be a no-fault divorce.

KATHERINE: Does it actually say "lady"?

DENNIS: It actually says a lot more than that. It says I was carrying on, humiliating you in front of family and friends. It says you hoped the marriage might continue. Hoped it might continue? You went to a lawyer. You kicked me out.

KATHERINE: You never stopped seeing her.

DENNIS: I did, Katherine. I *did* stop seeing her. (*Waving the document again.*) What do you mean by this?

KATHERINE: My *attorney* means just what he says. No-fault divorce. We divide the marital assets, right down the middle. *You* want a divorce. So, I'll take my half of the marital property.

DENNIS: *I* want a divorce? You could never stop being suspicious. You could never forgive me. This is revenge, Kath.

KATHERINE: This is the law, Dennis.

DENNIS: Kath, why does it have to be like this? I want us to be friends.

KATHERINE: You have what you want. But you want to be friends—and you want all the money, too. Take what you get, Dennis. I didn't tell any of our friends what a jerk you are or what kind of a whore you've taken up with—oh, yes, don't say a thing. Our friends want the details. They want me to tell them how awful you are. They want to cluck and be sympathetic—and all they want in return are a few damning details. Did he bring her to your home? Did he fuck her in your bed?

DENNIS: You know that's not true. You know I wouldn't do anything like that.

KATHERINE: I know what I *could* do. I wouldn't have to say much. Just a tear, a catch in my throat, a few juicy details, and that would be confirmation of how terribly wronged I've been. Do you know how much attention I could get if I would just share my devastation? I'm not your wife anymore, Dennis. I'm not even your friend. And I'm taking half of the marital property. (*A beat. She picks up a wooden box.*) The chess set is yours. You always beat me, anyway.

DENNIS: I told you the truth. I never made excuses.

KATHERINE: There are no excuses.

DENNIS: There are no excuses.

KATHERINE: Stop seeing her. Say you'll stop seeing her and come home. Why can't you just come home?

DENNIS: (*After a long pause.*) I tried. *We* tried. It didn't work. Not for me. Not for you.

(*He drops his keys on the table and exits. Still holding the chess set, she watches the door as the lights fade slowly to black.*)

Then Ben not only reveals his awareness of Jenny's affair,

but releases her to pursue her new love and announces that he has accepted a job in Chicago, where his daughter and her partner have joined a women's theatre company.

(*As the lights rise, JENNY is lying on a couch, one hand over her eyes.*)

JENNY: (*Calling off, weakly.*) Oh, Ben. Now I really know why I never drink scotch.

(*BEN enters, carrying a fizzing glass of Bromo Seltzer.*)

BEN: Here. Drink it while it's still fizzing. All of it.

JENNY: (*Drinking some.*) That's enough.

BEN: I've told you time and again, the only way to avoid a hangover is to get up in the middle of the night and wash down three aspirins with a glass of Bromo. (*A beat.*) Drink it all.

JENNY: In the middle of the night I was too drunk to know I was going to *have* a hangover

BEN: You certainly didn't want to sleep. You decided you wanted to dance.

JENNY: I don't remember anything but how sweet you were.

BEN: If we'd made love, it would have been because you'd had too much to drink. It would have been because you're sad.

JENNY: I'm *not* sad. You're right about my work. It's just a setback.

BEN: You're sad because you're in love with someone else, and I haven't let you tell me.

JENNY: I tell you everything. One way or another.

BEN: You've fallen in love with someone else. It's Dennis, isn't it?

JENNY: (*Quietly.*) Dennis. It *was* Dennis. I'm sorry. It's over.

BEN: No. It's not. (*A beat.*) Making love one last time—for old time's sake—for old Ben's sake—that would have been wrong.

JENNY: Ben. It's over. And I'm sorry.

BEN: I didn't have a chance to tell you last night. I've made some decisions. Sometimes the current takes you, and you just have to let go.

JENNY: But I wouldn't—

BEN: (*Sharply.*) Jenny! I'm not talking about you. I'm talking about *me*. (*She shrinks back.*) I've thought about that day. When I couldn't stop death from taking its course.

JENNY: What are you saying?

BEN: I'm leaving. *I'm* leaving.

JENNY: Ben. I haven't seen him in weeks.

BEN: I need to move on. *You* need to move on. (*A beat.*) I have an interview with the Maritime Museum in Chicago next week.

JENNY: (*Indignant.*) How could you do that without telling me?

BEN: (*Gently.*) Jenny. I need something new. I can't keep looking out across the Detroit River at Windsor, seeing cars driving back and forth in the sunshine, seeing that current, waiting for the ice to form again.

JENNY: I'm not someone you tried to save!

BEN: (*Quietly.*) And I'm not Dennis. Am I?

(*The lights fade slowly to black.*)

The play ended with two intertwined scenes. One showed the lovers together for the first time—in Japan, where Dennis has been headhunted by the Japanese auto parts corporation, and where Jenny is working with a master of Japanese woodcut art. The other scene dramatized Ben's visit to the embittered Katherine to give her an unexpected gift: as museum director, he has access to the papers of the bootlegger about whom she's been writing. Ironically, the bootlegger, smuggling liquor from Canada long ago by driving across the frozen surface of the Detroit River, had fallen through the ice and narrowly escaped with his life. I recalled my satisfaction in coming up with this echo during a later draft of the play.

(*As the lights rise, BEN enters the lobby. He checks the numbers on the brass plate, picks up the telephone, punches buttons, and waits.*)

BEN: Hello? Mrs. MacLeod? (*Pause.*) It's Ben Ziehl. (*Pause.*) I know. I've come anyway. I've brought you sort of a gift.

(*After a moment, he sits on a bench beside the telephone. The lights rise dimly on JENNY and DENNIS's apartment, minimally suggested by typically Oriental set pieces and decorations. JENNY and DENNIS sit at a low table, backs to the audience, arms around each other, heads together, looking leisurely through a photograph album and drinking sake. A Go game board sits on the table.*)

DENNIS: That's my father when he was a boy in Glasgow. And that's my mother, with the bow in her hair.

JENNY: She's beautiful. She looks like you.

(*KATHERINE comes to the door of the lobby, pauses, then comes outside where BEN is seated, letting the door shut behind her. He rises.*)

KATHERINE: Hello, Ben. I'm sorry. I don't know what we can say to each other. I told you not to come.

BEN: I came because I know you're writing about Prohibition in Detroit—about bootleggers.

KATHERINE: You know about my book. Because your wife told you after my husband told her. They talked about us. In their secret meetings. In bed, I suppose. Did she tell you I prefer red wine to white? That I'm a lousy chess player, but they left me the damned chess set, anyway?

BEN: Please. I thought we could talk. Do we have to do it here in the lobby?

KATHERINE: I hate that people I don't know *know* things about me. That they talk about me.

BEN: It's the end of intimacy. (*A beat.*) At least Jenny and Dennis won't be saying anything about us for a while. Not in this hemisphere, anyway.

KATHERINE: (*Bitterly.*) They've *really* run away now. Leaving us to face the music. (*A beat.*) Why shouldn't they be punished for what they did? It's like a joke on us!

BEN: Were you happier when you thought Dennis was in trouble at Chrysler? When Jenny lost the sculpture commission?

KATHERINE: (*Vehemently.*) Yes! You're damn right I was! You see. We can only say things that will make each other feel bad.

BEN: I know your friend—Marvin Dietrich. The former bootlegger you're writing about. He's on the Board of Directors at the Maritime Museum. Don't you think that's funny? Ironic, anyway.

KATHERINE: He's a remarkable man.

BEN: May I come in?

(*She shrugs and lets BEN follow her inside. In the Yokohama apartment, JENNY and DENNIS are dancing in each other's arms, without music, but in perfect time. After a few moments, they stop and he holds her at arms' length.*)

DENNIS: I can't believe how happy I am.

JENNY: Did you think we should be punished? That we should feel guilty and miserable?

DENNIS: Yes. But, instead, here we are. With a view of Mount Fuji. An adventure. Because of your wonderful art.

JENNY: Because you kept me supplied with Matsu ball-bearings. And because the Matsu people thought you were wasted at Chrysler.

DENNIS: Lucky.

JENNY: We are. (*A beat.*) I imagined you with me. Like

this. Together, in some exotic place. I was afraid it would never happen. Anywhere.

DENNIS: I tried not to let it happen. I really did.

JENNY: I know. So did I.

DENNIS: Katherine doesn't believe that.

JENNY: I think Ben does.

DENNIS: Because it happened to him once. Because that's the way he feels about you.

JENNY: Yes.

DENNIS: *(A beat.)* Maybe we didn't try hard enough.

JENNY: Could you have done anything different?

DENNIS: No.

(*The lights fade on them and rise on the condo as KATHERINE and BEN enter. Some furniture and decorations have been removed, but the chessboard remains on the table, with a game in progress, next to a copy of KATHERINE's manuscript and a legal pad with a pen lying on it.*)

KATHERINE: Dennis wouldn't even get an attorney. He was angry at first, and then he said, all right—whatever I wanted. Then he ran away. *They* did.

BEN: So it should only take the minimum period—three months.

KATHERINE: I need more time than that. (*A beat.*) What did you bring? Can I get you a glass of wine? I'm having some.

BEN: No. Nothing, thanks. (*He continues as she gets a glass of wine for herself.*) Marvin had a fundraiser for the museum. Very posh. At the Detroit Yacht Club. And we were talking. About you—that's right—and your private business. But he likes your book. About him. About the Purple Gang.

KATHERINE: He said he liked the texture. The way I went after the details. But he was very reluctant to give me anything beyond what I could find in public sources.

BEN: He kept a diary. When he was a sixteen-year-old rumrunner. And he's going to let you use it. He says it will make your book. He says it will make *you.*

KATHERINE: These days, I feel as if making *me* is a project that would have to start from the ground up. (*Looking at him.*) I can't imagine how you're dealing with this, especially after what happened to you with that poor man on the ice.

BEN: See. There. You know things, too. (*After a pause.*) Marvin and I talked about that, too. Just before he got out of the bootlegging business, he and one of his pals were driving across the Detroit River on the ice with a load of liquor. Late at night, no lights. They hit a patch of thin ice and broke through. Marvin managed to get out of the car. His friend didn't. Marvin said he had to walk on the ice for a quarter of a mile, soaked to the skin, freezing, to get home to Detroit. (*A beat.*) That was his gift to me. (*Holding up the manila envelope.*) This is his gift to you. He liked the idea of my telling you about it. It'll make a good section for your book.

KATHERINE: He never told me about a diary.

BEN: He likes keeping things to himself.

KATHERINE: But he also said he wants the details to be right.

BEN: And here they are.

(*Handing her the envelope.*)

KATHERINE: I wonder if you'd feel like giving me this if you knew what I'd done.

BEN: You're getting the divorce on your own terms. You said Dennis agreed to it. You shouldn't feel guilty about that.

KATHERINE: Guilty? What do I have to feel guilty about? I didn't want a divorce. I want them to hurt. (*A beat.*) I wrote to Chrysler about them. Anonymously. I'm probably the one who got them to cancel your wife's sculpture commission. Who got Dennis in trouble with the board. (*A beat.*) How do you feel about helping me with my book now?

BEN: (*After a moment or two.*) As it turns out, you didn't really hurt them, did you?

KATHERINE: I wanted to. I still want to.

BEN: They tried, you know. To stop seeing each other. I believe Jenny when she tells me that.

KATHERINE: And I believe Dennis. I guess. (*A beat.*) If I let myself start thinking about it when I go to bed at night, I can't go to sleep. (*A beat.*) It doesn't matter, does it? I'm here. You're here. And they're not.

BEN: But we're none of us at the bottom of the Detroit River. (*A beat.*) In any case, I won't be here long. I'm running away, too. I've got a new job at a museum in Chicago.

KATHERINE: It's not that easy for me. I'm only part-time as a copy-editor at the *Free Press*. That doesn't add up to much career-mobility.

BEN: After the book comes out, that'll change.

KATHERINE: It had better. (*A beat.*) I'm sorry. I don't like whining. Least of all to you.

BEN: Who in the world better?

(*He gets up to leave. The lights rise on the kitchen, where JENNY and DENNIS are dancing again. After a short time, she kisses him, then, letting go of him, cheerfully, shows him her sketchpad.*)

DENNIS: (*Admiringly.*) Your first sculpture. With the fish-tie and the playing cards. The one that caught Mr. Kasahara's eye. That is so beautiful, Jenny. It's Ben, isn't it? It's what you love about him. It's what I love about you.

(*Without answering, she kisses him again, and they resume dancing to their silent music. In the condo, KATHERINE finishes her wine and puts the glass on the table.*)

BEN: Finish your book, Katherine. Be famous. Get your divorce as fast as you can. Run away if you have to.

KATHERINE: I will. I am. As fast as I'm able.

BEN: (*Indicating the chessboard.*) Maybe you'll turn into a better chess player.

KATHERINE: I hate the game. (*Quickly, she sweeps the pieces into their box and folds the board, then picks them up and holds them out to BEN.*) Take it. My gift to you.

(*After looking at her for a moment, he does take it.*)

BEN: Thank you. Take care of yourself, Katherine.

KATHERINE: Oh, I will. I guess we all will. (*A beat.*) It's just not fair.

BEN: Love isn't fair. It's like death. It takes you when you least expect it. You can fight it. But when it's real, there's nothing you can do except let yourself go.

(*They shake hands. BEN exits. She pours another glass of wine, then sits, opens the envelope, takes out an old diary, and begins to read. After a few moments, she throws the diary to the floor as BEN appears in the lobby. He remains there while KATHERINE sits looking straight ahead, and JENNY and DENNIS continue to dance as the lights fade slowly to black.*)

As the lights dimmed, a silence fell along with the darkness, like a collective intake of breath. Then, as the lights rose again and the cast appeared to take their bows, applause began, growing in volume beyond any hopes I might have admitted to myself. And, around me, the crowd rose in a standing ovation, "bravos" resounding amid the clapping of hands. Beside me, Andrea, too, had risen, and was looking down at me, smiling, her gray eyes wide. Larry, like me, remained fixed in his seat. But Larry wasn't smiling.

26

After the bows and the cast's recognition of Ed, and after they waved me to my feet to more applause, I was borne in the crush of the crowd toward the lobby. Ahead of me, Andrea followed as Larry shouldered his way up the center aisle.

She turned quickly to me and said, "I'm sorry. We won't be able to stay for the party." Then the two of them disappeared, leaving me surrounded by well-wishing audience members to whom gracious responses were required.

What had happened? Had Larry discovered what Andrea and I were up to? Was the man, to use another homely expression beloved of my mother, not as green as he was cabbage-looking? Had Andrea said something to him? Or was he just irritated by the play's success? One way or another, Larry and Andrea's absence reduced the number of moving parts in an offstage drama that had become uncomfortably complicated. I decided the best thing I could do for now was give myself up to what seemed, after all, like a triumphant evening.

My old teacher, Aaron Golden, shouldered his way through the crowd. He embraced me, then took hold of my arms and looked up at me. "Well, Dennis," he said, "you've come a long way since your attempt to translate Racine."

"Thanks, Aaron," I said. "Coming from someone who's seen my early fumbling, your praise is welcome."

"Your play works," Golden said. "Aside from a couple of anachronisms and things that have changed since you left the city, it's right on the money, dramatically speaking."

"You'll have to email me any notes you may have."

"I will." Golden stepped back. "I wish I could stay for the festivities, but I'm not getting any younger, and I don't hold my liquor as well as I used to."

After a few farewell words, we shook hands and Golden walked off into the crowd and out of the building. No professor, current or former, I thought, could resist a critical word or two. And few students, whether they wanted to admit it or not, could deny the criticism was valid.

The after-show reception was to take place in the McGregor Memorial Center, the spectacular centerpiece of the Community Arts Complex and another place where I remembered having attended lecture classes. After a short time milling around among the people in the theatre lobby, accepting compliments and smiling for iPhone photos and videos, I accompanied Ed and the cast upstairs for the easy walk across campus in the cool evening air. Nowhere in the knots of people around us could I spot Wily Fox. I wondered briefly why the man seemed so disinclined to talk to someone whose play he professed to admire and whose career he'd obviously helped. Then, as with Andrea and Larry, I decided that was a subject best faced on another day.

As I walked next to Ed among cast and crew, I raised

my hand to check our progress. Then I raised my voice to thank them all for their work, adding, "I really saw the parts coming together, relating to each other in a way I hadn't before. I've only seen two other productions, one in a fairly small black box in Chicago, then the off-Broadway version a year later. Each of those prompted some useful rewriting. Now this production seems like the final version—of the script, at least."

"That's good news," Ed said. "I'm happy to know we did it justice. And I don't want to jinx us, but Terry DeVere took time to congratulate me before he left to write his review. Same for Anne Albert from the *News*. They almost never do that."

We all agreed fingers should be crossed and further speculation curbed. Then we continued our short trek to McGregor.

When we got there, I somehow wound up standing close enough to Rachel to smell her perfume. I couldn't place the fragrance, but it was undeniably effective. She was wearing what she'd probably call (complete with caps) a *Little Green Dress* and strappy high heels Deirdre would identify—also in caps—as *Come-Fuck-Me Pumps*.

Scrubbed of her stage makeup and looking fresh-faced and lithe, she raised her eyebrows and canted her head. "So, I guess you had classes in all these campus buildings?"

"I did," I said. "Back in the day. Most of them have been around much longer than I have." Rachel laughed at this allusion to the disparity in our ages, and I went on. "Old Main, State Hall, the Ed Building. I even had the lecture part of a Sociology class right here in McGregor. About the brainwashing of American GIs during the Korean... What did they call it? Not war —"

"Conflict," she supplied, smiling, and narrowing her green eyes.

"Very good," I said. "Talented, intelligent, *and* well-read."

"Don't forget *good to look at*." She laughed with an appropriate degree of self-mockery and touched her mop of red hair, tied back in a simple but impressive after-show ponytail.

"Hard to forget in that dress and those shoes," I said, raising my glass in acknowledgement.

"I'm glad you're paying attention." She raised her own glass.

I glanced around us. "Do you know Dean Fox?"

"Wily?" she said, frowning. "Why do you ask?"

"He's apparently one of the main reasons why this production is happening. But every time I try to talk with him, he disappears. Like now." I gestured with my glass. "He seems to have something better to do than hang around for the after-party."

Rachel chuckled. "For a second, I thought you were implying something about him and me."

Mildly surprised, I said, "Why would you think that?"

"Wily has an eye for the ladies. Maybe he had a hot date after the show." Rachel looked down, then back at me. "He has hit on me, in fact."

"Well, if he has an eye for the ladies, I'm not surprised he'd have an eye for you."

Rachel smiled and sipped at her drink. "And how about you? Are your eyes still directed elsewhere?"

"You know I'm leaving town in a day or two."

"I've also noticed the tall blonde with the goon for a husband."

I hesitated for a moment, then said, "They're old friends. I knew them in graduate school. Out East."

"Sorry. I may have misread things. But I know time is short." This was the least actor-ish thing she had said since we had met. It certainly made her even more attractive.

"Time is always short," I said. "Actors and directors usually have their eye on the next show, even on opening night of the current one. What's next on your list?"

"*Oklahoma*," she acknowledged. "Auditions are in a couple of weeks."

"Let me guess," I said. "You're going for Ado Annie."

I couldn't tell in the fluorescent lighting if she had colored slightly. But she did say, "*Touché*," with a performer's becoming smile.

I tilted my head at the crowd around us. "I need to do my duty and engage the paying customers. You gave a wonderful performance. Thanks for that. And we *will* stay in touch."

She gave a little bow. "Till then," she said, and walked away toward where Mark and Paul were talking with Carey, the costumer. I gave them all a little wave, then turned to work the room.

27

I was euphoric as I left the Cass Café sometime after one in the morning. The cast and crew had repaired to the place after the more genteel McGregor reception ended, and almost everyone had phones or iPads at the ready to check the online reviews.

Ed and I had sat at a smaller table next to the main group, trying to preserve a little professional detachment and gamely resisting the impulse to check our own phones. "However they turn out," I told my director, "I know what a great job you all did with the show. The production is everything I could have hoped for."

Ed had thanked me, but noted dryly, "We all know the game. The reviews sell tickets. And from then on, they wind up being clips you can use or clips you can't use."

I couldn't resist asking him what was next on his agenda. Ed shrugged and said, "You know how it is. One thing after another. Not much time to savor success—or whine about failure. I'll be getting ready to take last winter's production of *Anne Frank* to the American College Theatre Regionals. Sorry we can't take your show, but we have to start planning way ahead of time."

"I know how it works," I said. "No need for apology. You have to go with a known quantity."

Before we could talk further, raucous cheers rose from the group clustered around the main table. Then they all surrounded Ed and me for triumphant hugs and, in Rachel's case, an impressively prolonged kiss for me, featuring a pleasantly assertive tongue. "Your loss," she whispered as she broke away.

Both the *News* and the *Free Press* had weighed in with raves for the production, the play, and the playwright, though each reviewer had a predictable nit or two to pick. Walking their wits, as George observes in *Who's Afraid of Virginia Woolf*. But nothing harmful. I texted as much to Eileen, noting as I did so that Deirdre had been unable to resist wishing me a broken leg, probably both literal and figurative. Keeping her casting hopes open, no doubt. I also told Eileen to hang in there until I could properly dedicate myself to cheering her up.

I put away my phone and splurged on a couple of bottles of Veuve Clicquot to toast our success, so by the time we were ready to leave, amid a chorus of well-wishes, I was more than a little buzzed. After hearing admonitions from Ed that the cast should be ready for the next evening's performance, I left them all to find their way to their various destinations and started off on foot toward the Inn.

The streets were surprisingly dark and deserted for a Friday night near campus. Just as I reached Kirby and turned toward Woodward and the Q-Line construction zone, I registered that someone was following me, or at least was walking behind me. Rachel? I wondered idly. I was so close to my destination, though, that I decided not to look around. Then I heard the footsteps quickening, and my chance to glance behind me was lost.

Almost simultaneously I heard a distorted voice —"You fucking asshole!"— then something struck my head with stunning force, driving me to my knees, at this point feeling more shock than pain. The flow of time became viscous, improbably slow. Here I am, I thought, at the peak of my career, women buzzing around me, about to be killed in a city where muggings are a cliché.

Desperate, I managed to twist toward my attacker just in time to see a looming dark form, large head covered with a ski mask, starting to swing something at me again. In stop motion, like a Claymation figure, I threw my left arm in front of my face and fell back so that the blow glanced off my forearm. Then I grabbed the object with my right hand and yanked on it. Surprisingly, whatever it was came loose.

Now, even though dazed, I had the initiative—and whatever it was I'd been hit with. All sharp angles in my hand. I found an unexpected reserve of energy and pushed myself up just as my assailant leaned down toward me. I swung the weapon weakly, striking his head with a surprising *clack*.

"Get away from me!" I shouted, sinking back to my knees.

Again, the slurred, guttural voice: "You asshole! Think you know everything!"

A heavy foot slammed into my ribs, driving me back to the sidewalk, and the weapon—a two-by-four, I thought fleetingly—clattered away. Helpless, I curled into a fetal position, expecting a further assault; but to my surprise, all that came was a sound somewhere between a snarl and a groan, followed by the sound of heavy, but receding, footfalls.

I lay there, as yet feeling no pain, my head wet with what had to be blood, and my senses fluttering, a sound like water rushing in my ears. In the silence that followed, one thought floated through my head: the enraged attacker might have had a Tidewater accent, distinctly un-Midwestern in any case. That could only mean Larry. I drifted off to the sound of a woman's soft voice saying, "Oh, you poor thing."

Then I heard car doors slamming and a powerful engine starting, followed by the screech of tires.

DETROIT II

When I finally resumed a semblance of rational thought, I found myself seated on a padded chair in the Emergency Room at Detroit Receiving Hospital, a place to which my past life in the city had thankfully never brought me.

After x-raying my head and forearm, and pronouncing me lucky not to have a fractured skull, a broken arm, or pronounced symptoms of serious concussion, the ER doctor had put a few stitches in my scalp, and a nurse covered them with a large adhesive bandage.

"You'll hurt for a while." The doctor, a brown-skinned young man named Sirsat, had an accent that was pure Detroit. "Both your head and arm. But you shouldn't need more than aspirin or acetaminophen."

"Beats being dead," I said, managing something like a grin. Everything I did seemed to come with a built-in time-lag.

Apparently, two Wayne State campus police officers had brought me to the ER then passed me off to another pair of Detroit city cops. Both were in their late twenties or early thirties, a trim African American who introduced himself as Officer Dooley, and a plump and pretty Hispanic woman whose nametag read "Hernandez."

Officer Hernandez looked down at me. "Anyone you'd like us to notify, Mr.—?"

"McCutcheon," I supplied, my voice sounding muffled and distorted, like a message from somewhere outside me. After a moment trying to decide which hemisphere of my skull hurt least, I added, "I'm from out of town. Pennsylvania. I used to live here years ago. But I'd just as soon get back to my bed and breakfast place. I can let people know in the morning. I should feel better then." This relatively coherent speech probably took me twice as long to deliver as it might have a few hours earlier.

Officer Dooley spoke up. "If this guy was masked, there's no point in having you look at mug shots. He was big, you said? Black? White?" In the fluorescent glare of the ER, I noted a small scar that created a gap on one side of Dooley's moustache.

"Big," I agreed. "Tall, not fat. I'm pretty sure he was white."

"How come?" Hernandez asked.

"Something," I said, struggling for coherence. "Something about his voice."

"So, what brings you to Detroit?" Dooley said.

I gave them a quick, expurgated account of my visit, ending with the previous night's reception, opening performance, after-party, the Cass Café gathering, and the subsequent mugging.

"Congrats on the play," Dooley said. "Too bad somebody didn't just drop you at your hotel."

"Seemed way too close to need a ride." I felt as though my head was balancing uneasily on my neck, and there still seemed to be a delay in my conversion of thought into speech.

Hernandez said, "So, I guess if you're from out of town, you won't have had a chance to make any enemies." The merciless fluorescents revealed tiny sprinkles of blackheads on the wings of her nostrils.

Again, after what I hoped was a thoughtful hesitation, I spoke carefully. "I think it must have been a random attack." Mentioning Larry could only complicate life for me, Andrea, the university—everyone. I went on, hoping to head off any further discussion of enemies. "If he planned to rob me, he must have decided it wasn't worth it after I got the weapon."

"Yeah," Hernandez agreed. "We'll check it out. But he probably had gloves on."

Dooley cocked his head like every TV cop who pauses on his way out the door to say, *Oh, just one more thing.* What he actually said was, "What about the woman?"

And, like every guilty suspect who answers a question with a question, I said, "Woman?"

Hernandez took it up. "The Wayne State guys said they were alerted to the mugging by a woman. They heard her shouting, 'Help him! Help him!' "

"I might have heard a woman's voice," I said. "But I was blacking out. I didn't see any woman. What about the Wayne State police? Did they see her?"

"Not very well," Dooley said. "They just saw her disappearing down the street at about the time they saw you on the ground."

I was reluctant to give any hint that might identify Andrea, or even Rachel. "Did they get any description at all? She may have saved my life."

"Could be," Hernandez said. "But one of the campus officers went after her. He said she sort of glided off around a corner—then disappeared. He said she didn't make a sound apart from her original call for help. No footsteps. Nothing. Said it seemed kinda creepy."

"She must have been at a gathering, a wedding or something," Dooley added.

"Or an opening night party," Hernandez put in.

Dooley went on. "They said she was wearing some sort of long silvery dress. Old-fashioned looking. Anything ring a bell?"

I felt a shiver go through me. "No," I said. "No bell. She must have been a good Samaritan who didn't want to get involved."

"Well," Hernandez said, "we don't have a lot to go on. Unless we find your Samaritan, or someone else who saw this guy."

"Can you remember if he said anything else?" Dooley asked, pen poised over his notebook. "Or was it just what you told us to begin with?"

"That was it." I closed my eyes against the fluorescent lighting. " 'You fucking asshole.' Then, 'You asshole.' But I was too dazed to register much of anything."

Dooley flipped his notebook shut. "Well, we'll get back to you if anything develops. Sorry you had to go through this, especially on what shoulda been a happy occasion. You can take a cab back to your hotel whenever the doc says you're good to go."

I thanked the cops, then sank back in the plastic-covered hospital chair. As I did so, I heard Hernandez in the hallway, speaking in an undertone to her partner. "What do you think?"

Dooley snorted. "I guess the mugger must've had something against assholes."

And who could argue with that? I thought. My only amendment to Dooley's observation would be, *louder, faster, funnier*.

2

When I woke the next morning at the Inn, my head was bisected by a line of pain that had me reaching for the bottle of acetaminophen Dr. Sirsat gave me when I left the hospital. My upper left forearm was purple and red, colors that would have looked fine in the sky at sunset, but not so great on a human appendage.

I had been visited by dreams through the night, waking and drifting off so many times I could scarcely distinguish one state from the other. Most of the dreams featured curtain-shrouded rooms, with unsettling sounds and movement coming from the darkest corners. Whatever lurked there I never saw, but the possibility of seeing it filled me with dread.

Other dreams, unsurprisingly, were odd, slow-motion recapitulations of the assault, always on a deserted street and always conveying a sense of my own helplessness before the menacing attacker, whose weapon struck me repeatedly with blows that, in the real world, would have been fatal. And when, as had actually happened, I managed to seize the two-by-four, I could feel the texture of the wood and its sharp edges; but my own attempts to inflict harm on the shadowy figure were weak and without effect.

Thinking about all this made me break out in a sweat and intensified my headache. After washing down three pills with a glass of water, I recalled the previous night's actual events in a scatter of images that refused to cohere beyond the main episodes. First, the hugely successful opening of the play. Then the beating.

The masked mugger must have been Larry Durant. Somehow, the blockhead learned—or guessed—about me and Andrea. Had she told him? Taunted him? Something made them leave unceremoniously at the end of the show. The one thing I knew was that I wouldn't accuse Larry. I didn't actually feel I deserved the attack. I just didn't want to face the complications; being beaten up was humiliating enough.

Then, to quote Officer Dooley, "What about the woman?"

I looked around the room. For what? Could I seriously believe some spirit was following me? The female Samaritan must have been Andrea. Or Rachel. Or a completely random woman in a long dress whose description just happened to match both the young woman I saw in the doorway to my room that first day or the other young woman in the Degas painting who captured my imagination with her resemblance to the ghost—*the ghost*, I was calling it now—and to Andrea herself.

I decided to distract myself with routine. I went to the bathroom, winced at the reflection of my bandage-swathed head, then brushed my teeth and shaved gingerly, after which I took a hot bath, keeping the bandage as dry as possible. Then I got out, toweled off, and put on the plush robe provided by the Inn.

I left the bathroom just in time to hear my computer ping with an incoming email message. Crossing the room and bringing the screen to life, I saw the message was from Deirdre, with the subject line, "Swept Away?" She had obviously been researching the production and no doubt more besides, so instead of deleting her message, I sat down and read it.

"*Swept Away?*" she began without salutation. "Don't make me laugh. You've never been swept away. You're always too busy thinking when you should be doing. Probably doing when you should be thinking, too, but never swept away. You're like some kind of Martian, a pod-person visiting Earth and imitating the inhabitants so you can write about them. I suppose I have to congratulate you on the great reviews. Easy to get when all you have to do is ransack my private life for material, even though no one could play it as well as I could. Fuck you very much."

I deleted the message. And, almost comically, as if she and Deirdre were somehow synchronized, I got a phone call from Eileen.

Not wasting time on a greeting, she said, "Ben Talbot."

After a beat, I said, "You don't sound like Ben Talbot."

"I don't look like him, either, wiseass. But I did hang out with him at UC-Santa Cruz."

"Never mind about your brushes with stardom," I said, sounding more aggressive than I intended. "What I want to know is how you're doing. Has Maxine come to her senses?"

After a brief silence, she answered, her voice revealing her discomfort. "I suppose her parents would say she has. And at this point I guess she would agree. No doubt the fiancé—Diether—is happy, too. That leaves me as odd-woman-out, emphasis on *odd*."

"*I* still love you." I realized I wasn't just saying so to comfort her. Then, to lighten the tone, I added, "No matter how odd you are."

"Blighted romance makes strange bedfellows," she said. She went on quickly, "Back to Ben Talbot. His last three movies have made big bucks, in case you haven't noticed."

"And this means something to me because—?"

"Don't be an idiot. You know why. I've read your reviews. I'll be happy to pass *Swept Away* along to Ben. He could play either of the men."

"I'll just be glad to get out of Detroit alive."

"You and everyone else in the city." Eileen waited for a second or two. "So, what's the deal?"

I filled her in on the deal—Andrea, Larry, the mugging. Then I paused, knowing what to expect.

"I told you to stick with the redhead. Are you all right?"

"Other than the headache and the bruised arm."

"You clown," Eileen said softly. "But don't worry about it. Just regard it as a lesson learned. And stay away from the lovely Andrea and her hubby. Keep your eye on the prize. Ben Talbot."

"Okay, I will." I couldn't really take it all in.

"And take care of yourself." Without waiting for a response, she broke the connection. I realized I had embarrassed her by speaking to her vulnerability.

Before I could think further, I heard my computer signal the arrival of a new email message, this one from Ed Friend, headed "Congrats!" Obviously, the events of the night before had not reached the level of news. Just another Detroit mugging, another anonymous job for the

ER.

Ed's message was full of good cheer. "Hi, Dennis," it began. "Well, you and Chekhov, eh? The reviews are just as enthusiastic as they seemed last night. I won't go into what they said—I'll leave you to savor them for yourself when the papers arrive. What I will say is how much I admire *Swept Away*. You're a hell of a writer. And everyone here feels the same. Talk around the department is that we should move the production upstairs to the big space. That would—will—take some figuring, not to mention restaging, especially with my *Ann Frank* involvement and questions about availability of cast members. But at least the talk is going on. And Genevieve agrees.

"We can kick it around tonight after the show—or before, if you like. I've been asked to do some interviews with the papers and radio stations, maybe even TV, and it would probably be good if you could be there, too. Answer this or give me a call. Congrats! Ed"

Before I could do more than marvel at this news and briefly consider how I'd explain my injuries, I heard a quiet knock from outside the room. Tying my robe a bit more tightly, I crossed to the door and opened it, revealing a smiling Latrece.

As she noted my robe, my damp hair, and the bandage on my head, her smile faded to a look of concern. "Mr. McCutcheon," she said, "I apologize for disturbing you. I'm not on duty today. But I didn't want you to have to wait for breakfast to see your wonderful reviews, so I thought I'd bring you the *Free Press*. I also printed a couple of online TV and radio reviews."

"Thanks, Latrece. That's really lovely of you, especially

on your day off." I took the paper and printed sheets from her.

"I had to be downtown anyway," she said. She directed her eyes again at my bandaged head. "I hope you're all right. It wasn't something that happened here at the Inn, was it?"

I shook my head carefully, trying not to register the pain that lanced through it. "No, no," I said. "Just a minor post-opening mishap." I realized Latrece would learn I'd been mugged, but I was finding conversation difficult in the light of Eileen's assertions about staying away from Andrea—and Larry—and her optimistic introduction of Ben Talbot's interest in the play. She would just have to put my equivocation down to my two-by-four-induced headache.

"Glad to hear it," she said. "Like I told you, if there is such a thing as a ghost here, she's a gentle one who'd never hurt anyone. She'd look out for you. And you look out for yourself, too."

"I'll be fine," I said. "I'll be out for coffee soon."

She smiled and nodded. "Robert and the weekend staff will keep it hot for you." Then, as she turned to leave, she noticed something on the floor. "What's this?" she said, bending to pick up a small rectangle of cardboard. Glancing at it, she said, "That's beautiful. You must have dropped it when you came in last night."

She handed me the postcard and walked away. I glanced down at the blank side. Nothing written there. Then I turned it over and looked at the picture. It was a DIA reproduction of the Degas painting, *Violinist and Young Woman.*

I closed the door and walked back into the room. I set

the card down next to my laptop, tossed my robe onto the bed, and got dressed. Then I came back to my computer, sat down, and gazed at the postcard. How could it have gotten there? If Andrea had come to the Inn during the night, or this morning, Latrece—or someone—would have known and mentioned it. Was I back to thinking about a ghost?

I breathed deeply, trying to decide what I might do. The postcard lay before me. The young woman in the gray dress, oblivious to the musician, looked off at something unseen. In a way, Deirdre was right. I was an observer, my responses often coming too many beats after the call to action. But the one action I could always take, however late, was to write.

I looked over my shoulder, where the woman in the postcard might be looking, toward the door to my room. Nothing. Nothing I could see. Nonetheless, I spoke to the closed door, behind which something might have saved me. "Thank you," I said.

And somewhere outside the room I heard another sound, like the plucking of a violin string. Chekhov, indeed.

Resisting the urge to investigate the noise, I sat down with the *Free Press* and the other stuff. As I had noted at the Cass Café, the notices were uniformly favorable except for the few innocuous reservations that established their critical *bona fides*. Terry DeVere, the *Free Press* reviewer, went so far as to wonder why *Swept Away* hadn't been picked up by Richard Corwin, the producer who'd given it a two-month run in New York. Money, of course, I answered silently. At the time, I had been pathetically grateful the producer had been willing to stage the show at all. Then I'd allowed myself the foolish luxury of hope, until after opening night.

To be sure, Corwin had said, "If we'd gotten one or two more good reviews, we could have parlayed that into another month or so to see if the show caught fire. But the *Times* had a couple of snotty sentences and *New York Magazine* was pretty bland—and of course the *New Yorker* took no notice at all. Maybe next time."

Next time, I had thought. What next time? But I had set myself right away to revising the script, and now hope was stirring again in Motown. Great reviews and a hairsbreadth escape from death. I realized I had better get back to Ed right away and tell him to count me in for the interviews, no matter how uncoordinated my right and left hemispheres might be. Not quite feeling up to a phone call, I tapped out an affirmative reply to Ed's email message, then settled back in the armchair to leaf through the newspaper, concentrating as best I could on the latest genuinely hopeful articles about the Tigers' and Red Wings' playoff chances, and the usual jaundiced assessment of what might befall the Lions.

And then I saw the inch or so headlined "Campus Mugging." The piece mentioned an attack on an unidentified out-of-town visitor, assistance by campus police, and ongoing investigation by the City of Detroit's finest. I hoped that might be the end of it. Then I realized, with another flash of lightning between my frontal lobes, that I ought to check to see that Andrea was safe. Who knew what else Larry might have done?

While I considered how I might go about contacting Andrea on a Saturday without involving Larry, my cellphone vibrated, signaling an incoming call. I checked the screen. Ed Friend. I clicked the talk button.

"I hope you're up and not too badly hung over," Ed began.

I grunted ambiguously, not wanting to get into the mugging just yet. "Up for what?" I said.

"Turns out Terry DeVere wants to talk to us this morning. I told him he could meet us at the Inn and talk over coffee and pastries. That okay?"

I gently blew out an invisible candle. "Let the wild rumpus commence."

"I'm in my office," Ed said. "I'll be there directly. Terry should arrive within the hour."

After disconnecting from Ed, I stood up too quickly and had to prop myself on the arm of the chair for a few seconds. Then I switched on the ringtone on my phone, which I'd carefully switched off before the show. The simple action seemed to demand more energy than disarming a bomb. When my head cleared a bit, I decided not to take anything with me for the interview. Anything DeVere needed beyond talk, he could get from Google, or I could email it to him. The fewer moving parts, the better.

I went into the bathroom and checked myself in the mirror. I decided I would attract fewer questions from DeVere if I removed the bandage. I got a fingernail under the adhesive and pried it off, careful not to interfere with the stitches in my scalp. Aside from yanking out more hair than I would have wished, the operation was a success. I gingerly brushed my fingers over my hair to conceal the stitches as best I could. The result wasn't wonderful, but it was better than the bandage and would have to do.

3

"Jesus," Ed Friend said, eyeing my head, "you really did take a beating. Hell of a way to end a triumphant evening in the theatre."

So much for concealing the evidence, I thought.

We were seated at one of the Inn's breakfast tables. Besides his mug of coffee, Ed had a cheese Danish, a banana, and a dish of blueberries on the plate in front of him. With my head still occupying more of my attention than I had hoped, I stuck with coffee and two more acetaminophen.

I had given Ed no more than bare details about the assault, figuring that approach was better than concocting something that might come back to haunt me later. *Haunt*, I thought ruefully. All I needed was a ghost complicating the rest of the story.

"Imagine how I'd be feeling now if the show had bombed," I said.

"Yeah," Ed acknowledged. "I'd be pretty bummed about that, even without getting whacked by a baseball bat. I should have dropped you back here."

Two-by-four, I thought, though I didn't bother to correct Ed. "I only had a few blocks to walk," I said. "What were the odds?"

"Obviously pretty good," Ed said. "I'm just glad it wasn't any more serious."

From behind the desk, Latrece's weekend relief, Robert, watched us as if Ed might have been sent to launch a follow-up attack on his injured guest. Catching me glancing at him, Robert flashed a gap-toothed smile.

"Terry doesn't usually do next-day pieces," Ed said around a mouthful of banana. "But I guess an excellent review compounded by a mugging makes for good copy. Shouldn't hurt box-office, either." Ed discarded his banana peel and grimaced. "Sorry to sound so cheerful about your misfortune. But you do seem to have gotten through it intact. I hope they catch the guy."

"Do you think DeVere will know about the mugging?" I asked. "After all, the story in the *Free Press* didn't mention my name."

"Maybe not," Ed said. "We'll soon see. By the way, Genevieve sends her best. I left a message for Wily Fox about the interviews. Who knows where he's gotten himself to?"

I felt my stomach lurch as I thought about negotiating a newspaper interview without getting into detail about what I thought had actually happened the night before. Given the latest developments, I was no longer in such a rush to contact Wily Fox.

But what about Andrea? Not having heard from her was beginning to make me feel uneasy. Ed's presence was a welcome distraction from further speculation, so I let him guide the conversation to topics that might come up during the interview.

Terry DeVere walked into the room about fifteen minutes late, accompanied by a photographer wearing a many-pocketed khaki vest and a couple of cameras dangling from his neck.

"Sorry for the delay," DeVere said in his precise east coast diction. "I stopped off to pick up Everett. Thought we'd get a few shots to go with the interview."

After the ritual of handshakes and introductions, we repaired to my room in Owen House, where we were less likely to be interrupted than in the breakfast room of the main building. Once we were settled, Everett Traynor, the photographer, a thirtyish African-American man with a flattop and shaved temples, said, "Don't pay me no never-mind. I'll get my pics while y'all make conversation."

"And I'll just record us," DeVere said, setting his phone on the padded luggage bench at the end of the bed. Then, just when I was beginning to think my removal of the bandage had worked, the reviewer added, "What happened to your head?"

"Detroit," I said. "I ran into a mugger on the way back from the Cass Café. The *Free Press* actually had a police-blotter item about it this morning."

"Well," DeVere said, "I guess I'll have to include it in my story, but I'll try not to make a meal of it for the good of your play—and the city. Was it a robbery?"

"No. Maybe just somebody working out hostility." Equivocal or not, I realized this response was accurate, at least. "It was over in less than a minute. All in all, I was pretty lucky."

DeVere went on to ask several obvious and relevant questions about the mugging, and I answered them thoroughly, without mentioning the Durants. After all, I couldn't be sure Larry had been the attacker. And I certainly wasn't going to introduce the supernatural. Ten minutes later, I felt relieved that the subject had been broached and, evidently, put behind us.

After that, the conversation went well, punctuated by the click of Everett's shutter and directed subtly by the experienced DeVere. They dealt with my background in Detroit, my writing habits and aspirations, rehashing a considerable amount of information covered in my public Q and A, but with more personal details.

After some incisive questions concerning my career at Brixton, DeVere said, "Well, Dennis, after this production, I predict you won't have to worry much about your tenure situation."

"I'll relay your opinion to the TPC," I said, trying to sound as humorous as the pain in my skull would allow.

DeVere grinned. Then, showing a sensitivity one might not expect from a tough reviewer, he said, "Maybe we can move out to the breakfast room for our talk with Ed and let you rest for a bit."

"Suits me," Ed said. He looked at me. "I'll see you tonight at the theatre if you feel up to it."

I thanked DeVere, Ed, and Everett, and within minutes was lying on the bed on top of the covers, blinds drawn, shoes kicked off, with a couple of additional painkillers inside me. I couldn't have cared less about poltergeists or apparitions. And even though I still felt uneasy about not having called Andrea, I decided that could wait until my head stopped pulsing.

4

I must have fallen asleep, because the next thing I knew the telephone was ringing on the nightstand beside me, making me jump and sending another stab of pain through my skull. I noted by the clock next to the phone that about half an hour had passed since I had lain down; then I picked up the receiver and spoke carefully, as if my voice might trigger a further shock. "Hello?"

"Sorry to disturb you, Mr. McCutcheon." The soft baritone wasn't quite in the James Earl Jones register, but pretty close. "This is Robert on the front desk. You have a visitor. Should I send him over to your room, or would you prefer to see him in the breakfast area?"

Visitor? Could it be another reporter? Ed? Larry Durant? Dean Fox? "Did he give a name?"

"He's from the police." Robert's voice was free of inflection.

This information hung for a few seconds in the electronic void. For various reasons, I felt a shiver of guilt. Then I said, "I guess you'd better send him over to my room."

I replaced the receiver and got out of bed, put on my shoes, and walked into the bathroom. Deciding against more painkillers, I sloshed some water on my face and rubbed my hands over my eyes. Surprisingly, this actually made me feel better. By the time I had toweled myself off, I heard a soft but authoritative knock.

I opened the door. Given Detroit's current demographic, I was unsurprised to see my visitor was African American. I was, however, startled to see that the cop, rather than being in uniform, was wearing what looked like a tailored grey suit with an understated stripe, a lime-green shirt, a narrow tie in muted pink, and stylish brown chukka boots in smooth-grained leather. The man looked fortyish, with the beginnings of a paunch, and his dark-skinned forehead gleamed below his graying, close-cut hair.

"I'm Sergeant Lindenbrook," he said, the timbre of his voice coming closer to Darth Vader than Robert's. "And you'd be Mr. Dennis McCutcheon." He extended his hand, and we shook. Firm grip, slightly sandpapery feel.

"Come on in," I said, gesturing toward the room's armchair. Lindenbrook sat and I took the desk chair, realizing as I did that sitting came as a relief. "I didn't expect a mugging would rate this level of response." Trying for a noncommittal tone, I added, "Did you catch the guy?"

Lindenbrook's mouth twitched in what might have been a smile. "We've spoken with Officers Dooley and Hernandez about your case, and it's still under active investigation. You're a little higher profile than our usual victims." He fished his cellphone from a pocket and said, "You don't mind if I record our conversation, just for accuracy's sake?"

I thought for a second, feeling a bit uneasy. "I suppose not," I finally said. "Go ahead."

"Good." Lindenbrook clicked on the record button. "This'll make things simpler. I just have some follow-up questions on a possibly related matter."

The detective paused, as if reluctant to say more, so I said, "Related matter?" I, too, waited to see what all this parroting might produce.

Lindenbrook looked at me impassively, no doubt used to this sort of verbal poker. He finally said, "First off, you told Dooley and Hernandez you figured you were attacked by some random mugger. That right?"

I felt something stir inside at the question. I seemed to be reeling from one narrative to another—academic novel, showbiz saga, ghost story, trashy romance, and now an episode of *Law and Order*. Then I reminded myself that, though I was the victim here, I wasn't necessarily innocent, and that I had better focus. "Well," I said, "the guy was wearing a ski mask and gloves, and he attacked me from behind, so what can I say?"

"Took a while for you to say *that*," Lindenbrook said, passing a finger across his neatly-trimmed moustache.

I allowed myself a ration of indignation, righteous or not. "I'm not really tracking too well right now," I said, gesturing at the stitches on my scalp. "And I already said as much to the officers at the hospital, Dooley and, and—"

"Hernandez," Lindenbrook supplied. "So, just to make sure, you're saying you didn't know your assailant?"

"I'm not sure why you'd think I would have."

Lindenbrook allowed another obviously tactical measure of silence, then said, "You wouldn't happen to be acquainted with a couple named Durant, would you?"

A thrill of shock passed through me. I decided to play for time. "Squeak," I said.

Lindenbrook's head tilted back slightly in a pretty good single take. "Come again?"

"Cat and mouse," I said, with what I hoped was a disarming smile. "And I guess I'm the mouse."

"That's right." Lindenbrook nodded. "You're a playwright. Good with dialogue." He paused. "So, I take it you do know the Durants?"

Deciding I might as well get on with it, I said, "They were my next-door neighbors years ago when I was in graduate school out East. I was surprised to run into them here in Detroit. They read about my coming to Wayne State for my play and took me out to dinner. At Fishbone's."

"Good food there." Lindenbrook grinned, then pressed on. "Mrs. Durant's a fine-looking woman."

This all seemed to be moving too quickly. "She is," I said. "Always has been."

"So," Lindenbrook said. "Could it be you somehow got crosswise with Mr. Durant, maybe over his fine-looking wife, and that this so-called mugging wasn't so random after all?"

"Jesus." I felt blood surging to my face. "I'm the *victim*. Of a masked attack. If you suspect Larry Durant, why don't you ask *him*?"

Lindenbrook gave me one of those opaque stares. "I'd love to," he said at last. "But Mr. Durant's in no position to answer. He's dead."

5

All I could do was stare at Lindenbrook, my jangled synapses unable to process the information. And Lindenbrook was far from providing any assistance. I saw now that his presence had nothing to do with my being a "high profile" victim. Finally, I managed to say, "Dead? How?"

"A heavy blow to the head with a blunt instrument. A two-by-four, evidently. Like you say you were assaulted by."

Again, my brain felt vapor-locked. "But who could have done it?" I realized I was about to say something unwise, but I couldn't stop himself. "Someone attacked both of us?"

"Thought you might help with that," Lindenbrook said, his dark eyes fixed on me. "You did say you took your attacker's weapon and retaliated. Maybe in the heat of the moment, you hit him a lot harder than you thought."

"I hit the guy—the mugger—once," I said, more loudly than I'd intended. "And I don't think I hit him more than a glancing blow. I was pretty dazed, just managed to get up from my knees. Then he took the two-by-four—or whatever it was—kicked me in the stomach, and ran off. I fell down again and heard a car drive away." I paused, breathing rapidly. "Where did Larry die?"

"At home. In Indian Village. His wife—widow—Andrea, says they got home right after seeing your play. I guess they sat with you during the performance. That right?"

"That's true," I said. "They didn't stay for the party. I got the impression Larry wasn't happy about something."

Lindenbrook nodded, as if checking off an item on a mental list. "So, by the time they got home, Mrs. Durant says they were in the midst of an argument. About you, it appears. Mr. Durant stormed out of their house and drove off. Mrs. Durant says she was afraid he might have intended to confront you, so she tried calling you to warn you." Lindenbrook paused, waiting for a reaction from me.

"I turned my phone off during the play, like everyone else. I guess I forgot to turn it back on. I found that out this morning."

"That makes sense," Lindenbrook said. "So, unless we're dealing with some real unlikely coincidences, seems like the attack on you and Mr. Durant's death are connected."

I squeezed my eyes shut for a second, trying to concentrate, then opened them. "If that's true, and I hit him so hard, how did Larry—Mr. Durant—manage to get himself home?"

"I try not to make too many assumptions." Lindenbrook shrugged. "But there are two possibilities. One is that someone else got him home. That starts a whole other line of inquiry. The other is that symptoms of head injuries are hard to predict. He could have driven home, then collapsed when whatever happened inside his skull took effect. Dr. Sirsat at the E-room said delayed reactions like that aren't uncommon. It's called *slow bleed*.

And that's what Mrs. Durant said must have happened. But those are questions for the medical examiner."

I felt a surge of nausea. "Sirsat?" I finally managed. "That's another coincidence. He's the doctor who treated me."

"So he said." Lindenbrook cocked his head. "In my business, coincidences usually turn out to be significant."

"In mine, too," I said. "But I usually try to make them believable."

"Good policy."

"Look," I said, reflecting momentarily on all the interrogation scenes I'd watched on *Law & Order*, "are you here to arrest me or something? Should I be calling a lawyer?"

"That's up to you, of course." Lindenbrook's tone was a bit less cordial. "Right now, we're just hoping you can help us with our inquiries, as the saying goes."

"Look," I said again, my own voice hardening, "if you think I'm responsible for Larry Durant's death, you need to tell me. Then I can decide what I ought to do."

Lindenbrook nodded, his expression radiating what might have been real sympathy. "We're a ways from attributing responsibility. If you got attacked from behind, like you say, and tried to protect yourself—"

"*If?*" I said, trying to contain my irritation. "Did you find the weapon? The ski mask?"

"Found a two-by-four and a mask in Mr. Durant's vehicle."

"Then you should be able to find my blood on the two-by-four. I'll be happy to provide a sample."

Lindenbrook smiled. "That's good. But we already got that at Receiving, remember? Forensics has the weapon now."

"So, when will you make a decision?"

"Not my call," Lindenbrook said affably. "So far, the evidence seems to corroborate your account, so it's very likely we'll put this unfortunate event down to self-defense—an attack by a jealous husband with a weapon and your natural impulse to ward him off, and so forth. But I'm just a cop, not a prosecutor. The best support for your version is the campus officers who came to your aid—and Mrs. Durant, of course. That, and finding the weapon and the ski mask."

"My *version*?" I couldn't suppress my impatience.

Lindenbrook held up his palms in a calming gesture. "After the medical and forensics examiners weigh in, we should be in a position to say for sure. You can take some comfort from my being here alone. My partner's got a new kid and took a couple days family leave, and right now, this doesn't look like a high-priority investigation. You probably know money's tight in Detroit these days."

I sighed. "I can't say I take much comfort from the news that I may have killed someone."

"Sounds like he might not have left you much choice." Lindenbrook waved his cellphone. "Before I switch the recorder off, I just have to tell you to stick around the city until we get things squared away and so forth. Okay?"

"Fine," I said. "I have the show to attend. And some press interviews."

Lindenbrook frowned. "I'd be a little, let's say *circumspect*, in communicating with the press about this matter."

"It's not something I feel like talking about."

"I hear you." Lindenbrook clicked off the phone's

recorder and got to his feet. "I'll be in touch." He pocketed his phone, then took out his wallet and handed me his card. "In case you want to get in touch first."

Before Lindenbrook reached the door, I couldn't resist. "One question," I said.

Lindenbrook turned back. "What's that?" he said, holding up his phone, presumably to record the exchange.

I forged ahead anyway. "This must have been pretty traumatic for Mrs. Durant. I mean, having to deal with it all by herself. How's she holding up?"

Lindenbrook tilted his head back and pursed his lips as if considering how much to reveal. "She seems to be doing okay," he said, finally looking at me. "Fortunately for her, she had some assistance from a neighbor. Guy happened to be out for an early morning bike ride. Saw Mr. Durant on the ground outside the house. Apparently, Mrs. Durant had fallen asleep, so he woke her, then helped her with calling 911. Said she was pretty distraught."

I felt a strange surge of unease. "Neighbor?"

"From up the street. Checked out. Good Samaritan situation, I guess." Lindenbrook shrugged. "They do turn up from time to time."

I hesitated a beat, then said, "Did the neighbor have a name?"

"Of course." Lindenbrook squinted at me. "Fox. Bill Fox. William. And by the way"—grinning—"that was *three* questions. Take care now." He nodded, pocketed his phone, then turned and walked out, shutting the door behind him.

After the detective left the room, I sat for several minutes trying to decide how many coincidences were too many. And I wondered what I might have said that I wouldn't want recorded. I also felt a heavy sense of guilt, while at the same time feeling unconvinced that my feeble attempt to defend myself could have caused Larry Durant's death. And the helpful neighbor, William Fox? What was going on here?

6

I finally decided I could no longer put off calling Andrea. Before doing so, though, I checked my laptop for emails and found nothing from her. I then looked at the record of recent calls on my cellphone. Nothing. So she evidently hadn't tried to call me last night, despite what Lindenbrook had said.

Well, here goes, I thought, and punched in her number. Ring followed ring, and just as I decided I would have to record a message, she was on the line.

"Dennis. It's me." Her voice was quiet and careful-sounding. She had returned to the childlike affectlessness I had noticed when I first re-encountered her. "I suppose you've heard. About Larry."

I waited, but she said no more. Finally, I spoke. "I have. I just had a visit from a Detroit cop named Sergeant Lindenbrook. I'm really sorry. Are you okay?"

"I'm holding up." I waited, and at last she spoke again. "I'm sorry, too. I felt I had to tell the police about you, about Larry being jealous and out of control."

"Did he do anything to you?" More silence. "For God's sake," I said. "What is it?"

"He yelled about you and me all the way home from the theatre," she said. "Then he ran out of the house and drove off. I thought you'd probably be surrounded by people, so I wasn't too worried. I guess I thought he'd just drive around and blow off steam. But I tried to call and warn you just in case."

"I had my phone turned off."

"That makes sense."

I couldn't resist saying, "I just checked my recent calls, and there's no record of one from you."

Another brief silence, then she said, "I was upset. I must have misdialed. Anyway, I didn't get through."

I decided to put off pursuing the question of the phone call. In any case, something seemed strange about the timing. How long could Larry have been waiting to spot me on the way back to the Inn? "Did you try calling Larry after he drove off?"

Again, I counted the seconds before she answered. "I didn't feel like talking to him. I hoped he'd cool off and come to his senses."

"I was attacked last night on the way home from the Cass Café." For some reason, I didn't feel like volunteering much more. I finally said, "I thought it might be a random mugging. He hit me with a two-by-four."

"My God," she said. "Are you all right?"

"The campus police took me to the hospital. Receiving. I needed stitches in my scalp. I was treated by the same doctor who apparently attended to Larry later on."

"I'm glad you're all right." She went on. "Do you think it might have been Larry? You didn't recognize him?"

"The mugger was wearing a ski-mask." I waited, unwilling to volunteer more. This all felt very strange. Why was I being so cagy?

"When Larry got home," she said, "he must have

gotten out of the car and collapsed in the driveway. I never got to talk to him." I heard her take a deep breath. "The police found a ski-mask and a—piece of wood in the car."

This entire recital came in that strangely emotionless childlike voice. I tried to imagine the look in her gray eyes. It all seemed more chilling than any of Deirdre's over-the-top histrionic tantrums. I had difficulty forming a coherent response, though at least her account seemed to confirm that Larry had been my attacker. Not that the information was as reassuring as I might have expected.

I took a deep breath of my own. "I'm really sorry. I got the two-by-four away from him—the guy—for a second or two and took a swing. I only hit him once. Then he grabbed it back from me and ran off. He didn't seem badly hurt. He had enough strength to kick me before he left." I mentally debated with myself about mentioning the woman who might have been on the scene but decided that was something for a later conversation. And what about Lindenbrook's Indian Village *Good Samaritan*? Instead of going there, I said, "I was defending myself. I had no time to think. I was dazed and confused. I certainly never meant to do him any harm. I feel terrible about this."

"Don't." Her voice was barely audible at first, then gained in volume. "He came after *you*. He could have killed *you*."

"Not that I hadn't given him reason." I realized how whiny I must sound. "I apologize," I said. "I know what an ordeal you must have had since last night. Would you like me to drive over to your place?" The suggestion was stupid, I realized, but I couldn't resist hearing what she would say. If it was yes, I could always invent a reason not to come.

Again, her response was time-delayed. "That probably wouldn't be a good idea right now. You must still be feeling the effects of being attacked. And we wouldn't want to give the police any ideas."

"Ideas?" I said. How stupid could I get away with seeming?

This time she answered quickly. "That there was anything going on between us, other than Larry's jealousy and possessiveness."

But something *was* going on between us, I thought. Or had been. "If you say so," I said, trying not to sound as irked as I felt. My emotions had become as jumbled as my logic.

She seemed to catch my tone. "It's just that I have so much to think about right now. The funeral arrangements, things like that. I'm sure the police will see you were only trying to protect yourself. We can talk more when things calm down."

Things like that, I thought. Like a two-million-dollar insurance policy, if I remembered correctly from dinner at Fishbone's. And now that I considered our conversation, she seemed to be talking as if she were being overheard, as if someone else were there. The police? "I guess you're right," I said carefully. "I'll talk to you when things settle down."

"Thank you for understanding," she said. And the line went dead.

7

Mentally replaying my conversation with Andrea, I opened a new document on my laptop, titled it "A & L," and typed in as much of our exchange as I could recall. Then I did the same for my interrogation by Lindenbrook, for it had been an interrogation after all. Once I finished typing, I realized I had only one person I could talk to candidly about anything important in my life. So I dialed that person via FaceTime.

Eileen's face duly appeared on my computer screen, looking beautiful as always, allowing for a little puffiness around her eyes and the usual fisheye effect of the lens. My own appearance on the app always featured more nose and less chin than I preferred to see.

Eileen harrumphed. "You really did take a beating, didn't you?"

"It feels worse than it looks," I said.

She shook her head as if at an incorrigible child. "To what do I owe the honor of this celebrity encounter?"

"Larry's dead," I said flatly.

"What?" She frowned, uncomprehending. "Larry?"

"Yeah," I said, "Andrea's husband. Apparently when I got the two-by-four away from the guy and hit him with it—just once, and I didn't think very hard at that—

apparently it caused some sort of slow bleed in his head. Anyway, Larry's dead."

"All right," she said. "Give me the whole story. Don't leave anything out."

With the document I had just completed fresh in my mind, I gave her as detailed an account as I could manage. I described the mugging again, my questioning by Lindenbrook, the details I had gleaned about Larry's death, the various coincidences with Wily Fox, if that's who the Samaritan turned out to be, and my strange conversation with Andrea.

Throughout this recitation, Eileen regarded me steadily, and when I finished, she said, "A two-million-dollar insurance policy?"

"That's right," I said. "People do have corporate insurance policies."

"You moron," she said softly. "Get yourself a lawyer. And watch out for Andrea. And the so-called neighbor who just happened to be riding his bike past the Durants' house at the crucial moment, and who's also the guy who happened to recommend your play to the theatre department."

"We don't know that for sure," I said.

"For God's sake," she said. "This isn't a fucking mystery. You've been set up."

Eileen's quick response made me realize I had been refusing to pay attention to my own suspicions. But images of my encounters with Andrea kept intruding. *Not with anyone*, she had said, after we'd made love. I looked at Eileen's skeptical scowl. "Do you really think so?"

"Dennis," she said. "I know your brain's attached directly to your pecker. But try to focus. Get a lawyer."

Part of me—Eileen wouldn't hesitate to identify which part—still wanted to argue. "The detective—Lindenbrook—said I probably didn't need one. That it looks like self-defense."

"That's not the fucking point," she said. "Have you stopped to consider that you may not have been responsible at all?"

"What?" No. I hadn't stopped to consider any such possibility.

"You need a keeper, Buster Bean. And I happen to be available."

"Well, you certainly are a keeper."

She shook her head pityingly. "Get a fucking lawyer."

Eileen disappeared from the screen. I looked at the computer but saw no answer there. This was all moving too quickly for my ill-functioning brain.

8

"I wanted to talk to you all before the show." I looked around me at the cast and crew. "You've probably read or heard something about what happened last night, and I don't want it to be a distraction for you."

Ed Friend said, "You don't have to worry, Dennis. They'll stay focused."

"This is Detroit," Rachel said. "Quite a few of us have had brushes with crime, even if we haven't been mugged."

"We're just glad to know you're okay," Paul added to a general chorus of assent.

I nodded in acknowledgement, careful not to let my head fall off. "Unfortunately," I said, "it turns out to be more complicated. I got the weapon away from the attacker and managed to hit him before he ran off."

"Good for you," Anna said, and this time the vocal response was even more positive, with some clapping.

I held up a hand for quiet. "The problem is—and I haven't even told Ed this up till now, for which I apologize—the problem is, even though he was wearing a ski mask, subsequent events have pointed to the attacker's being someone I knew." This got a ripple of surprise from the group, and an ambiguous look from Ed, but I plowed ahead. "Evidently, he was angry at what he thought was a relationship between me and his wife. I'd known her—and him—back East, years ago. And now he's dead, possibly from my hitting him in self-defense."

Ed said, "Jesus." Otherwise, no one made a sound.

"I wanted you all to know," I went on, "just to keep rumors to a minimum. I'm sorry to put this on you just before the show, but you'll understand, I'm pretty shaken up myself."

At this point Ed stepped in. "All right, guys. Time to get your heads in the game." He clapped his hands. "Let's go."

Cast and crew moved off to their various pre-show locations, buzzing amongst themselves. Before she and Anna disappeared into the wings toward their dressing-room, Rachel caught my eye. She gave me a half-smile and shook her head as if regarding a naughty child, a lot like the last look I had gotten from Eileen.

When we were alone, Ed, too, favored me with a parental frown. "I wish you'd given me a heads-up on this a little sooner," he said.

I spread my hands and shrugged. "I'm sorry. The cop—a Sergeant Lindenbrook—said I had to be careful about telling anyone. And it took me a while just to process the situation. In fact, I'm still working on that. But I decided all of you ought to know."

"Okay," Ed said. "How's your head?"

"It hurts. But at least I'm alive."

This hung between us for a few seconds. Then Ed touched my shoulder. "Well, go on out there and try to enjoy the show."

We shook hands, and Ed went off in the direction of the dressing-rooms, no doubt to see if the four cast members really were focused on the business at hand. I started for the stage left door leading to the auditorium. But before I got there, I heard footsteps behind me and a soft voice.

"Dennis? Can I have a second?"

I turned to see Carey, the costume designer. Tonight, her hair in braids, she was wearing yellow ballet slippers and red dungarees over a rainbow-striped, long-sleeved tee-shirt. But her expression was anything but festive.

"What's up?" I said.

"I've been meaning to tell you about something." Her mouth twitched nervously. "And now, with all the stress you must be feeling, I just have to say it."

I waited without speaking, unable to predict what might be coming.

"The ghost," she said. "I know that first day at the Inn you saw something."

"I've never mentioned that," I said carefully, "except to Ed."

"It was a prank," she said. "Everyone knows the Inn's supposed to be haunted, so I was asked to set it up—just to break the tension of staging a new show. I pulled a Victorian outfit from wardrobe and asked one of the second-year acting students to sneak up to the door of your room and give you something to take your mind off pre-opening jitters."

The revelation caused me to revisit the tremor I had felt when the young woman appeared at my door. "So how did she disappear without a trace?"

"It's an old building," she said. "There's a little door under the stairway to the second floor. You know, like in *Harry Potter*?" She gave a quick smile. "Well, I just wanted you to know."

She turned to leave, but I said, "Wait up." She faced me again. "You said you were asked to set it up. By whom?"

"Oh," she said. "I thought you'd figure that out right away. By the same person who recommended your show to the department. Dean Fox."

9

I stared at the head on my mug of Newcastle Brown, trying to decide on the best way to begin. Rachel and I were seated at a tiny table in the crowded confines of the Circa 1890 Saloon on Cass Avenue, a Law School hangout she had recommended as being unlikely to bring us attention from her usual crowd.

"So," she said, her stage-trained voice penetrating the noise around us, "to what do I owe this special attention?" She was wearing a green scoop-necked leotard, a flippy black skirt, and her cowboy boots. As at the opening-night reception, her face was scrubbed clean of stage makeup, making her look young and vulnerable. She took a sip from her own pint of Pilsner Urquell. "Given your situation, I know you can't have designs on what passes for my virtue."

"Wily Fox," I said.

She fixed me with her green-eyed stare and frowned. "He prefers Bill," she said.

"That's what I understand from the police, though he told me I could call him Wily."

"The police?" She looked genuinely puzzled. "What do you mean?"

"I'll tell you in a minute," I said. "But I have a couple of questions first." She sat back waiting, and I continued. "Is he a bike rider?"

She nodded. "He's all about staying in shape. Has a really expensive racing bike—two or three thousand dollars. He rides to campus and back a few times a week, decked out in the full regalia—skin-tight shorts and shirt, special shoes, fancy helmet. Showers and changes into his dean's finery."

"So where does he ride to campus from? Do you know?"

"He has a place in Indian Village." She looked at me steadily for a beat. "And, yes, I've been there. A College of Fine Arts cocktail party."

I registered this with an uneasy sensation in my stomach. "And what about his board membership at the DIA?"

"What about it?"

"I guess his fine arts background makes it logical."

"That, and his way with wealthy donors." She paused. "Especially female donors of a certain age."

"Any problems you know of?" Seeing her quizzical expression, I spread my hands and shrugged. "I'm just trying to figure out why he'd recommend my play."

She registered momentary indignation. "Anybody would recommend it," she said. "It's a wonderful play. I mean that."

"And you're wonderful in it." I smiled. "I mean that."

"I've heard rumors about Fox," she said. "About financial irregularities. Missing art objects. Not that I really know about his being involved in anything. I'm just a student, after all."

"And what about at the university?"

She gave a little snort. "The usual, for a ladies' man. Inappropriate relationships with students. Innuendo. Nothing that's stuck—so far. And even though I may be trying out for Ado Annie, I'm not about to fall for some Ali Hakim in real life."

I smiled and took a swallow from my mug. "I take it that means you don't see me as either Ali or Jud Fry."

She cocked her head. "It doesn't mean I've fallen for you, either."

"I guess I deserved that."

"Don't worry," she said, and laughed. "You're Curly all the way—even if you don't have any curls." I laughed, too, but then Rachel looked serious. "Enough with the *Oklahoma* innuendo. What's the point of all the Wily Fox questions?"

I played for time, swirling the Newcastle Brown in my mug. "I thought he preferred Bill." But I saw she had had enough of repartee. "I'm not entirely sure," I admitted. "But however good it may be, I'm pretty sure our friend the dean recommended my play for reasons I know nothing about. And he's been strangely reluctant to talk to me since I got here. Now, with Larry Durant's death—in Indian Village—I find out that not only does Fox live there, too, but he was the Good Samaritan who happened by in the middle of the night to help Andrea Durant cope with the emergency. And tonight, Carey told me Fox had her set up a prank to make me think I'd seen a ghost at the inn."

"A ghost?" Rachel looked as if she were trying to suppress a laugh.

"According to Carey, Fox asked her to have a student masquerade as one of the ghosts that are rumored to haunt the place. Supposedly as a tension-breaker. I wasn't tense until I thought I'd seen a ghost."

"What an odd thing for him to do."

"That's not all." I described the apparent presence of a woman during the mugging, followed by her mysterious disappearance.

"You'd been hit on the head," Rachel said. "Maybe you hallucinated."

"The campus cops said they caught a glimpse of her, too. You have to admit, that seems like a lot of coincidences, even for the fevered imagination of a playwright."

Rachel took a few seconds before responding. "But aren't you—I'm sorry to put it like this—aren't *you* the one who hit this Durant guy? And you *were* somehow involved with his wife. Even from a distance I could see that."

"You're right. I just feel as if there's something more happening here. And I need to figure it out."

Rachel reached out and laid a hand on the table. "If I can help, just let me know."

I covered her hand with one of my own. "You've already helped, Rachel." I leaned back and drank what was left in my mug. "Now I'd better see you back to your place. You need your rest for tomorrow's matinee."

10

Rachel kissed me warmly at the front door of her Second Avenue flat, and I felt a moment's pang before leaving her. But I wasn't about to complicate my life any further, so I simply asked her to keep our evening's conversation confidential and wished her goodnight.

Despite the attack, I wasn't particularly apprehensive as I approached the Inn. The streets were still relatively populated with Saturday night bar crawlers. As I walked, I thought about Carey's revelation and my various other brushes lately with the supernatural, including the apparition—or whatever it was—at the battlefield in Gettysburg. On the face of it, I realized, they didn't exactly make me look like the most reliable of witnesses. But witness to what? That was the question. And what about the inexplicable things I had seen and heard since that first day? That was another question. Even a fake ghost could stir the imagination.

Having made my way across the construction zone on Woodward, I walked down Ferry and into the parking lot of Owen House. Reflexively, I checked the window of my room. Nothing stirred behind the curtains.

On impulse, I stopped in at the main building, where I found Robert behind the desk reading Walter Mosley's *A*

Little Yellow Dog. Next to him on the counter lay an economics textbook. Robert glanced up and said, "Evening, Mister McCutcheon."

"Evening," I said. "Shouldn't you be off by now?"

Robert grinned, revealing the gap between his top front teeth. "Working a double shift," he said. "Got to pay for books and tuition." He gestured at the textbook on the counter. "Gonna have to get back to homework soon. But I have to take a break now and then. Helps keep me awake."

Pointing at the novel, I said, "Good book. Mosley makes LA in the forties and fifties come alive."

Robert nodded. "He sure makes you feel that, even if you're way too young to know for sure. I just read *Devil in a Blue Dress.* Good movie, too. Denzel. Don Cheadle."

"You're right. Mouse is one scary character."

"Book's better than the movie, though," Robert said. "I like the way Mosley writes."

"Me, too. Can I ask a favor?"

"Just say the word." Robert put down his book.

"Can you make sure no calls get sent through to my room? I'll collect messages in the morning."

"You got it."

"Thanks, Robert. And good luck with economics; class and tuition bills."

I handed Robert a ten from my wallet, then left him with Walter Mosley and walked back to Owen House.

Once back in my room, I settled at the desk chair and turned on my phone, which I had switched off for the performance and left that way for my conversation with Rachel. I listened to voicemails from both the *News* and *Free Press* requesting interviews or statements. Then I switched the phone off again and tried to think of something I could do. Finally, despite the lateness of the hour, I could decide on nothing better than calling Eileen. She certainly seemed to be my lifeline, I thought, as I woke my computer, set up a Face Time call, and watched the screen

As if she had been waiting for the call, Eileen appeared almost immediately, looking unaccountably fresh and beautiful, all things considered. Without preamble, she raised her eyebrows and said, "So? Have you gotten a lawyer yet?"

"I told you. I may not need one. Besides, the only one I really know of in town represented my black-sheep cousin Randy a couple of times. That was a long time ago. And neither of those worked out well. Being guilty didn't help him. He wound up in Jackson Prison."

"Where is he now?"

"Somewhere on the West Coast. The last I heard from him, he said he had AIDS. His story was always *wrong place, wrong time.*"

"Maybe it runs in the family."

"Maybe. But I've found out a few things since we last spoke. So let's forget the lawyer for right now."

Eileen blew out a non-existent candle, reminding me again how synchronized our habits had become. "Okay. Fill me in on the latest plot twists."

I checked my watch. "I'm sorry it's so late. Maybe you'd rather hear all this tomorrow?"

"Talk."

"You're sure? What about Maxine? Any new developments?"

Eileen's lips compressed for a moment. "I don't feel

like getting into that."

"What if I don't feel like talking either?"

Her scowl transformed into a good-humored sneer. "That'll be the day. You called me. I didn't sit up past my bedtime to unburden myself about *my* problems. Quit stalling."

I started talking, filling her in on my conversations with Carey and Rachel. She listened without saying a word. As I finished my account, she finally spoke. "Rachel sounds like a clever girl."

"Good-looking, too. But definitely hetero."

Eileen flashed one of her smart-assed smiles. "Everything's negotiable."

I fixed her with what I hoped was a disconcerting stare. "I'll have to remember that."

"Ho-ho," she said. Then, becoming serious, she went on. "The shit's going to hit the fan tomorrow. Once the media connect the mugging and Durant's death, they'll be all over it. And you."

With a twinge of unease, I said, "I told the cast and crew tonight, just so they wouldn't be blindsided by the press. But I can't see this being the kind of story that would rate much coverage."

"Dennis, Dennis," she said, "your heart's in the right place. I wish I could say the same thing about your brain. The porch-light's on, but nobody's home."

"Hey," I said, "I do have a head injury, after all."

She shook her head. "You'd better get some rest. You'll need it. By the way," she added, "I did try to call you earlier. I assume you turned your phone off for the show."

"I did. And it'll be off again once we're done here."

"Leave it like that," she said.

"You don't have any immediate thoughts? Ideas?"

"I have plenty of thoughts—and ideas," she said. "But I'm going to leave it for tomorrow. I'll talk to you after your matinee. I have a couple of errands to run first."

"Errands?"

"We can talk about that after the show."

"Very mysterious."

"You bet."

I shook my head. "You're quite the tricky little minx."

Even on the less-than-perfect definition of the computer screen, I could see Eileen's expression darken. "Maybe there are ghosts there, after all."

"What do you mean?"

"*Little minx*. That's what my dear Uncle Landon called me just before he—as we put it in our quaint Southern way—*interfered* with me."

"I'm sorry. I didn't mean—" I didn't know what I didn't mean.

Eileen waved a hand in front of her face. "Perish the thought," she said, emphasizing her Southern accent.

To lighten the tone, I said, "Sounds as if you're channeling Scarlett O'Hara—or Doc Holliday."

She grinned. "I'm your huckleberry."

"I live in hope."

She looked at me steadily from the screen until I felt my neck growing warm. Then she quoted another of Val Kilmer's memorable lines from *Tombstone*. "Well—an enchanted moment."

Feeling the need to re-establish our usual tone, I said, "I'll enchant *you*."

"*I* live in hope. Well, I have things to do. You can go rest up for your obligations to the media. I'll see you later."

The screen went black. I turned the phone off, but watched it for a while anyway, wondering what had just happened.

▍▍

I awoke at around seven a.m., brushed my teeth, shaved and bathed, then dressed for the day in a blue oxford-cloth shirt, tan corduroy jeans, and brown Pikolinos slip-ons. If I didn't feel good, I could at least look presentable. I found a copy of the *Free Press* outside my door, then roused my computer, but decided against turning on my phone.

I shook out the *Free Press* and glanced at the front page below the fold, where a brief article was headlined, WSU VISITING PLAYWRIGHT NAMED IN TRIANGLE, SUSPICIOUS DEATH. A small picture accompanied the story, obviously from the previous day's interview with Terry DeVere. At the end of the piece, the reader was referred to DeVere's interview in the entertainment section.

Eileen was right, I thought. The shit has officially hit the fan.

The *Freep* story covered the facts without undue embellishment, naming me, Andrea, and Larry, but omitting any mention of Wily Fox. It also described the show's highly successful opening, alluding to DeVere's enthusiastic review. The closest the article came to speculation was a reference to unnamed police sources noting that the deceased might have sustained a fatal injury during an attack on the playwright, but cautioning that further action on the incident would await the medical examiner's report.

I sighed. Then I used the house phone to call the front desk and told Robert to continue holding my calls.

"You got lots of messages out here," Robert said. "Reporters camped out, too. You want me to bring your messages to you?"

"Thanks," I said, "but I'll get them when I come to breakfast."

"I'll be glad to bring you over some coffee and rolls," Robert said. "Give you a little nourishment before you face the mob."

"That would be great. Thanks." I replaced the receiver.

I switched on my cellphone, revealing messages from more press and media reporters, which I decided against listening to.

I also had a voicemail from Dr. Finsterwald. The familiar creaking tones, like that of a superannuated adolescent, sounded worried, as usual. "Dennis, this is Raymond Finsterwald. I'd meant to call and congratulate you on the success of your play. Now I find myself hoping you haven't managed to cause yourself and the university trouble that can't be remedied. Please do what you must to resolve your problems and get your focus back to academe, where you belong. You can consider this as representing the view of Dean Rimmer, too."

I switched off the phone again. The eyes of Brixton were upon me.

Minutes later, I opened the door in response to a soft knock, revealing Robert with a tray bearing coffee and rolls, which he set down on the table next to the armchair; he also dropped a sheaf of phone messages on the bed. I thanked him, fished another ten from my wallet, and gave it to him.

Robert grinned, winked at me, and made the bill disappear. "Judging by the number of people in the breakfast room and the parking lot," he said, pausing in the doorway before leaving, "you're probably about to be ganged up on by a bunch of reporters with a bunch of questions." He closed the door behind him.

I sat in the armchair, deciding to concentrate on coffee and croissants for a while before facing either the press gang or the matinee.

12

Having done all I could to ward off the press on my way to the theatre, pleading the imminent start of the matinee, I was hoping they might have dispersed by the time the performance ended. But when I left the theatre that afternoon after congratulating the cast and crew on another strong effort under difficult conditions, I was assailed again by the phalanx of media people.

They surrounded me with their flashing teeth and well-coiffed hair, their incessant and repetitious questions, their cameras clicking and whirring like cicadas, and their microphones pointed like defective light-sabers. Well, I thought wryly, a few weeks ago this was the kind of attention I thought I wanted. Unfortunately, my play was only a sidebar to the main story.

"Please," I finally said, trying to keep moving forward, "I told you all back at the Inn this morning, I have nothing to say beyond that I was attacked on the street. I sympathize with your need to ask questions. There's just not much to add right now, not till I hear more from the police."

One of the reporters, I couldn't tell from which medium, said, "Do you expect to be charged in Mr. Durant's death?"

Still moving through the human barricade, I said, "I've told you already, I was trying to defend myself against a masked attacker. I had no idea who it was. And I hope that'll be clear in the light of the evidence."

Another reporter waved a microphone or a cellphone. "Do you think this will hurt your career? Or will the notoriety help?"

I had a moment to think about the turn-away attendance at the matinee, and my having relinquished my own seat to stand at the back of the house. Then I said, "I don't care about that at the moment. A man's death is more important than my ambitions, or even this production, though all those talented people deserve to have their work seen and appreciated for itself. Now, please, I've answered as many questions as I can. I'd be grateful for a little privacy."

Another face, another spray-on tan, another waving microphone. "Have you spoken with Mrs. Durant? Will you be seeing her soon? Are you in love with her?"

Good questions, except for the last one I thought, as I shouldered my way forward, but not ones I could answer, except for the last one, even if I wanted to, which I didn't. "Please," I said, "give me a little breathing space."

And with all the *How do you feels*? and *What was in your minds*? echoing around me, I made my way across Woodward toward my home away from home. Arriving at Owen House, I climbed the porch stairs, vaguely noticing a little red Mustang with rental plates parked a few spaces away from my SUV. I hoped it wasn't some enterprising reporter who'd managed to get an editor to pop for the expense.

Once inside, I closed the door of my room behind me

and experienced the mingled sense of relief and shame I sometimes felt when exiting the stage after botching a scene. I knew I hadn't said anything horribly damaging to myself or anyone else, but the reporters had evoked one of those dreams where I was naked amid a crowd of clothed gawkers.

I sat down at the desk chair and touched the pad on my laptop. The screen revealed a plethora of emails, only one of which caught my attention. It was from Deirdre, and the subject line said, "READ THIS, D-MAN." I would have deleted it unread, but she had used one of her pet names for me from happier days, such as they'd been.

I scrolled down to the text. "D-Man," it said, "Funny how success can turn to crap, isn't it? What can you expect when you're led around by Little D?" Maybe I should have deleted it, I thought, but I read on. "I knew that bitch was after you when I first laid eyes on her. But I do have to say, no matter how much of a dog you are, you wouldn't do physical harm to anyone if you could avoid it. Hang in there, you moron. Your XD."

Wonders, I decided, might never cease. I was diverted from further speculation on the state of Deirdre's mind by a percussive knock. The rhythm—*shave and a haircut, two bits*—was somehow familiar, but not the sharpness of the rapping.

I crossed the room and opened the door, then jerked back in shock and involuntarily said, "Jesus."

"I thought you were a confirmed atheist." Eileen stood there grinning, wearing an orange silk blouse, black jeans, and a pair of black suede boots. She was holding a sizable paper bag in one hand. The other held a two-by-four, which she'd obviously used to announce herself.

"I'm more of an agnostic," I said. "But you know that."

"You looked like you'd seen a ghost."

"Ho-ho." I took a moment. "So that's your Mustang outside?"

"Rental. I needed some wheels."

"What the hell are you doing here?"

"I said you need a keeper, didn't I? So I got a cheap flight out of Philly, landed at Detroit Metro." Eileen put her arms around me, not really hampered by the sack or the two-by-four, and I realized how much I had missed the fresh scent of whatever soap it was she used. She kissed my cheek, then stepped back and looked up at me.

"When did you get here?" I said. "And where are you staying?"

"I'm staying right here. I arrived too late to see your matinee performance. Sorry. I rented the Mustang and ran a few errands. What's the matter? Aren't you glad to see me?"

"Of *course* I am. You can't imagine."

"Then how about letting me in?"

"Provided you lay down the two-by-four."

"Ho-ho," she said. "We'll see how you behave."

I stood aside to let her enter. She glanced around the room, set down the bag on the luggage bench and flipped the two-by-four onto the bed, then sank into the armchair.

"You look pretty fresh after traveling."

She smiled. "I'll take that as a compliment." She nodded at the door. "I had a shower and changed after checking in. According to Robert on the desk, you're pretty well under siege by the press."

"That's an understatement. I also had a voicemail from Finsterwald this morning. I've been put on notice to"—I switched to our department chair's voice—"'resolve my problems quickly and return to academe.'" I met her eyes. "How did you get him to let you go?"

She shook her head. "I talked to him this morning on the way to Philly. I don't have a class till Tuesday, and I called Durwood and sweet-talked him into helping a fellow Southerner by giving my students a take-home assignment."

"After the freshman comp exam, I'm surprised you managed to talk Durwood into anything."

"I think he's a little afraid of me."

"No doubt. I'm afraid of you, too. But Finsterwald's a tougher sell."

"I told Finsterwald I was headed for Chicago."

"Chicago?"

"What he doesn't know won't hurt either of us. I said I had some location research to do there at the request of—"

"Don't tell me," I said. "Ben Talbot."

"Some people," Eileen said, "are impressed by movie stars. Fortunately, that includes Finsterwald. Though maybe not intellectually superior playwrights who moonlight as accused killers."

"It was self-defense."

"That's what they all say."

I sighed in mingled exasperation and relief. "I am glad to see you." I indicated the bed. "So, what's the deal with the two-by? If it's a joke, it's in pretty bad taste, all things considered."

"It's not a joke. It's more of a visual aid. I told you last night I had things to do. I stopped and did a little shopping on my way here." She rose from the chair and moved to the luggage bench, where she rustled around in the paper bag, coming up with a whitish helmet of some sort and what looked like a piece of black wool. She held up the helmet. "This is a Giro *Trinity* bike helmet in matte titanium. The shell is polycarbonate, and it has a liner to absorb impact. Expanded polystyrene. Costs about fifty bucks."

"And you need this why?"

"Who do you know around here who's a bike rider?" She pulled on the helmet and fastened it below her chin. She then shook out the piece of black fabric, which proved to be a ski-mask of the kind favored by bank robbers in the movies. She pulled it on over the helmet, tugging it down to cover everything but her eyes. Then she retrieved the two-by-four from the bed and tossed it to me. Her covered head, its size increased by the helmet, and the feel of the wood in my hands momentarily thrust me back into the scene of two nights before. I looked glassily at Eileen. "Hit me," she said.

"Hit you?"

"Don't just repeat me like a parrot. That's cheap television dialogue. You said you hit this guy a glancing blow. Clock me just like that."

"You're sure?"

"For fifty bucks and change I'm more than sure."

"Okay," I said. "Here goes." I ducked down to get the right angle and swiped the two-by-four at Eileen's head. It struck her with a *clack* I instantly recognized was just like the clumsy blow I had landed on my attacker. "That was it," I said. Then, seeing her stagger backward, I tossed aside the weapon and added, "Are you all right?"

She pulled off the mask and the helmet and dropped them on the rack. "Jesus," she said, "that was a bell-ringer.

He's lucky he had the helmet and the mask. He obviously knew what he was doing."

"So, you really think it wasn't Larry who attacked me? That it was Fox I hit?"

"No shit, Sherlock. Or should I say Dr. Watson? Thank goodness you have Professor Moriarty on the case."

"I'm trying to work this thing through."

"I told you. It was a setup. You said Larry Durant had an unusually large head, didn't you?"

"Yeah. My former housemate Arnie Rivkin used to call him The Blockhead."

"And the helmet under the ski-mask made you think Larry was the attacker. That and the suggestion of Larry's accent. Don't forget, Fox is a theatre guy."

"You're saying Andrea and Fox worked all this out ahead of time? She got him to bring me out here just to be seduced and look as if I killed Larry in self-defense? So who killed Larry?"

Eileen snorted. "Duh. *They* did, of course. Look, Dennis. You told me this guy Fox is probably in trouble at both the university and the DIA. And Andrea hated her husband. Who just happened to have—what?—a two-million-dollar life insurance policy."

I shook my head. "Sex and money," I said.

"They make the world go 'round."

"And I'm the patsy."

"Somebody has to be in every well-laid plan." Eileen ⸳⸳⸳ged. "You have to hand it to them, though. If the plan ⸳⸳dy wins. They get the money and, ⸳ other. You get off on self-defense—"

⸳ing I didn't do."

⸳tails. You also get great reviews—and

maybe a movie contract."

"Jesus Christ," I said. "The only one who loses is Larry."

"Somebody has to in every well-laid plan."

"If the cops decide I killed Larry in self-defense, Andrea and Fox must think I'll be so relieved to be in the clear that I won't go after them. Even if I somehow figure out they did it."

"Sounds about right."

"So the theory is that one or both of them killed Larry in Indian Village and stashed him somewhere. Then Fox drives Larry's car back to campus and attacks me, lets me hit his well-protected head, and takes off back to Indian Village."

"Where they haul the body out of wherever they've stashed it, probably right in the car, and stage Fox's discovery of Larry's collapse—or whatever—and call 911. Very neat." Eileen plopped down in the armchair again. "And please don't tell me that woman was asleep at home."

I moved the helmet and ski-mask off the bench and perched there, feeling suddenly weary. "You've solved a murder, Professor Moriarty."

"*We* solved it. *You* gathered the evidence. You just didn't want to believe it." She smiled at me without her usual irony. "We're a team."

"Okay," I conceded. "Now what do we do?"

She leaned forward in the armchair, no longer smiling. "We need to wait till the DPD says you acted in self-defense."

"But it wasn't Larry who attacked me!"

"So far, they think it was. And we don't want tl

accusing you of manslaughter—or worse still, murder."

"The point is," I said, realizing as I spoke how relieved I was not to be a killer, "somebody murdered that poor schnook. And we ought to do something."

"It's all in the timing," Eileen said. "If they decide you killed the guy in self-defense, they'll release the body, and you can bet Andrea will have him cremated faster than a knife-fight in a phone booth."

"Knife fight in a phone booth?"

"I *am* from the South, you know." Eileen grinned. "And I thought I told you about needless repetition. Anyway, once the body's gone, Andrea and Fox will be pretty nearly untouchable. There'll be no way to nail them."

"That means we need to talk to Lindenbrook as soon as he tells me I'm in the clear. Maybe we can set *them* up. The question is, how? We need a plan."

"Well, you said it. Money and sex."

"And the greatest of these is money." I felt a surge of excitement. "Maybe we can convince Lindenbrook not to release the body right away. They can say they need to finish a tox-screen or something. Then I can get in touch with Andrea and Fox and tell them I know what they've done, and that I want a piece of the two-million-dollar insurance settlement to keep quiet."

"I like it. Maybe we can get Lindenbrook to let you wear a wire and meet them—make them admit everything"

"Sounds a little TV-ish, doesn't it?"

Eileen shrugged. "Life imitates commercial art."

"Could be dangerous," I said. "Considering what they've done already."

"True." She nodded. "It would have to be in a public

place. The more crowded the better."

"The DIA would seem like poetic justice."

"But the DIA is huge. Who knows how electronics would work in there? And it would be hard to hide cops."

"Maybe the Cass Café. Then the cops could park an unmarked van nearby. Poetic justice, too."

"Maybe we ought to convince the cops we're right," she said, "and let them decide how to play it."

"I can't believe you've come all the way out here, that you're even doing this."

Eileen shrugged. "You may have noticed I don't have that many people I care about."

I snorted. "You may have noticed I don't either."

"It hasn't escaped my attention," she said. "You ever think it might be related to your hanging around with me?"

This hung in the space between us for several seconds. Then I said, "It's pretty close to suppertime. Maybe we ought to go somewhere and relax over food and drink, then let you get some sleep. We've done enough for today."

"We'll have to go separately and *happen* to run into each other. That'll give us a fighting chance to avoid the press."

"Do you have someplace in mind?"

"You're the Detroit guy. Nothing too exotic. Or vegetarian."

I moved to my computer and checked nearby restaurants. After a few minutes I said, "Let's try Harry's. It's on Clifford just off Woodward toward downtown. I've never been there, but it looks popular enough so we can lose ourselves in the crowd."

13

Harry's was located near where Woodward crossed over I-75. When Eileen and I at last managed to find parking places for our respective vehicles and *happened* to run into each other, we learned that the place was, in fact, crowded.

A big noisy sports bar with square columns and multiple flat-screens broadcasting multiple sporting events, Harry's was a good spot in which to lose ourselves. We found a small table near a column and realized quickly that quiet conversation was unlikely. But that was all right because no one was listening except our tee-shirted waitress.

We ordered draft beers, and when the waitress returned with them, I built a burger with cheddar, house-smoked bacon, and chipotle mayo, and added an order of fried pickle chips in place of French fries, while Eileen settled for a shrimp and cheddar grits appetizer.

"You can share my pickle chips," I said.

"I'm just happy you picked a place with shrimp 'n' grits."

As we waited for our order and sipped the beer, I told Eileen about my unexpectedly pleasant email message from Deirdre. "That woman zags when you figure she'll

263

zig," Eileen said. "But then your boyish charm eventually works on all the ladies, doesn't it?"

Even though it hurt, I waggled my eyebrows. "*All* the ladies?"

She made a face at me. "You wish."

As I was considering an appropriately snotty comeback, my phone, which I'd left on vibrate, came to life in my pocket. I checked the number. "It's Andrea," I said, and pushed my chair back. "I'd better take this outside where I can hear."

Eileen wagged a finger. "Careful what you say."

On the way out of the bar, I pressed talk and said, "I'm at dinner. I'm going to find a quiet spot." Once outside on the relatively peaceful sidewalk, I said, "I'm surprised to hear from you."

"I just wanted to find out how you were doing." Even with the hollow electronic reception of the cellphone, Andrea's flat little-girl voice was immediately recognizable.

"I guess I'm doing all right for someone who may have killed a man."

Was that a gasp I'd heard? "I know the police won't charge you with anything," she said carefully.

"Maybe not." I tried to keep my own tone neutral. When she said nothing, I decided to up the ante. "You never told me you knew Wily Fox."

Another brief silence followed, which she broke by saying, "Bill Fox is a neighbor." She obviously wasn't going to call him Wily. "And we met him at a DIA reception."

She apparently wasn't going to volunteer anything more, so I said, "You mean you didn't have anything to do with his recommending my play to the theatre department?"

Her little silences suggested she might be checking with someone else before speaking. Had she switched me on speaker? Was Fox there and listening? She finally said, "I may have mentioned something about you. I'm sorry. I should have told you."

I decided to push a bit. "Speaking of the DIA, I understand Fox may be in some kind of trouble there. Something financial."

"I, uh—" She apparently had nothing more to say.

I went on. "And Wayne State may have him in their sights, too. He's apparently been pushing the harassment envelope."

After a few moments, she said, "None of that has anything to do with me—or Larry's death. Why are you being so unpleasant all of a sudden? And hostile? After what we've shared."

"Sorry," I said. "My head's still a little fuzzy." I tacked another way. "How are *you* feeling?"

This got a quicker response. "I'm all right, I guess. I suppose I'm still in shock."

I pressed. "But you wanted out of the marriage. And now you stand to be rich."

"Rich?" she said, almost inaudibly.

"At Fishbone's I thought Larry said he had a two-million-dollar life insurance policy."

"Oh," she said. "I guess. But first they'll have to release the—Larry's body. For the funeral. And then I'll need to contact the company. I'm sure there are lots of formalities. Anyway, I just called to find out if you were okay."

I responded to this relative outpouring with a terse, "I am, pretty much. But I'd better get back to my table. My dinner's waiting."

Another brief silence. Then she said, "Take care."

Before I could ask her if she missed me, she broke the connection. I walked back into the bar and sat down across from Eileen. My burger was waiting at my place, as were the fried pickle chips, into which Eileen had obviously made inroads. She had ordered two more drafts.

"So," she said, around a mouthful of shrimp and grits, "did the McCutcheon charm work wonders?"

"Not so's you'd notice." While eating my burger I filled her in on my conversation with Andrea, noting my suspicion that Fox might have been present and listening.

"Good," she said. "Sounds like you've given them something to worry about."

"I hope so."

She reached over and took another of my fried pickles. "You'd better have a few of these while they're still available. They're pretty good. Then let's finish up here and get back to the Inn. I could use a decent night's sleep. Detective work takes a lot out of a body."

14

As on the previous morning, I rose around eight a.m., performed my usual bathroom routine, then dressed in blue jeans, a long-sleeved purple tee-shirt, and my Pikolinos. Not long after, I heard Eileen's usual *shave-and-a-haircut* knock and let her in. She, too, was ready to meet the world, looking lean and lovely in her black jeans and black suede boots, varying yesterday's look with a blouse in green silk that Rachel would have approved.

She was balancing a tray with coffee, pastries, and fresh fruit, which she set down on the table by the armchair. "I picked these up so we could avoid any chance encounters with reporters in the breakfast room. I don't think they've connected us yet. A couple of them asked me if I'd seen or talked to you. I gave them blank looks."

"That's great," I said, picking up the carafe. "I'll pour."

"Slept well," she said in answer to my unasked question. "No ghosts."

"Me, too. Sound sleep, no wraiths, no poltergeists." I poured cream in my coffee and took a sip. It was hot and strong. "I'm also feeling less like a used piñata, which is all to the good."

I switched on the radio to WRCJ-FM, and for a while we sat in companionable silence, listening to a guitar concerto by Joaquin Rodrigo while eating croissants and drinking our coffee. From early in our acquaintance, despite our penchant for smartassed repartee, both of us had valued each other's ability to know when to shut up for a while.

As the concerto reached its climax, the house phone rang. I clicked off the radio and picked up the receiver. "Robert?" I said.

"It's Latrece. Robert's probably getting ready to sleep his way through his Econ class after sitting behind the front desk here all weekend."

"Sorry, Latrece," I said. "Days and nights are starting to run into each other. Too many things going on."

"I hear you," she said. "And I'm sorry to bother you. But you got visitors. Police. They're on their way over there right now, so I wanted to give you a heads-up."

I thanked her and replaced the receiver. "Curtain up," I said to Eileen, who dropped into the armchair. As I spoke, I heard a knock at the door. I crossed the room and opened it to reveal the imposing figure of Sergeant Lindenbrook. Today, his tailored suit was brown with a fine red stripe and the shirt was lavender, but he was wearing the same muted pink tie and his chukka boots. Almost hidden behind Lindenbrook was a short white woman with close-cut blonde hair. She was wearing black low-heeled shoes and an outfit that looked to me like a vintage denim leisure suit.

"My partner," Lindenbrook said after I showed the two of them into the room. "Detective Claudine Dreyfus, meet Mr. Dennis McCutcheon."

"Morning," Dreyfus said in a high-pitched, tired-sounding voice.

Both detectives looked quizzically at me, then at Eileen. "This is Dr. Eileen Moriarty," I said, "my office-mate at Brixton University. She flew in to provide moral support."

Lindenbrook and Dreyfus introduced themselves, shaking hands with Eileen. Lindenbrook turned to me. "You do have a knack for attracting pleasant-looking ladies, Mr. McCutcheon."

"I'm not so sure they're all as pleasant as they look," Eileen said. "Me included."

"You two are out and about early," I said.

Lindenbrook shrugged. "Wheels of justice always turnin'."

"Sorry, we've already had coffee and pastries," Eileen said. "If we'd known you were coming, we'd have provided some for you."

"No problem," Dreyfus said. "We've already made a Dunkin' Donut stop. Got to keep up the cop traditions." She passed a hand over her mouth, presumably checking for powdered sugar.

"Sit down." I gestured to the few choices of seating. After the detectives were settled, I sat in the desk chair and looked at them. "Congratulations," I said to Dreyfus, "on the new baby."

"Three-year-old," she said. "We adopted. But thanks."

Lindenbrook stuck his chin out in the general direction of campus. "Afternoon show go well yesterday?"

"Not bad, all things considered. I guess we can't complain about the press coverage."

Lindenbrook gave a gravelly chuckle. "Guess not. At least you didn't shoot your mouth off."

"So," I said, "to what do I owe the pleasure? Visitors

are usually announced from the front desk."

"This is more of an official visit," Dreyfus said, her voice almost rising to a squeak at the end.

"Front desks sometimes make an exception for us." Lindenbrook worked his Darth Vader timbre.

"Besides," Dreyfus said, "you didn't seem too surprised, so I figure Latrece managed to warn you anyway."

I looked from her to Lindenbrook. "Is this where I get good-cop, bad-cop?"

"This is where you get good *news*," Lindenbrook said. "ME's and Forensics reports came in, so we thought you'd like to know. Looks like self-defense on your part, like I told you before. One or two inconsistencies in the details, but that's not unusual. Cases are never perfect."

I felt a knot loosen inside me. Then a sense of uneasiness returned. "I guess that is good news," I said.

Lindenbrook snorted. "You *guess*?"

A thought struck me. "Did your ME do a tox-screen?"

Now it was Dreyfus's turn to snort. "No need for a tox-screen. We know what killed him. And who."

"I suppose that means you'll be releasing the body," Eileen put in.

"Pretty soon," Dreyfus said. "Let the woman bury her husband. Cremate him, whatever."

"Cremate him," I repeated without inflection.

Lindenbrook squinted at him. "You got a problem with that?"

"We both have a problem with it," Eileen said. "Don't we, Dennis?"

"We do."

Dreyfus shot a look at me, then turned back to Eileen.

"Don't tell me you're a forensics expert."

Eileen smiled sweetly. "Film scholar," she said.

Dreyfus took a breath. "You got something to say, go ahead and say it."

For answer, Eileen rose from the armchair and crossed to the luggage bench where Dreyfus was perched. The detective moved her feet aside. Eileen reached under the bench, then stepped back with the paper bag in one hand and the two-by-four in the other.

"Whoa." Lindenbrook started to rise. "What's that for?" he said, pointing at the two-by-four.

"Relax," I said. "It's for demonstration purposes."

Lindenbrook sat down again. "What you plan to demonstrate?"

"A phony mugging," Eileen said. She set the two-by-four on the bed and withdrew the bicycle helmet and the ski-mask from the bag. She held them out to me. "Your turn this time."

"Please," I said, waving her off. "One more shot to the head and my porchlight may go out for good."

She pulled on the helmet. "Don't ever say I'm not willing to suffer for my art."

15

After Eileen and I had finished our performance, set aside the props, and explained our theory on the hows and whys of Larry Durant's death, Lindenbrook and Dreyfus exchanged looks like a couple of poker players who had just checked their hole-cards.

Dreyfus finally spoke, addressing me. "As things stand, this would be a closed case. Seems like most guys in your position would be happy to let well-enough alone."

"I thought about it," I said, my head buzzing a little, as if Eileen had hit me, rather than the other way around. "But I—*we*—figured you guys ought to decide what to do."

"If anything," Eileen added.

"So," Lindenbrook said, "you're telling us that Fox is in some kind of trouble at the DIA."

"The rumor is misuse of donations," I said, "and possible removal of artwork from DIA storage. Apparently, there's lots of stuff in the basement over there that may be easy to pilfer with the right kind of access."

Dreyfus jumped in. "Misuse. Removal. Pilfering. You're saying the guy's a thief. And a killer."

"And that Andrea Durant stands to inherit two million dollars through Larry's corporate life insurance." Eileen snapped her fingers. "All their money troubles vanish, and they end up with each other."

"Ain't love grand?" Lindenbrook said.

Eileen continued. "We don't have definitive proof, obviously. But Dennis is willing—and in a position—to help you try to get some."

"How's that?" Lindenbrook asked.

"I'll get in touch with them," I said, "and tell them I want to talk about what I think happened."

Eileen broke in. "Then when they meet, he can wear a wire, demand a share of the two million, and get them to admit what they've done."

"And on the stolen art question," I said, "the only time I was at Andrea's house, she showed me a sketch that could be a study for a painting by Edward Hopper. She said she found it at a gallery, but it could be something she got from Fox."

"You never said anything about that." Eileen's tone was mildly accusatory.

"It just occurred to me," I said by way of apology. Then I turned to the two detectives. "Anyway, if it is a Hopper, it's worth a lot of money."

Dreyfus hummed thoughtfully. "Speaking of money, what you two are proposing wouldn't be cheap. Approval for a wire. Setup for eavesdropping. Maybe phone-taps. Extra manpower, extra vehicles, possible overtime."

"And a tox-screen of the body," I said.

Eileen nodded. "Dennis said Larry Durant was a big guy. Who knows how they managed to whack him with a two-by-four without a struggle."

Lindenbrook shook his head. "You heard Claudine. This is Detroit. Everything's about budget these days.

I spread my hands and shrugged. "I can't imagine a

tox-screen is all that costly."

"Let's not get ahead of ourselves," Dreyfus said. "What happens if Fox and Andrea tell Dennis here to take a hike?"

"That's up to you guys and your bosses," Eileen said. "It's no skin off our noses. We're just trying to help."

Lindenbrook inclined his head at his partner. "I guess we can check with the guys in Fraud and Embezzlement, see if there's anything to this."

Dreyfus shrugged. "Let's do it."

"So I'm in the clear on Larry's death?" I said.

"Didn't say that." Dreyfus fixed me with a cop stare. "Like John told you before, you never know what the DA's gonna do. Case is still open till it's closed."

"But don't worry," Lindenbrook said. "One way or another, you folks can probably get out of here in a few days. Maybe a week."

Eileen snorted. "So the good news isn't exactly ready for a press release."

And I said, "That means our proposal makes even more sense."

The detectives got to their feet as if choreographed. "We'll have to get back to you," Lindenbrook said. "Anything develops in the meantime, you got my card."

Eileen and I rose, too. "Suit yourselves," Eileen said. "You just have to remember one thing."

"What's that?" Dreyfus asked.

"If you release Larry's body to Andrea, all this'll be academic. That woman will have it run through a crematorium faster than a one-legged man comes in second in an ass-kicking competition."

After the detectives left, I shook my head at Eileen. "You and your mouthful of cheese grits. Didn't exactly have them in stitches."

"Do we care?" she said. "They're the ones who don't know whether to wind their ass or scratch their watch. And by the way, congratulations. No matter how reluctant those guys are to do their jobs, it's nice to know you're in the clear."

"You heard Dreyfus. Case is still open till it's closed."

Eileen snorted. "Bullshit. That's just cop intimidation. It's all over but the shouting here."

"The scandal may sink my tenure. Rimmer's waiting to pounce like a big, fat Cheshire Cat."

"Fuck Rimmer."

"Let's leave that unenviable pursuit to the lovely Corrine. Anyway," I added, "thanks. For everything. You're one true friend."

Eileen deflected this drift toward sentiment. "Now we can move on to further opportunities. Ben Talbot. Off-Broadway. Hollywood."

"And getting your books launched properly. I plan to throw you one hell of a party."

"Let's concentrate on getting out of here first," she said.

"When are you due to fly home?"

"I bought a one-way ticket," she said. "I figured we could drive home together in your Highlander."

"That's the second-best news I've gotten today."

Eileen gave one of her full-throated laughs. "Let's get out of here for a while," she said. "I feel the need for some fresh air."

I peered out through the curtains over the desk. "Looks like it might rain. How about a visit to the DIA? It's worth the time."

"Why not?" she said. "Seems like I ought to check out the scene where some of the crimes took place."

"Good. You can go first so we're not seen leaving together."

Eileen checked the parking lot through the curtains. "Maybe we're overestimating the media's fascination. Or their willingness to get wet waiting for you to appear. The parking lot looks empty."

"Humor me," I said. "I'll meet you on the lower floor by the Renee Sintenis donkey statue. Just ask someone. It's a favorite rendezvous for patrons. I used to love it when I was a kid. And please, no jackass jokes."

"I'll try to restrain myself," she said. "But you never know when a jackass may present itself for commentary."

16

After Eileen left the inn, I waited for five minutes or so, then walked out into the empty parking lot. Fifteen minutes of fame, I thought. Nonetheless, I took a circuitous path through a misty drizzle around the back of the DIA, finally climbing the broad stairs toward the front entrance. Seeing Eileen there gave me a little jolt of pleasure. But why was she standing outside in the rain? Then I realized.

"Well," she said good-humoredly, "it turns out a jackass has presented itself—or himself."

"Sorry," I said. "I forgot they were closed on Mondays. I guess I'm still a little addled. I thought we might be able to drop by their administrative offices and create a little havoc on the subject of Fox's misbehavior."

"Maybe we can work that in tomorrow," Eileen said. "And I had my heart set on scoping out the Rivera murals in person. I took a look at them last night in the brochure on my nightstand. Very impressive. Made me think of Marlon Brando in *Viva Zapata!*"

"I'm sure that would have made Diego very happy."

She laughed. "At least they didn't remind me of Leo Carrillo in *Viva Villa!*"

"Very funny."

"'Not a fan of Pancho and Cisco?"

"Can't recall."

She shot me a look. "I'm not sure how long I'll let you play the addled brain card, Buster."

"Believe me," I said, "it's not a card I plan to play any longer than I have to." I stuck out my hand, my palm up. "The rain looks like it's letting up. Maybe I can show you a bit of the campus."

"I'm easy," she said. "I'd enjoy seeing the haunts of Baby Dennis. Or is *haunts* an uncomfortable term?"

"Well, now we know there *was* no haunt," I said. "Just another Wily Fox illusion. But I do wish I could've shown you the Degas painting, *Violinist and Young Woman*. I did get an eerie feeling when I saw it."

"With Andrea," she said. "Maybe I don't need to retrace those particular steps."

"Maybe not."

Side by side, we set off on a leisurely meander around campus, during which I regaled Eileen with stories from my Detroit years and my checkered educational experiences. Fortunately, the rain held off, and the low-hanging clouds kept the temperature pleasantly cool for a stroll.

Finally, Eileen said, "Enough. How about some lunch? All this reminiscing on the hoof works up an appetite."

"As long as we missed the DIA, why don't I take you to the Cass Café? It has a pretty nice gallery and the food's fine, too."

Once at the Café, Eileen duly admired the artwork, which leaned heavily toward the contemporary. I settled for a bowl of roasted curry lentil soup. Eileen ordered the rosemary chicken salad. I decided against telling her that she had duplicated Andrea's lunch order of the previous week.

17

On the way back to the Inn, we walked separately again, though I noted as I had earlier, that the press seemed to have moved on to other crimes and misdemeanors. The parking lot remained blessedly deserted.

Eileen was waiting in the parlor. "Back to headquarters?" she said.

"Back to headquarters," I agreed, and led the way to my room, where Eileen took her accustomed position in the armchair and I took mine at the desk.

Leaning back in the chair, I felt my phone vibrate. I took it out and checked the caller. Andrea. With a hollow sensation in my stomach, I showed the screen to Eileen, who said, "Didn't see that coming."

I clicked talk, then put the call on speaker. Andrea's breathy voice came through immediately. "Dennis, I'm worried."

"About what?"

"I just heard from the police. A Sergeant Lindenbrook. He said they've decided you must have acted in self-defense, which is wonderful news. But he also said they can't release Larry's body. Not yet."

I exchanged a look with Eileen, who gave me a thumbs-up. "What are you worried about?" I said to

Andrea. "It must be some kind of formality."

"I'm worried about Bill Fox," she said. "I think it has something to do with him."

"So." I paused for effect. "He's not there now?"

"No. Of course not."

"I thought you said he'd helped you."

"No," she said quickly. "I mean, he was there when Larry collapsed, and he called 911. But—I'm not sure how to put this—he may have had something to do with—I don't know." She fell silent for a few seconds, then said, "I'm afraid he may be obsessed with me in some way."

Again, I looked at Eileen, who stifled a snort of derision. "Obsessed?" I said.

"I don't know." Andrea's voice fell almost to a whisper. "I hope I can depend on you for support. Our relationship means a lot to me." After another beat, she said, "In every way."

I tried to think of what to say, settling for, "That's good to know. What do you want me to do?"

"I'm not sure," she said. "I'm afraid Bill Fox will try to get in touch with you."

"For what?" I said.

"I don't know," she said quickly. "Just be there for me. Sorry—I have to go." The screen flashed *call ended.*

"Well," I said to Eileen, "what do you think about that?"

Eileen passed a hand across her mouth, then said, "I'd like to slap that woman to sleep and then slap her for sleepin'. She's slipperier than a Mississippi sturgeon. She's obviously figured out something's up and she's trying to play both ends against the middle. You or Fox, she'll take whoever comes out on top. So to speak."

"Be that as it may," I said, "the good news is that Lindenbrook and Dreyfus have evidently decided our theory on Larry's death may not be totally nuts."

"Or at least," Eileen said, "like your friend Andrea, they're hedging their bets."

"All we can do is wait for their next move. But they have postponed releasing the body. That's something."

"You should probably give them a call and let them know what we've heard from the *femme fatale*."

I failed to suppress the thought that Eileen's tone seemed to convey something not unlike jealousy. "You're right," I said neutrally. I took Lindenbrook's card from my wallet and thumbed the number into my phone.

"Put it on speaker," Eileen said.

I did so in time to hear Lindenbrook's deep voice saying, "I'm listening. Don't waste your chance."

"I hear you've decided to hold onto Larry's body," I said.

"How'd you hear that?"

"Andrea called and told me. She's obviously worried."

"Hmmm. Interesting."

"So," I said, "does this mean you want me to get them to incriminate themselves?"

"It does mean we checked with the Fraud people," Lindenbrook said, "and found out they got their eye on Mr. Fox."

The high-pitched voice of Claudine Dreyfus chimed in from the background. "If you're going to talk to them, we need to work out a script for you, have you call them in a controlled environment."

"This could be dangerous," Lindenbrook said. "And you're an amateur here."

"He's a playwright!" Eileen said loudly enough to carry to both detectives. "And an actor. Scripts are what he does."

"Don't forget," Dreyfus said in the background, "if you two are right, Fox and Mrs. Durant have already killed someone."

"That's right," Lindenbrook added. "We got to ensure your safety."

"But if I don't call from my cell, or the room phone here," I added, "they're bound to get suspicious."

Lindenbrook wasn't budging. "We got to follow our procedures," he said, "especially when department money's involved."

"So, what's the plan?" I said.

"Maybe if you tell them it's a twofer," Eileen put in, "you can get a deal."

A brief silence followed, punctuated by an inaudible exchange between the detectives. Eileen rolled her eyes. Lindenbrook finally came back on the line. "All right," he said. "Your call from Mrs. Durant could move things along. You sit tight while we check with our superiors. We'll get back to you."

Eileen broke in again. "We do have to get back to our jobs, you know. This is costing *us* money, too."

"I hear you," Lindenbrook said. "We appreciate your patience."

"It's a limited commodity," I said.

Dreyfus's emphatic soprano grated through the speaker. "We'll be in touch!" The line went dead.

"That went well," I said.

Eileen shook her head. "Maybe we should just head back to Brixton, let all these folks play their own hands.

Especially since you're not about to be charged with anything."

"But that translates into a win for Fox."

"And your lady-friend."

"And I wind up legally responsible for Larry's death, whether they charge me or not. It just doesn't seem right."

"Can't argue."

"We ought to do something."

"So let's drive to Andrea's neighborhood and watch her place, see what they may be up to."

"A stakeout?" I clicked my tongue dubiously. "The cops certainly wouldn't be pleased."

"So what?" Eileen was almost bouncing in her chair. "Right now, they're not even sure they have anything to investigate. Or whether it'll break the budget. And Fox and Andrea don't know about me—or my rental car. You can sit in the back seat and be inconspicuous."

"I have a better idea," I said, catching her enthusiasm. "Let's keep your Mustang in reserve. No one knows about it yet. We'll leave here separately, and you can park around the block from Andrea's house. I'll pick you up unobtrusively in my SUV. The rear windows are tinted, so you can sit in the back seat where you won't be seen."

"I'm not sure we need all this logistical tom-foolery. The reporters have pretty much evaporated."

"Humor me," I said. "Besides, I'm not really worried about reporters at this point. I'll park close enough to the house so if Andrea and Fox do happen to see me it'll give them something to worry about."

"Stir up the anthill," Eileen said. "Let's do it."

We both took deep breaths. I felt a slight queasiness under the adrenaline rush. "Let's be careful out there," I

said. "This isn't a movie."
    "Not yet," she said.

18

"Well," Eileen said from her unobtrusive crouch in the rear seat of the SUV, "so much for Moriarty and McCutcheon, consulting detectives. So far, the only thing I've registered is that you do a nice job of parallel parking."

"Something you and my father would have agreed on."

We had been sitting half a block away from Andrea's Tudor place for the better part of three hours, peering through a fine mist of rain for the past twenty minutes. The late Larry's big Chrysler Town and Country was parked in the driveway, but it was the most interesting sight we had seen, other than a couple of young mothers walking side by side pushing strollers prior to the turn in the weather.

On the plus side, we'd listened to a fine selection of instrumental music on WRCJ-FM as selected by the station's classical DJ Dr. Dave Wagner. But we had seen no evidence of suspicious activity. We had certainly observed no sign that our presence had created any unease on the part of the suspected conspirators, though Eileen insisted she had seen a curtain twitch behind an upstairs window.

I shifted behind the steering wheel to glance back at her. "Let's hope they're watching and worrying."

"We can hope," she said. "But as I believe Ashley

Wilkes allowed in *Gone with the Wind*, you can grab three wishes in one hand and a piece of crap in the other and see which hand fills up first."

"Don't forget, Miz Scarlett," I said, "this was your idea. And I believe Margaret Mitchell's spinning in her grave as we speak."

"*I'll think about that tomorrow.*" Eileen gave it her best Vivien Leigh Atlanta-by-way-of-the-Royal-Academy drawl. "I guess as long as we're wishing, maybe we can hope Lindenbrook and Dreyfus will get their act together."

"Frankly," I said, shooting for Clark Gable, "I'm not sure they give a damn. Meanwhile, here's my idea. Let's go pick up your Mustang around the block. Then we'll head back to Harry's and get you another fix of shrimp and grits. Even classical music wears thin after a while."

"Not a bad thought." Eileen massaged the intersections of her neck and shoulders. "We heard from Andrea while we were at Harry's last night. Maybe we'll luck out again."

"Well, the rain's let up." I turned on the Toyota's ignition. "And at least the shrimp and grits are a sure thing."

19

As things turned out, Eileen and I both enjoyed Harry's shrimp and grits, washed down with a couple of Bell's *Oberons* at the recommendation of our waitress, Patti. But even though I'd left my cellphone on the table in a spirit of hopefulness, good food and drink was as lucky as we got.

As we drained our second beers, I said, "If we're going to head back to the inn, you leave first. I'll take care of the bill."

Eileen shook her head. "I can pay my way."

"Forget it," I said. "This was my invitation. Besides, I already owe you plenty for schlepping all the way out here. Plane fare, car rental, lodging. Not to mention the bicycle helmet. And saving my ass."

"Fine," she conceded. "But I figure we're safer if we leave together. I'm pretty sure, at this point, nobody cares."

"This from the woman who wanted to take me shark fishing in a flat-bottomed boat. Humor me," I said, waving my credit card at the waitress. "Our not attracting attention together still makes you my secret weapon."

"Okay. I'll meet you back at the ranch."

After paying the check, I watched as Eileen left the bar, then waited a few minutes before leaving myself. I had parked my SUV a couple of blocks away, and while I walked back to it, I decided we might be better off abandoning our attempts to trap Fox and Andrea. After all, I had been let off the hook for Larry's death, even if I was held technically responsible. And who knew? Maybe Eileen and I were wrong. Maybe I *had* killed Larry.

Nearing my Toyota, I noticed a big Chrysler Town and Country parked behind me. The sight gave me a sudden feeling of unease. As I rounded the front of my vehicle and clicked the remote to open the door, the driver's door of the T & C swung open, dispelling any doubt that it was Larry Durant's. Wily Fox emerged, resplendent in what looked like Calvin Klein jeans and a white cashmere sweater over a lavender t-shirt. A gray blazer and stylish gray loafers completed the ensemble. His black hair was swept up from his scalp in the expensive style of the self-congratulatory pundit who presided over *Morning Joe* on MSNBC. The associate dean gave me a half-smile, keeping his radiant capped teeth in reserve, and said, "We need to talk."

I froze, suddenly unsure of myself, and said, "About what?"

Fox's half-smile vanished. "Don't waste time acting dumb," he said. "Let's take a drive."

I glanced at the big Chrysler, playing for time. "Does Andrea know you have her car?"

"Of course," Fox said. "But we'll take yours."

"Where?"

"Somewhere private, where we can chinwag in confidence."

Just what I don't want to do, I thought. Aloud, I said, "I'd rather we wagged our chins somewhere public. What about Harry's? It's handy. And no one will overhear us."

"I don't think so." Fox clicked the T & C's key and the trunk popped open. "I'm going to need you to open the back hatch of your Highlander and transfer something from Larry's car. Well, it's really Andrea's car now."

I felt a chill go through me. "Transfer what?"

"Not to worry," Fox said. "It's just my bicycle. But be careful with it. It was expensive."

"Why should I put it in my car?"

"Because I asked you so nicely." Fox reached into the right-hand pocket of his blazer and, hand still concealed, pointed something at me. "I am glad to see you, Dennis. I also have a gun in my pocket. It's small-caliber, but more than lethal enough to do the job. So why don't you move the bike? Then we'll get in your Japanese SUV and find a place to talk."

I didn't move. "Does Andrea know about this?"

"What do *you* think?"

"I think that's not an answer."

Fox ignored this. "Give me your car key."

"If I don't, you're not going to shoot me here on a public street."

"This is Detroit." Fox's mouth twitched, not even a half-smile. "You willing to bet your life? Like Larry?"

I felt my stomach lurch. I knew I should do something, but I couldn't make myself take action.

Fox held out his left hand. "The key."

I gave the car key to him. Fox opened the Toyota's rear hatch and motioned me toward the T & C's commodious trunk. The bike was an expensive one, just as Rachel had reported. I lifted it, finding it light, but ungainly.

"Be careful," Fox said. "In ten years, that model will be

a collector's item." He fished two blankets from the T & C, then closed the trunk. "Stow it and cover it with this blanket."

Without comment, I moved the awkward burden into the Highlander, tossed the blanket over it, and closed the hatch.

"What's the other blanket for?" I asked, more to buy time than because I really wanted to know the answer.

"All in good time," Fox said.

Trying to keep my hand from trembling, I reached out for my remote. Fox, however, held onto it. "I thought you wanted me to drive," I said.

"We both know your Highlander starts with a push-button." Fox shook the fob. "I'll just hang onto this for the time being."

I got into the driver's seat of my vehicle. Walking quickly to the passenger's side, Fox opened the door, tossed the second blanket onto the rear seats, and got in. He used both hands to buckle his seatbelt. Before I could react, had I considered doing so, Fox pocketed my fob with his left hand and used his right hand to remove a small pistol from inside his blazer. No doubt Eileen could have identified the make and caliber.

"Click it or ticket," Fox said. "Then drive."

I fastened my seatbelt and started the car. "Where to?" I said, trying to keep my voice steady despite feeling I was headed for an inevitable conclusion.

"Belle Isle. Andrea tells me it's one of your favorite places."

20

As I drove along Jefferson toward the MacArthur Bridge, I realized that Fox probably didn't want to talk. Or wag his chin. He just wanted a secluded spot to get rid of a nuisance. And from my adolescent years, I knew the island was full of secluded spots, probably more so now that access to it required payment and so much of it had fallen into disuse. If only Lindenbrook and Dreyfus had taken some initiative about giving me a wire to wear and a way to arrange a public meeting. If only I hadn't talked Eileen into our not leaving Harry's together.

I had to make some sort of effort, though. "If you cut me in on the two million insurance settlement," I said, "I'll go back East and concentrate on writing. You and Andrea can get on with whatever it is you have in mind. The police have decided I killed Larry in self-defense."

"Cut you in?" Fox said, leaning sidewise in the passenger's seat as if we were on a pleasure drive. "Thank goodness the dialogue in your play is a bit snappier. But I suppose you *are* under stress."

"Dramaturgy aside," I managed, "the offer stands."

Fox scratched the side of his nose with the pistol's short barrel. "As it happens," he said, "I'm a little pressed, financially speaking. I can't afford to share." He waved the gun. "Pull over here."

"I thought we were driving over to the island."

"Don't argue," Fox said, a tinge of exasperation in his voice. "Just pull over."

I did as I was told, parking the Highlander at the curb. As luck—or Fox's knowledge of the neighborhood—would have it, Jefferson was deserted at this point, so I had no opportunity to signal any passer-by, even if I had been inclined to risk being shot.

Fox reached in a blazer pocket and pulled out a double-looped plastic zip-tie, the kind of cheap restraint cops often used in place of metal handcuffs. "Put them on," he said.

"I can't drive with cuffs on," I said.

"Let me worry about that." Fox made a slight motion with his pistol.

Feeling more and more despair, I slipped my hands into the cuffs, after which Fox reached over and pulled them tight.

"Now what?" I said, trying to keep a quaver out of my voice.

Fox reached back into his pocket, this time with-drawing a black ball gag with a collar. "Open wide," he said.

I leaned away from Fox. "This is crazy." How could this be happening? I suddenly realized that what I had said to Eileen was absolutely true. This wasn't a movie, wasn't a story. It was real.

Fox jabbed the gun into my ribs. "Do it." I complied, and Fox thrust the black rubber ball into my mouth. While I was trying not to retch, Fox set the pistol down and quickly secured the collar around my neck. Shit, I thought, why hadn't I done something? "Good boy," Fox said. He opened the passenger's door, then quickly walked around the Highlander and opened both the driver's and rear doors. "Now get in back there and lie on the floor."

I did as I was told, jamming myself in behind the front seats, surrendering to the apparent inevitable. I could feel hope running out of me like water from a leaky pitcher. Fox dragged the second blanket off the rear seat and threw it over me. In the sudden darkness, my senses seemed heightened. I felt the distinct nubby textures of the floor mats and the scratch of the blanket, registered the mingled smells of wool and rubber and synthetic fibers. Again, I had to resist the impulse to retch.

"If you move, or try to attract attention," Fox said, "I'll shoot the bridge attendant. Then I'll shoot you. I'm a little on edge, and you've become a pain in the ass, so don't count on civilized behavior."

I heard the Highlander's doors slam, then the sound of the engine coming to life. I felt the vehicle moving away from the curb. Pretzeled between the front and rear seats, I envisioned Fox driving across the bridge to the gatehouse, barely slowing to wave a pass-card at the attendant, who would hardly register what he looked like. I imagined the river sparkling, beautifully indifferent in the fading light, and downstream, the Ren Cen and the Ambassador Bridge. I felt an ironic pang as I recalled the lines in my play in which Ben, the maritime museum director, describes seeing cars moving along the river in Windsor as he fails to save a man's life. I knew I should have given some sign of distress, but I did nothing, telling myself I did so for the safety of the bridge attendant, if there even was anyone on duty.

I realized again that, since its conversion from city park to state park, with consequent admission charges where entrance had once been free, the island would be even more deserted than it had been in my youth. I pictured Eileen back at the Inn, wondering what had become of me, probably feeling pissed off.

"Comfy back there?" Fox sounded cheerful, as if we were on a pleasant excursion. I didn't make a sound. Fuck Fox and the bicycle he rode in on. Or, more likely, the one he would ride home on.

After what seemed like an impossibly long time, the Highlander came to a stop and the engine went silent, except for its customary ticking as it cooled. I heard the front door open and close; then the rear door opened and the blanket was removed. "Out," Fox said.

I made an undignified backward scramble out of the SUV, barking my shins, and managed to get to my feet, swaying unsteadily as I looked around me. Fox regarded me from a safe distance, gun in hand. We had come to rest in a little parking lot. A few picnic benches were scattered here and there amid fairly dense tree cover. The place would be a pleasant spot for a picnic on most days. Now, in the rapidly gathering dusk, it simply looked like the end of the line.

21

"Turn around," Fox said.

I did so, and Fox quickly freed me from the ball gag, tossing it aside onto a picnic table. "So," I said, testing for play in the cuffs around my wrists and finding none, "we weren't really looking for a place to talk, were we?"

"Not really. Yet here you are, talking. Would you like me to strap on the ball gag again?"

"The bridge attendant will be able to identify you, even if you did have me stashed between the seats."

"Maybe there wasn't a bridge attendant." He let that sit for a moment, then said, "As it happened, she barely registered me. All she saw was the park pass. And your Highlander."

"You're probably on surveillance cameras."

"Surveillance cameras?" Fox laughed. "This is Detroit, buddy boy. The city can barely afford streetlights."

Pushing on, I said, "How do you figure on getting away with a second murder?" I felt my ears buzzing as if my head were enclosed in a plastic bubble. "You won't have a fall guy this time. Wouldn't it be simpler to make some arrangement with me?"

"I—we—thought we *had* an arrangement," Fox said. "I work things out so you get your play produced. Good reviews are an unexpected bonus for you. You get to screw the lovely Andrea—a real bonus, I think you'd agree. I take care of the jealous Larry and make it look like you did it, even though it's *me* he's jealous of, instead of you. And we're kind enough to get you cleared into the bargain." He had dropped his cool pose and was working himself into real irritation. "But you couldn't let well enough alone. You think we didn't see you skulking around the house this afternoon? Then you call Andrea and let her know your suspicions about the two of us. It looked like only a matter of time before you said something to that idiot detective Lindenbrook and his stupid dyke partner." Switching back to a semblance of cool, he concluded, "In short, you've turned out to be a real disappointment."

I took the plunge. "I did talk to them. They're probably paying a visit to Andrea right now. Why do you think they haven't released Larry's body? They don't want you cremating it before they can continue investigating."

"They've already decided you killed Larry in self-defense. So it's time for a pre-emptive strike."

"I don't understand."

"You wouldn't, would you? You're overcome by guilt and remorse. You killed your lover's husband. So you decide to end it all."

Standing near one of the picnic tables, I was acutely aware of the small dark opening in the barrel of Fox's pistol. "And how am I planning to end it all?" I said, unable to suppress a shudder.

Fox reached inside his blazer and withdrew a small kitchen knife, like something you might use to slice carrots. The blade gleamed despite the failing light, and it certainly looked as if it could do real damage. "You're going to slash your wrists. I took the liberty of procuring this utensil unobtrusively from the Inn's breakfast room while you were at Harry's. I let them know how disappointed I was to have missed you. I also typed and printed *this* at the guest office station while I was there." He set the knife down on the picnic table and took out a folded sheet of typing paper from which he read: "I can't live with this any longer. Larry didn't deserve what I did to him." He looked at me, the half-smile returning from wherever it had gone. "Very Sophoclean, wouldn't you say? Fraught with *peripeteia*. Succinct, too."

"You really are a sociopath, you know?"

Fox's smile moved up a notch. "It's easier than being an associate dean."

"And you expect me to sign your suicide note?"

"No need." Fox held up the sheet of paper. "I had several specimens of your signature from the paperwork about your production. One of the perks of being associate dean. Or a sociopath. And I had plenty of time to practice. It wasn't so tough. Now, let's get serious." Fox threw the knife down between us and gestured at it with the pistol. "Pick it up. I need your fingerprints on it."

I did so. "How are you going to deal with your DIA problems?"

Fox laughed, a sound so casually dismissive that it made me increasingly sick. "You don't know how things work, do you? When I solve my temporary financial bind, I'll just make things right with the DIA. This is Detroit. Embezzlement and bribery are indoor sports. Nobody needs a scandal getting in the way of fundraising. And I have a lovely fan-club of lavender-haired old ladies."

Trying to keep the edge of desperation from my voice,

I said, "And what about the artwork?"

Fox gave another snort of derision. "I've earned the few things I've taken. They'll never even miss them."

"The Hopper sketch?"

For the first time, Fox seemed a touch discomposed. "Andrea shouldn't have shown you that. It was a mistake. She likes pretty things. I suppose she just couldn't resist. But we'll resolve that issue, too. Nothing for *you* to worry about."

"Except being dead."

"Look on the bright side. I really do like your play. Maybe it'll have a posthumous celebrity. One way or another, your worries will be over." He gestured with the pistol again. "We can start the final scene any time you're ready."

"How do you expect me to cut myself with handcuffs on?"

"I don't." Fox reached into a pocket again. He took out a bottle of pills and rattled them. "Oxycodone," he said. "You'll swallow a generous dose. It should take effect pretty quickly. Then I'll do the honors with the knife. I'll use the knife to cut off the cuffs. The knife-wounds will obscure the cuff-marks. I'm willing to wait, though. You won't feel a thing. Not much, anyway. You can think of Socrates." Fox smiled indulgently. "Pretty thoughtful of me to provide the oxy, eh? You won't even suffer. Much."

Still playing for time, I said, "Is that how you handled Larry? Got him dazed and confused?"

Fox flashed a feral-looking smile. "You have to admit, it's better than knowing what's coming. He never knew what hit him."

"But I'll know," I said. "And what if I won't take the

oxy? What if I don't let you slice me up?" My heart was beating rapidly, and my legs felt weak.

"I'll just have to shoot you." Fox said this with no evident concern.

Keep talking, I thought. "How will you explain that?"

"I won't be on the scene. I'll be pedaling back to Indian Village on my bike. Sometimes onstage, you have to improvise. You ought to know that. And, after all, this is Detroit. I can always get another gun." Fox waved the pistol ominously.

I looked at the knife in my hand, my brain filling with random thoughts. The email from Deirdre popped into my head. *"You're always too busy thinking when you should be doing. Probably doing when you should be thinking, too, but never swept away. You're like some kind of Martian, a pod-person visiting Earth and imitating the inhabitants so you can write about them."* I thought of Fox returning to his cozy office in Old Main after disposing of his latest problem. Or returning to bed with Andrea. Then, out of nowhere, my brain plucked a line from the Brando cinematic fiasco *One-Eyed Jacks—"Lookit here what's happenin' to Romeo."*—spoken by Ben Johnson just before Karl Malden smashes Brando's gun-hand with the butt end of a rifle. Or maybe a shotgun.

"Let's get on with it, McCutcheon. Do you want the pills or not?" Fox sounded impatient, on the point of action. "If so, you'd better drop the knife."

And suddenly, the image of Old Main took me back to my long-ago fencing class, in which my nemesis Lionel had beaten me by ignoring the aesthetics of the art and attacking opponents like a berserker. Without further thought, I let out a roar, began waving my arms as wildly as the handcuffs allowed, and plunged toward Fox, pointing the knife as I moved.

I heard a noise and felt something strike my left arm the way a branch might when you run blindly through trees. I bowled into Fox, knocking him back into the picnic table. Then I realized I was on my knees in front of the other man, who had fallen back against the tabletop. And I became vaguely aware of the parking lot filling with light and the sound of an engine. I was no longer holding the knife, and my left arm seemed weak and useless.

I glanced at my arm. The sleeve of my jacket was covered with blood, and I suddenly felt a wave of nausea.

"You son of a bitch." Fox's voice sounded distant and strained. "You've stabbed me."

I looked in front of me, my vision tunneling, and saw the knife projecting from Fox's stomach, staining the immaculate white of his cashmere sweater with a swath of scarlet.

"You son of a bitch," Fox repeated with effort. "Do you know how much I paid for this sweater?" I saw he was still holding the pistol, which he was struggling to raise. "Now I *am* going to shoot you."

"No, you're not!" A familiar voice, like the bright light, came from behind me and to one side, but I couldn't manage to turn toward it. "Drop it!"

Could it really be Eileen? I leaned down, bracing myself on my right hand, which I saw was bleeding, too. The knife, I thought.

"Don't!" The voice behind me sounded frantic, but I couldn't manage to lift my head toward Fox. Then the parking lot echoed with the sound of an explosion that could only have been from another firearm, and I tumbled forward among wet leaves.

"Dennis? Are you all right?"

The voice was, indeed, Eileen's. Fighting to stay conscious, I said, "I'm going to need a new jacket."

"Never mind your jacket. You idiot."

From somewhere, a Harrison Ford line from *Random Hearts* floated into my mind, but I wasn't sure I had managed to actually say it out loud. *"You're supposed to be nice to me. I've been shot."*

The distant sound of sirens was the last thing I registered before darkness closed over me like Fox's blanket.

22

I opened my eyes to find myself on a gurney in a fast-moving ambulance. I had a bandage wrapped tightly around the upper part of my left arm and an IV tube taped to my right. I was also hooked up to a vital-signs monitor and, in descending order of importance, had a big bandage on my right hand. I felt no pain, very likely thanks to whatever was flowing through the IV line. Better than Fox's Oxycodone, especially given the planned end result.

A brown-skinned EMT with short black hair and a bushy moustache sat next to me and leaned in. "How you doing, my friend?" The accent was Hispanic.

"You tell me." I had some difficulty forming the words, as if the ball gag were back in my mouth.

"Your vitals are fine, and you're okay enough to give me a comeback. That's good."

"Where's Eileen?"

"You got me there, buddy. If she's the first thing you ask about, she's probably on the way to meet you at the hospital. You in any pain?"

"No. Whatever you're pumping into me is doing its job. I'm a little groggy, though." I knew I needed to learn something else, but my eyelids wanted to close. With an effort I said, "What about the other guy?"

The EMT shook his head. "Don't know 'bout that. I'm focused on you."

"You must have some idea."

"All I can say is, didn't look good." The ambulance swerved, then came to a halt. "Here we are."

I let my eyes close.

When I opened them, after a dreamless and indeterminate interval, I was confronted by a sight I had hoped never to see again, and the sound of a familiar voice.

"All things considered, I can't say I'm surprised to see you." Dr. Sirsat, the young ER physician who had treated me just days earlier, gave me a gleaming smile. "Though we don't really encourage repeat business."

I felt a bit more clear-headed, enough so to be aware of a pang in my left arm and a twinge in my bandaged right palm. "Same guy put me here both times," I said. "Do you know what happened to him?"

Dr. Sirsat's mouth twitched unhappily. "He had both a knife and a gunshot wound. I'm afraid he expired on arrival."

Despite what Fox had nearly done to me, I took no pleasure in the news. "Which wound did it?" I managed.

"That's hard to say. The combination was certainly fatal. We did what we could, but it was too little, too late."

I took a deep breath. "I know you all do your best to save everyone. But he had it coming, if anyone ever did."

The young doctor's face remained impassive. "Your own gunshot wound was what we call through-and-through. It should heal relatively quickly, without any future impairment. The cut on your hand is minor. We'll probably release you quite soon."

"That's good news. I thought I was done for."

"You've been very fortunate," Sirsat said. "Twice now. I hope not to see you again." He smiled. "Unless it's at the theatre. My wife and I plan to see your play on Friday."

"I'm not sure I'll be there," I said. "But I'll make sure you get complimentary tickets."

"You're very kind."

"I appreciate all you've done." I eyed the door of the room. "Do you know anything about my friend, Eileen? Professor Moriarty. Is she all right?"

"She's fine. She's talking to a pair of detectives down the hall. From what I've overheard, she may well have saved your life."

23

"Looks like your pal here saved your life." Lindenbrook, dressed nattily as usual, wearing his favorite pink tie, smiled down at me from where he, Dreyfus, Dr. Sirsat, and Eileen stood around the bed.

"But how?" I said.

Dreyfus, enunciating as if she were addressing a none-too-bright child, said, "She shot the son of a bitch before he could shoot you again."

"Of course," Lindenbrook said, "that was apparently after you stabbed him."

"No," I said. I looked at Eileen, who smiled back at him, and I thought, what a beautiful woman.

"No, what?" Dreyfus said.

I shifted as best he could in the bed. "I mean," I addressed Eileen, "where did you get a gun?"

"Brought it with me," she said, "in my checked luggage. Then had it in the trunk of the Mustang. Figured it might come in handy in case I ran into a shark." She gave me a familiar impish grin. "I did, and it did."

I looked at Lindenbrook. "She's not in trouble for having it?"

The detective shook his head. "Nope. She has a concealed carry permit. We checked."

Eileen grinned at me. "Law and order, every time," she said.

"How did you manage to find us on Belle Isle?" I persisted.

"You didn't really think I'd go right back to the Inn?" Eileen spread her hands. "I watched you from a distance. I'd never seen Fox, but I figured who it was when I saw the Town and Country, and you stowing the bike in your Highlander. I thought about intervening right then, but I decided to follow you in the Mustang. I almost lost you a couple of times. I'm sorry it got so far out of control, but I did get there on time."

I waved off the apology. "If you'd done what I told you to do, I'd be dead. You saved me."

"You pretty much saved yourself." She looked at me steadily, without emotion. "I just finished the job."

"She called *us*, too," Dreyfus said. "Told us where you were."

"And with who," Lindenbrook said.

"Whom." Dreyfus grinned at him.

Lindenbrook gave her a look. "Sorry it took us so long. Besides, we got a little sidetracked by Mrs. Durant. She called to warn us about Fox. Said he frightened her. Didn't know what he might do next."

Eileen made a rude sound. "I've never even met the woman, but from all I've heard, if her lips are moving, she's lying."

"One way or another," Lindenbrook said, "ya'll are just lucky this Fox kept yapping at Mr. McCutcheon like some James Bond villain. People we usually deal with want to put a cap in you, they just do it." He made a pistol of his right hand. "Bang."

"I guess it's a white thing, Al." Dreyfus gave him a reasonable facsimile of Eileen's impish smile, then turned to us. "All of you folks are way too verbal and articulate for your own good," she said. "Why you write plays, I guess."

"Sounds as if you need some privacy." Dr. Sirsat moved toward the door. "And I *am* on ER duty."

"Before you go," Lindenbrook said, "how's your patient here?"

"We've replaced his blood loss, filled him with painkiller. But we want to keep him overnight, get him fully hydrated. He should be able to leave in the morning." The doctor looked at me. "You'll have to take it easy for a bit, of course."

"Thanks again," I said.

"My job, my pleasure." So saying, Sirsat left the room.

"So," I said to Lindenbrook. "Al. First time we've heard your first name. Short for Albert? Alvin?"

Lindenbrook gave Dreyfus what I assumed was a *lesbro* look. "Aloysius," he finally said. "I prefer Sergeant."

"Relative to Mrs. Durant," Dreyfus said, looking unabashed, "we did finally get permission for you to wear a wire."

"Fox is dead," I said. "He admitted everything *he* did, but nothing that really incriminated Andrea."

"And now he's not around to add anything to the story." Eileen expelled a breath in disgust. "So why would Andrea admit anything?"

"We don't have much to go on," Lindenbrook agreed. "The forensics and medical reports still might support your having killed Larry Durant in self-defense."

"What?" I tried to lean forward in outrage, but the combination of the wounded arm and the cut hand meant

I couldn't quite manage it. "What about the tox scan?"

Lindenbrook shrugged. "Might never get one of those."

"And we only have your word and circumstantial evidence to back up your story about Fox." Dreyfus gave me a cop stare.

"So what are you saying?" Eileen demanded. "You think I flew to Detroit because Dennis and I are part of some plot to lure Fox to Belle Isle and kill him? You think *I* put Dennis in handcuffs? Took the knife from the inn? Typed a fake suicide note? Planted the Oxycodone? Fox was the one with the gun. He shot Dennis, for God's sake. Not to mention smacking him on the head with a two-by-four!"

Lindenbrook made a calming gesture. "We're not accusing you of anything. So far as the story's told, both of you are heroes. Claudine's just pointing out the difficulty of pinning anything on Mrs. Durant."

"If you'd gotten quicker approval for a wire, Fox would probably still be alive," Eileen said, her voice rising, "and you'd have a case against *both* of them."

"I can't argue with that," Lindenbrook conceded. "Those are the conditions we have to work with."

"So you're telling us it isn't worth the trouble to go after Andrea," I said.

"And if we do nothing, she inherits two million bucks." Eileen gave a humorless laugh.

Dreyfus shrugged. "Up to you."

I looked at both detectives.

Lindenbrook shrugged in concurrence.

24

"Now that your roommate has come to your rescue, is your relationship with Mrs. Durant at an end?"

The question came from Lisa Felsen, a writer for *People Magazine*. On first seeing the press badge, Eileen had whispered to me, "We're in the big leagues now."

Not long out of the hospital, my arm still bandaged and throbbing and my hand still bandaged and twingeing, I was seated with Eileen, Ed Friend, and the cast and crew onstage at the Studio Theatre. Dr. Addante, mindful of good publicity for the show, had kindly agreed that the space would better accommodate a press conference than the breakfast room at the inn. Eileen and I could have done without the media, but living in the twenty-first century came with certain unavoidable costs. Ms. Felsen had let us know that she wasn't used to finding herself among the usual mob of reporters. *People* generally got exclusives, and she clearly planned on some future interview without the *hoi polloi*.

Having stalled for a few seconds, I said, "First of all, Professor Moriarty is my *office*-mate, my colleague, and my friend. Mrs. Durant was a friend from years ago, out East. I've seen her several times since coming to Detroit. I'll be returning home to Brixton in a day or so. I don't imagine I'll be seeing Mrs. Durant before I leave town."

The Felsen woman persisted. "So, you won't be attending services for Mr. Durant?"

I shook my head. "Mr. Durant's murder was tragic. But all things considered, I believe my attendance at his funeral would be inappropriate."

Another reporter took up the baton. "Are you and your roommate romantically involved?"

I deferred to Eileen, who said, "I'm not sure why all of you seem unable to grasp the distinction between *room*mate and *office*mate. Professor McCutcheon and I are faculty colleagues and good friends, which is why I came to Detroit when I learned he'd been injured in what appeared to be a street mugging."

The reporter took another tack. "How does it feel to be heroes and to escape death at the hands of a cold-blooded killer?"

"Well," I said, "Professor Moriarty is the real hero. I was just acting on blind instinct—self-preservation. And to be accurate, the man"—I avoided speaking Fox's name—"was trying to force me to kill *myself*."

"But he did kill Mr. Durant, didn't he?"

"If you haven't already gotten enough information on that, I'd suggest you address your question to the police." I glanced at the back of the auditorium, where Lindenbrook and Dreyfus were observing from a discreet distance. "I'm just happy to be here avoiding as many direct answers as I can."

This drew laughter, but was quickly followed by a question from a local television type. "Where did you learn to shoot, Professor Moriarty?"

"I'm from North Carolina," Eileen said, pouring honey

on her normal slight drawl. "My Grandpaw taught me to shoot almost as soon as I could walk. I'm glad I was able to use my weapon to thwart Dean Fox's intentions. But I have to say I fully support background checks and a ban on automatic weapons. I'm not interested in the NRA's loony Second Amendment agenda."

This caused a brief silence to fall. The media weren't interested in a political angle. Another reporter changed the subject. "Dennis," she said. "Larry DeVere of the *Free Press* has reported rumors that *Swept Away* is headed for a New York production next year. Can you confirm that?"

I had, in fact, heard from Richard Corwin, the producer behind the play's short Off-Broadway run. "Mr. DeVere is well-informed," I said. "I can confirm that discussions are underway to explore that possibility."

"And isn't Professor Moriarty a former film-school classmate of Ben Talbot, a genuine A-list star with his own production company? Is a movie version in the works?"

I shook my head. "Talk like that is way premature."

Eileen broke in. "Ben and I are good friends. He's certainly aware of Dennis's play, and I'll be more than happy to assist in furthering any possibility of a film. Or a West Coast stage production. But as Dennis suggested, those chickens are still in their eggs."

At this point, the *People* woman made a relatively unobtrusive exit, though not before raising her eyebrows at me, intimating that we hadn't seen the last of her.

The press corps eventually widened their net to include Ed Friend, the cast, and the crew as a sidebar to the main story. All of them, I noted gratefully, were pretty careful in their responses, as if taking their cue from my own reticence. I made sure to break in at one point to let everyone know how helpful Rachel had been in clarifying my own suspicions about Fox. This won me a smile from her and gave the press a chance to learn a few things about her and her acting ambitions. I was careful to praise everyone connected with the production and expressed my gratitude to both Ed and Genevieve Addante.

But since only Eileen and I were directly involved in the criminal aspects of the story, the questions inevitably doubled back to us, first becoming repetitious, then downright silly. I was afraid they would start asking the two of us about our favorite colors. I did, however, manage to put in a plug for Eileen's forthcoming books, and suggested a sidebar story might be in order.

At this point, Ed Friend intervened like any good director and called a halt to the proceedings. In the milling around that followed, I let Ed and the *Swept Away* ensemble know that I would be pleased to host a farewell party later that evening at the Cass Café. We set up the gathering for nine p.m., then everyone began straggling out of the theatre.

Not surprisingly, Ms. Felsen, the *People* correspondent, waylaid us in the lobby and arranged an interview with Eileen and me for the end of the week in Philadelphia, where she said she would be able to get usable photographs. That done, she swanned out of the theatre, sparing us any further badgering.

"You realize," Eileen said, "that what she's really after is an interview with Ben."

I made a face at her. "I'm aware."

"And," she added, "at this point, Ben's probably more interested in a film treatment of this murder fiasco than in a stage play."

I made another face. "You really know how to boost a guy's ego."

She smiled sweetly. "Boostin' men's egos is what I'm all about."

Lindenbrook and Dreyfus headed us off at the back of the auditorium. Both detectives had spruced up for the occasion, Lindenbrook varying his outfit with a canary yellow shirt and peach-colored tie, and Dreyfus wearing a charcoal gray jacket and skirt over a pink blouse.

"You don't want to take another shot at the wire, eh?" Lindenbrook said.

I shrugged. "Andrea's way too cagy for that, we figure."

"Cagy isn't the half of it," Eileen said.

"Well," Dreyfus said, "you win some, you lose some."

Lindenbrook stuck out his hand. "Looks like you and Professor Moriarty are headed for better things, anyway. You may as well forget about Mrs. Durant. Leave her to us."

"Yeah," Dreyfus said. "There's supposed to be no such thing as a perfect crime." She pointed two fingers at her eyes, then in the general direction of Indian Village. "We'll be watching her."

We shook hands with the detectives, me, gingerly with my bandaged right hand, after which Eileen said, "As Professor Harold Hill pointed out in *The Music Man*, 'That kinda girl ties knots no sailor ever knew.'"

Lindenbrook grinned. "Saw that the other night on AMC. Good movie." He gave a little wave. "Take care, you two."

As the detectives took their turn being surrounded by reporters, Eileen and I began making our way back to the inn. "I like your bit about the chickens," I said. "I may steal it."

"Feel free."

"And I admired your *chutzpah* in getting in a plea for gun control."

Eileen laughed. "I think it was A. B. Guthrie who said, 'The trouble with opportunity is that its name's usually wrote on its butt.' I didn't want to blow the chance."

I felt my phone vibrate in my pocket. Taking it out, I saw the call was from Andrea. I let Eileen know, then hit *talk* and *speaker*.

"Andrea," I said, and waited.

"Hello, Dennis." Despite my better judgment, her soft voice caused a subtle shift within me.

"Congratulations," I said. "You're finally free. And wealthy. Enjoy your Hopper sketch."

"It may not be a Hopper."

"I doubt very much if Wily Fox would have risked stealing a fake."

After a second or two she said, "Anyway, I'm glad you're all right. I was so worried."

"Were you?"

"Of course," she said, her tone opaque. "I realized too late how crazy Bill Fox was. And how dangerous."

"Yeah," I said. "I found out up close and personal." A thought struck me. "By the way, were you there on the street when I was attacked on opening night?"

"Of course not. How could you think that?"

"I just wondered." I recalled the woman's voice I'd heard saying, *Oh, you poor thing.* A mystery.

"Will I see you?" she asked eventually. "At Larry's memorial service?"

"Eileen and I are leaving tomorrow morning."

Again, she took a few seconds before speaking. "I'm so sorry about all this. I wish—"

I cut her off. "Don't wish. As my mother always said, 'If wishes were horses, beggars would ride.' " I ended the call and switched off my phone.

"Talk about *chutzpah*," Eileen said. Then she added, "So you thought she was there when Fox went upside your head on opening night?"

"I remember hearing a woman's voice. And the police said they caught a glimpse of a woman in a long dress disappearing just as they got to me."

"Well," Eileen said, "it was either Andrea or we're back to ghosts."

"We've got enough to think about without apparitions."

"The hell you say." She stopped walking to look at me with narrowed eyes. "You apparently had time or inclination to set up a practical joke from your hospital bed. I didn't want to mention it earlier, especially after you had a real near-death experience. Maybe you figured I'd think you'd come closer to the spirit world. Or are you going to plead diminished capacity?"

"What do you mean?"

"Come on, Dennis," she said. "When I got home from the hospital, I unlocked the door of my room. And just as I was ready to step inside, I heard a voice say, 'He needs you.' I turned around just in time to see a woman in a long dress backing away around the stairs. I covered the distance in nothing flat, but she'd disappeared. What's the trick? Another acting student? Or the same one?"

I felt a shiver go through me. "I couldn't begin to tell

you," I said.

"Well," she said, "I'll give you the benefit of the doubt. Being around you is suddenly like being in *Ghostbusters*."

I looked at her and tried a grin. "Who you gonna call?"

25

I shifted in the passenger seat of the Highlander, my left arm aching and my head feeling the after-effects of the previous night's gathering at the Cass Café. Behind the steering wheel, driving with her customary expertise, Eileen looked fresh and beautiful, not hung over at all. We'd been on the highway for half an hour or so, driving south on Interstate 75 on the way to I-80.

"I'm still seeing you in your party outfit," I said. "I can't get over it." Eileen had met me on the Inn's porch in a little black dress and heels that wouldn't have looked out of place on Corinne Rimmer.

She flashed me a smile. "I told you I stopped off to do some shopping when I got to town. It wasn't all bike helmets and two-by-fours. A girl likes to dress up now and again. And that seemed like the perfect time. I have to admit, though, when I was getting dressed in my room, I kept checking for Bill Murray."

Before I could figure out what to say, my phone pinged and I eyed the screen. Eileen shot me a questioning look.

"Deirdre," I said. I read the text aloud. *"Don't forget about your first leading lady when the time comes to cast your next production."*

Eileen snorted. "Talk about being haunted."

I typed a response to Deirdre, which I also read aloud. *"We'll get back to you."*

Eileen grinned. "The standard kiss-off for would-be auditioners. Very nice."

"Glad you approve."

"Nice party," Eileen said, returning to a more pleasant topic. "They like you. And Rachel's quite the fast filly."

"I can give you her number."

"What makes you think I don't have it already?"

"Congratulations."

She glanced at me. "Don't get your knickers in a knot. You think I'd two-time my *roommate*?"

"Ho-ho," I said. Then, to change the subject, I pointed out the billboard proclaiming Toledo as "The Glass Center of the World."

"Didn't realize Toledo was quite that fragile," Eileen said. "Or *central*, come to think of it."

"The great Midwest," I said. "Full of surprises. Like your dress."

"Speaking of surprises," she said quickly, "you still maintain you didn't set up my ghost sighting?"

"I swear."

"I asked Latrece about it and she was evasive, but she did say the place is rumored to be haunted. Same line she gave you."

"Who knows? Certainly not I." Moving on, I said, "I heard from Finsterwald before breakfast this morning."

"Me, too," she said. "He's not happy. But he had to concede that we've brought our little academic backwater a bounty of good publicity."

"Publicity, maybe. I'm not sure they'll agree it was good."

"Hey," Eileen said, "ink is ink."

"No doubt Dean Rimmer has already weighed in on our behalf," I said. "He always sees the big picture."

"No doubt you'll find Corinne Rimmer even more avid to have you provide her with guitar lessons, or whatever kind of lessons she has in mind."

"Why, Professor Moriarty, could it be I hear a touch of jealousy in your tone? You think I'd two-time my *roommate*?"

Steering the Highlander around a sweeping curve on the highway, she looked at me appraisingly. "I hope not," she said.

"You surprise me." I noted that Eileen's face was a little flushed.

"I haven't always been a lesbian," she said at last. "Uncle Landon soured me on men. But I had a thing for Ben Talbot once upon a time. Followed him all the way to London on his first big movie shoot."

"Now that *doesn't* surprise me quite so much. He must be pretty hot to make you pop for a Transatlantic flight. I can't wait to meet him. If I ever get to."

"We'll see," she said. After a moment she added, "Ben's a movie star. Like most men in his position, he thinks the sun comes up just to hear him crow. Most men, if it comes to that."

"Present company excepted, I hope."

"Jury's still out on that one." She glanced at me. "I haven't had much luck with women lately."

"Neither have I." We both laughed, then fell silent while she steered us onto I-80. She accelerated smoothly and tucked the Highlander into the right-hand lane behind a semi.

I took a deep breath. "You're my best friend. That's more important than anything."

She looked at me and raised her eyebrows. "You're my best friend, too. That's more important than anything." She laughed. "We sound like Seinfeld and Elaine discussing whether they can manage to combine *this* and *that*."

"And we know how well *that* worked out."

"Maybe we should stop along the way."

"You're the driver."

"I am, at that."

"How about Gettysburg? I can show you the battlefield. Maybe you'll see the guy with the musket."

"Then we can have a leisurely dinner. Discuss matters." She smiled mischievously. "I'll wear my dress."

"Are you serious? You know history shows I'm not very good at this."

She laughed again. "As they say in LA, 'Everything's negotiable.' Maybe we'll be swept away."

END

AUTHOR'S NOTE

My heartfelt thanks to wonderful writing friends and colleagues Richard Katrovas, Robert Eversz, and Peter Gooch, who read this novel through several drafts and made excellent suggestions that helped it grow into its current form. My wife and frequent collaborator Deborah Ann Percy not only served as invaluable critic and copy editor, but also allowed me to use material from our co-written play *Beyond Sex* (HP Publishing House, Bucharest, 2011) as the basis for the play by my protagonist that is central to the novel's action. I'm grateful to Nick Court-right, Kyle McCord, and Hillary Reyes, and David Hardin for excellent editorial and proofreading work, to Cameron Finch and Kelleen Cullison for the attractive interior design and layout, to Sarah Matyczyn's fine photo, which makes me look as good as I'm likely to, and to Jerry Fry, whose cover art offers a wonderful take on both the story and the setting. I'm also indebted to Stuart Dybek, Bonnie Jo Campbell, Robert Eversz, Steve Hamilton, and Joseph Heywood for their kind words about my work. My thanks to all of these. Any faults in the novel are purely my own.

The action of the book is largely set in Detroit, where—like my protagonist Dennis McCutcheon—I spent many of my formative years. Though I hope the city comes alive in my descriptions, I am solely responsible for taking a novelist's license here and there with places, chronology, geography, and other details. The small Pennsylvania town of Brixton and all its aspects are completely fictional. As for characters and action, they are products of my imagination and are not intended to represent any actual people or events.

ABOUT ATMOSPHERE PRESS

Atmosphere Press is an independent, full-service publisher for excellent books in all genres and for all audiences. Learn more about what we do at atmospherepress.com.

We encourage you to check out some of Atmosphere's latest releases, which are available at Amazon.com and via order from your local bookstore:

The Tattered Black Book, a novel by Lexy Duck
American Genes, a novel by Kirby Nielsen
The Red Castle, a novel by Noah Verhoeff
Newer Testaments, a novel by Philip Brunetti
All Things in Time, a novel by Sue Buyer
Hobson's Mischief, a novel by Caitlin Decatur
The Black-Marketer's Daughter, a novel by Suman Mallick
The Farthing Quest, a novel by Casey Bruce
This Side of Babylon, a novel by James Stoia
Within the Gray, a novel by Jenna Ashlyn
For a Better Life, a novel by Julia Reid Galosy
Where No Man Pursueth, a novel by Micheal E. Jimerson
Here's Waldo, a novel by Nick Olson
Tales of Little Egypt, a historical novel by James Gilbert
The Hidden Life, a novel by Robert Castle
Big Beasts, a novel by Patrick Scott
Alvarado, a novel by John W. Horton III
Nothing to Get Nostalgic About, a novel by Eddie Brophy
Whose Mary Kate, a novel by Jane Leclere Doyle

ABOUT THE AUTHOR

Arnold Johnston lives in Kalamazoo and South Haven, MI. His poetry, fiction, non-fiction, and translations have appeared widely in literary journals and anthologies. His plays, and others written in collaboration with his wife, Deborah Ann Percy, have won over 200 productions, as well as numerous awards and publication across the country and internationally; and they've written, co-written, edited, or translated some twenty books. Arnie's translations of Jacques Brel's songs have appeared in numerous musical revues nationwide, and are also featured on his CD, *Jacques Brel: I'm Here!* A performer-singer, Arnie has played many solo concerts and some 100 roles on stage, screen, and radio. He is a member of the Dramatists Guild, Poets & Writers, the Associated Writing Programs, and the American Literary Translators Association. He was chairman of the English Department (1997-2007) and taught creative writing for many years at Western Michigan University in the program he co-founded. He is now a full-time writer.

ALSO BY ARNOLD JOHNSTON

Fiction:

Swept Away, a novel.

The Witching Voice, A Novel from the Life of Robert Burns,
Wings Press, 2009.

Poetry:

Where We're Going, Where We've Been, FutureCycle Press,
2020.

Sonnets: Signs and Portents, Finishing Line Press, 2014.

What the Earth Taught Us, March Street Press, 1996.

Drama:

It's About Us, Eldridge Publishing, 2019 (with Deborah
Ann Percy).

Radiation: A Month of Sun-Days, HP Publishing, 2016
(with Deborah Ann Percy).

Rumpelstiltskin: The True Hero, Eldridge Publishing, 2013
(with Deborah Ann Percy).

Beyond Sex, HP Publishing, 2011 (with Deborah Ann
Percy).

Duets: Love is Strange, March Street Press, 2008 (with
Deborah Ann Percy).

The Art of the One-Act, New Issues Press, 2007 (edited
with Deborah Ann Percy).

Rasputin in New York, HP Publishing, 1999 (with Deborah
Ann Percy).

The Witching Voice: A Play About Robert Burns, WMU
Press, 1973.

Translations:

Epilogue, from Hristache Popescu's Romanian play *Epilog*, HP Publishing, 2011 (with Dona   Roşu and Deborah Ann Percy)

With C. S. Nicolăescu Plopşor Through the Ages, from Lucian Roşu's Romanian memoir *Cu C. S. Nicolăescu-Plopşor Prin Veac*. Editura Mica Valahie, 2004. (with Dona Roşu and Deborah Ann Percy)

Night of the Passions and *Sons of Cain*, from Hristache Popescu's Romanian plays *Noaptea Patimilor* and *Fii Lui Cain*, HP Publishing, 1999 (with Dona Roşu and Deborah Ann Percy)

Literary Criticism:

Of Earth and Darkness: The Novels of William Golding, University of Missouri Press, 1980.

CPSIA information can be obtained
at www.ICGtesting.com
Printed in the USA
BVHW031638220421
605632BV00007B/752